"How to Knock a Bravebird from Her Perch is a good quick read with sufficient detail and grit to make it a page turner."

— QBR: The Black Book Review

"I personally grew up about one hour from where Pecan was born, so I greatly appreciated the main character and really commend the author on capturing the dialect as used by the uneducated and poor black community of the time. This is a great read, hard to put down, and I wasn't disappointed at all in the end!"

— Onlinebookclub.org

"From the very first page, this story sucked me in. Simmons gives Pecan a strong voice, even as she struggles to find her own inner strength. The writing is lyrical and compelling, which kept me turning the pages during difficult and heartbreaking passages. Luckily for the reader, the story is about more than those terrible moments. There is a slow and beautiful process of self-discovery that allows Pecan to become Belinda, allows a lost, grieving child to become a strong, self-sufficient woman."

— Rebecca Kovar (Bookshelf Bombshells)

"How to Knock a Bravebird from Her Perch is not only dramatic and heartbreaking, it also encourages women to accept the past but do whatever it takes to change the future."

— Khamneithang Vaiphei (Goodreads & Amazon)

"Ms. Simmons has done a brilliant job of crafting a story that will stick with you for a long time.

— *AJ Arndt (AJ Arndt Book Blog)*

"This is a powerful read that sort of sneaks up on you if you aren't paying attention. I say that because you know going in that it's pretty much involving domestic violence but it's not overtly descriptive in the occurrences of that until the latter half of the book. This book is mostly about the struggle the victims go through making the decisions they have to make to allow themselves, & those they love, to be survivors."

— *Melanie (The Voices Within Unleashed)*

"D. Bryant Simmons is a writer and I mean that in the very sense of the word. The emotional connection was immediate. The characters were jumping off the page. (About Pecan's daughters) Each one was as interesting and delightful as the next. Pecan Morrow is a fighter and I mean that in every sense of the word."

—*Cedric Boyd, Author of The Good Wolf (Amazon)*

HOW TO KNOCK A BRAVEBIRD FROM HER PERCH

The First Novel in the Morrow Girls Series

D. BRYANT SIMMONS

Bravebird Publishing | Chicago | 2014

Cover Designer: Andrew Brown
Editor: Lauren I. Ruiz
Typesetter: D. Bryant Simmons

Bravebird Publishing
Chicago Ridge, IL 60415
info@bravebirdpublishing.com
www.bravebirdpublishing.com

Publisher's Cataloging-in-Publication Data
Bryant Simmons, D., 1983-
     How to knock a bravebird from her perch: the first novel in the
morrow girls series / D. Bryant Simmons.
        p. cm.
     Does not include index.
     ISBN 978-0-9857516-6-1
     1. African American women—Fiction. 2. African American
families—Fiction. 3. Mothers and daughters—Fiction.
I. Bryant Simmons, D. 1983-. II. Title.

Printed in the United States of America.
0 9 8 7 6 5 4 3 14

For all women who doubt their abilities.
Especially my mother.

I love you.

Contents

HOW TO KNOCK
A BRAVEBIRD
FROM HER PERCH

Prologue

T HE WIND CAME AND blew through town like never before on the day I was born. It was May 17, 1952, in Hattiesburg, Mississippi. When the nurse came around to tell my daddy I was here he whooped and hollered so loud everybody thought he was crazy. Hell, it took five nurses to convince him that it was okay to touch me. I wasn't real tiny like some babies, but he was a big man with big old hands. That's what I remember most about my daddy, his hands. Working man's hands. Big and ashy with blisters and dead skin. He was always apologizing for them, but me, I loved them.

Now from what I was told about the hospital, it was cold and it seemed like folks were screaming but they'd probably say it was me. My daddy said the doctor ain't even have to hit me, that I came out screaming just like he was. Only difference was he stopped after a while. He said that when they took me home I was still screaming and folks would come by and say, "Ooo what y'all doing to that child to make her scream like that?" He'd smile and say I was just gearing up to start singing, that I was practicing. Then he'd laugh in that way that put folks in the mind of a big friendly grizzly bear. Kind of laugh that made them at least wanna smile. That was my daddy. He had a voice like nails on sandpaper—scratchy and real deep. And he loved pecan pie almost as much as he loved me. That's how I got my name. My mama leaned toward Belinda so that's what's on the papers but growing up most folks called me Pecan. Because they say it was real obvious how much he loved me and I loved him.

I don't remember what my mama looked like, but folks say I look like her. Mostly on account of my shade of brown. Not too dark and not too light. Right in the middle. And my figure was like that too. Not too big and not too small. Not too tall and not short neither. I figured that's what they meant saying I looked like her. But my daddy used to say it was my eyes. He said they were the most beautiful eyes he ever saw. My mama's eyes...Was really the only thing he ever said about her. That she had real pretty eyes. The kind that bat at a man and make him do crazy things. Folks used to say that I had that power over him too. That I could just bat my eyes and make him do what I wanted. Course I never saw it like that. Never saw fit to even test it out.

Anyway, folks meant it as a good thing—saying I looked like my mama but it used to make me mad. What I wanna look like her for? She ain't do nothing. My daddy was the one did everything for me. Braided my hair. Taught me things.

When I was seven I'd figured some of it out by just listening when the grown folks talked. Most women were naturally giving people but my mama was only good at giving the men folks a good time. Being a wife and mother just wasn't her cup of tea. Broke my daddy's heart so bad he couldn't even say her name. So, I tried real hard not to bring it up but every so often I'd ask my daddy where my mama was and a few days later I'd get a letter from either New Orleans or Mobile. That's how I learned that Hattiesburg was right between New Orleans and Mobile. And she'd say how much fun she was having and how much she loved me. Never that she was coming home or that she missed me. Only that I shouldn't worry and that I was loved. Eventually I started to wonder why my mama's handwriting and my daddy's handwriting looked so much alike.

He worked for a lumber company, knocking down trees, but what he really did was fix things. Folks came from far and wide to have my daddy fix something of theirs. He never charged for it, just did it because he said it needed doing. When I was eight, we were sitting on the porch, watching folks go by and he explained it to me. He said, "Folks gotta get to work, they gotta eat, they gotta have them some clean clothes; that's why I do what I do. You gonna see. When you get to be a lady you gonna find a way to be useful too."

I nodded like I understood because I ain't wanna disappoint him, but I ain't have one clue what he was talking about. Me, useful? I couldn't see past being a kid.

Then when I got to be a teenager, talk turned from useful to proper. Not from my daddy, but from other folks in the neighborhood, folks at church. They were all worried about me because I was raised by a man. Worried I wouldn't make a proper wife to somebody. One of the deacons' wives took me aside one day and explained that ladies wore stockings. She said I was pretty enough, but if I wanted to find somebody to love me, I'd have to make myself look like a lady. Stockings and hairpins and pressing combs...my daddy just watched all nervous like from the hallway while I burned each one of my ears time and time again. But in the end everybody wanted to put they hands in my hair.

"Well look at you, girl!" They said. "Got some nice hair now, huh? Just gotta make sure you know how to cook and you gonna snatch up a man real quick!"

They were never satisfied. My daddy finally had to tell them, "Stop picking on her. She gonna be just fine."

I wasn't much in the kitchen. I could bake pretty good but real food was a different story. Didn't worry me too much because my daddy's stew and barbecue broke records. Him and his apron that said so. He called it his truth-telling apron because it said that he was working up some magic right there on the fabric. I'd watch him throw stuff together that ain't have no business being near each other and folks would suck it all down, and then look around for some more.

I was pretty good in school, though. Got good marks, was liked by most everybody. I was a good girl, folks said. All the way up until my last year...

A couple of us girls were standing around drinking soda pops when the bus from Biloxi pulled into town and sent dust flying every which way. A gritty storm cloud, swirling around me in my plaid dress that wasn't anything really special. The driver screeched to a stop and folks started to unload. This big guy strolled down the steps, pausing once his feet hit the dirt so he could look around at what was waiting for him. He was full of muscles, with a face like Smokey Robinson's, wearing a clean white shirt that was only buttoned up halfway so we could see what God had blessed him with. He tilted his hat down over his face to block out the sun. He'd gotten off the bus with a bunch of other folks but I don't remember them.

"Morning," he said, tipping his hat toward us.

"It ain't morning. It's almost two o'clock." LeAnn pointed to the clock over the general store and hurried after him. "Where you from?"

"Biloxi." He looked back over his shoulder, watching us giggling behind them. "What's so funny?"

"Ignore them." LeAnn dismissed us with a wave. She was real

friendly, like a welcome wagon for all the guys come through our town. We were her friends so that's what we called it. Friendly. Other folks called it something else. "So...how long you in town for?"

"Don't know." He looked her up and down, a grin just dying to get out. Men folk was always grinning at LeAnn. But then he did something that shocked all of us. He looked away from LeAnn and right at me. My heart just plain old stopped right there in the street. I couldn't stop smiling even though I knew I looked a fool. That was the beginning of me and Ricky.

RICKY HAD BEEN OUTTA school a few years but I still had to go so we had to wait until the end of the day to see each other. Sometimes he couldn't wait and he'd show up in the halls, just watching me. Made me feel special that he just wanted to look at me. My house was about a ten-minute walk across town from my school. Ricky walked me home every day and we'd talk about all the things he wanted to do. Mostly, how he was gonna do something nobody else could do. He was gonna beat Muhammad Ali. Of course I ain't have no idea who this Ali person was until he explained it to me. Ricky had a destiny and I believed him when he said it was gonna happen.

"The only difference between us is he Muslim. I got a pretty face just like him. I'm fast...see, quick...just like him." He swung at the air in front of us, running this way and that, kicking up dust from the road while my bag of books slapped up against his backside. "See. You see?"

"Yeah, I see."

"I met this man once. A boxing legend. And he say I got natural talent. That's why I'm gonna be the greatest. They just don't know it yet. You believe me, right, Pecan?"

"Yeah, I believe you."

"You believe I'm gonna be something?"

"Yeah." I nodded and couldn't help but blush every time he looked at me.

He stopped fighting the air long enough to pull me off to the side of the road. Nature made way for us. Smelling green way up in the trees and down low around the grass that whisked around my knees. Spring was just a few days away.

"R-Ricky, where we going?"

He ain't answer me just held tighter to my hand. We dodged a few branches and hopped over a fallen log then stopped. He dropped my bag on top of an annthill, not paying it no mind. Couldn't hear the road no more, just birds chirping and the wind. Most of my clothes were homemade and I did my own washing so I was looking around, thinking about all the stains I was gonna get on the bottom of my dress and in my stockings. But couldn't stay on that too long, the way Ricky was looking at me. Never stopped looking at me that way, not really. But back then just seeing him smiling dirty thoughts at me made me blush real hard. Here was this pretty Southern boy that was going someplace and he ain't make no secret about the fact he wanted me with him. He looked at me like he wanted to crawl up inside me and tear me apart. Scared me so that I started to back away. I backed up until my back was up against a tree. And Ricky ain't waste no time getting pressed up against my front. Wasn't nowhere for me to go. He was hard all over, his muscles and all. I could see them through his clothes because they were just that thin. But still I ain't expect to feel so much hardness.

"Um...Ricky?"

He sorta moaned and rubbed up against me. I hadn't been that close to a boy ever. The tangy sweetness of his sweat beat off his chest until it got all up in me. His legs between mine, his hot breath all over my neck. I knew what was coming next.

"Ricky, I-I...I can't."

"You can't what?" His lips parted into a smile and then he kissed me like I was all grown up and all I could do was blush. "You a good girl, ain't you, Pecan? Hmm? You know what I mean?"

I did. And I was. Not that I could say it. I just sorta nodded. And he kissed me again. His tongue big and wet, slid on top of mine then disappeared, leaving me breathless. He was moving down my body...to my neck, my chest. Taking the buttons one at a time until my brassiere was showing to all of outside.

"Ricky, stop!" I covered myself best I could.

"I just wanna look. I ain't gonna do nothing." He looked at me all innocent like. "Come on, Pecan. I swear."

"You swear?"

"Yeah, I said I swear." Ricky coaxed my arms down to my sides so he could see what I was hiding. Nothing special in my eyes. I'd known girls that had more to hide but Ricky got real hard and swollen pretty fast. Next thing I knew he was right back to squeezing up against me and growling up in my ear.

"Ricky, come on stop now."

With all his strength, he ain't have to try too hard to lift me up. And he ain't care none that the tree bark was scratching through the back of my dress. Just wanted to get me so my legs were wrapped around him. And before I knew it he was fumbling up under my dress.

"You feel that? Huh? Feel that? I know you do."

"Um...Ricky...You swore!"

This groan came from somewhere down deep inside him and he

pushed up off the tree so there was space between us. He did it even though he ain't want to, and watched me fix myself up. Put the buttons back in the right slots. Watched so hard I thought maybe he was gonna come back after me. But then he said, "Wanna be my girl?"

"Your girl?"

"Yeah. Unless you lying to me about being a good girl. You do this with every boy in town? Let them get all up on you?"

"No..."

"Aight, then. You gonna be my girl. My mama always said I should find me a good girl." He took my hand, grinning at me so I could see his pearly white teeth. "And you pretty too. Betcha know how to cook real good, don't you?"

"Not really."

"But you'd learn." He nudged me on. "You'd learn for me, wouldn't you, Pecan?"

I nodded and we walked the rest of the way to my house holding hands. We looked a hot mess—dusty and wrinkled and I was missing a barrette. Folks were staring but I ain't care. Not until I saw the look on my daddy's face.

"Where you been, Pecan?" His voice boomed down the dusty road and folks cut they eyes in my direction.

"At school." I couldn't even look at him, not because it was a lie or anything, just because I was afraid he'd think it was.

"Go on in the house and clean yourself up."

I did as I was told and by the time I came back out Ricky was gone. My daddy was sitting on the porch, chewing tobacco and nodding to folks as they came past. I never knew what he said to Ricky, but I knew he ain't like him too much.

My daddy was a talker, could out-talk anybody, but never with

Ricky. And that night over supper, he ain't even wanna talk to me much. All you could hear was the clink of forks and the crickets outside our front door. I wanted to say something. I hated the thought of him thinking I was a different girl than I was. I was a good girl. Most girls I knew had already had they first kiss and was working on other things. Not me. But I couldn't get the words to come out of my mouth. So we ate in silence for a while.

"From now on you come straight home from school. You walk with that girlfriend of yours that live down the street. You hear me?"

"Yes s-sir." I nodded, damn close to crying.

"If that boy wanna see you, he gotta ask me about it first. You hear me, Pecan?"

"Y-Y-Yes daddy."

'Course it wasn't really up to me. I passed on the message to Ricky and he just kinda smirked. Ain't stop him from showing up at the high school or following me and my girlfriends around town, whistling at our behinds. Wasn't no secret around town. Everybody knew Ricky had his eye on me. Some folks thought he had more than that. I could tell by the way they looked at me. But I was my daddy's girl. Wasn't about to do nothing that make him think bad of me. So, I kept my distance from Ricky. He had to settle for smiling at me and making faces from across the street.

We were never alone after that little thing in the woods. Must've gotten on his nerves real bad because one day he showed up at my house, flowers in hand. They were so fresh the roots were still on them.

My daddy met him out on the porch like Ricky wasn't good enough to come up in the house. Told him if he wanted to see me he could do it when everybody else did. Said Ricky wasn't gonna be running off with me.

Folks said it was just because I was his only chile, only girl. They said because of how my mama did him he wasn't gonna like nobody for me. But I'd never know if they were right or if it was more than that because the very next day my daddy died. They said he just fell over in the field when he was working. Heart attack. Just like that. One day he was there with me, the next he was gone. I thought maybe it was me. That I'd killed him by doing what I almost did with Ricky.

⁂

THE MISSISSIPPI HEAT HAD its run of Hattiesburg the day we put my daddy in the ground. It was so hot steam was rising off the grass around his grave. Muggy and damn near stifling the heat was. I got all pitted before we even got to the graveyard. Ricky was good. He held my hand through it all. Saying how he knew what I was feeling because he lost his mama that year too.

"Hold on, Pecan." He said. "Just hold on, baby. It's almost over."

The sun beamed down on top of that tiny little hill. Me and Ricky, the preacher, and half the town. The preacher read from his book and some of the pages flew out, heading toward the Mississippi. He ran after the missing pages, his little bitty legs leaping up in the air to catch them like they were really worth something. Ricky had to fight back a smile. He tried to hide it but I saw. I just ain't care. They lowered my daddy down that dark rectangle of a hole and I thought I was dying. Ricky said I was talking and swearing but I don't remember all that. I remember washing the dirt and grass stains outta my stockings and skirt and from under my nails. I remember crying to him, "I'm all alone now."

"N'all you ain't." He said in a husky whisper. "I'm a take care of you. You hear me, Pecan? You gone be just fine."

We were married before the end of the week.

1
Married Woman, Regular Man

WE WERE MARRIED ABOUT a week before Ricky let me in on his plan. Mississippi wasn't where it was happening with his boxing and he knew exactly where he wanted to go. Chicago. There was this famous boxing gym there where some guy had trained up under some other guy that used to be somebody. He said it was where he was supposed to be and I was his wife so that meant I was supposed to be there too. Not in the house I'd grown up in, where I'd lived with my daddy. So I packed up my things and off we went.

We lived in this rundown apartment that wasn't anything more than a bed and a sink. Was right next to the train tracks. Not the kind on the ground, the ones that run around on tall metal stilts. I hadn't seen anything like it until we moved to Chicago. The windows shook every time the train would run past. The hot water was always stingy, giving up only a few drops at a time. And there was a smell like dead cats from the minute you opened the door. I couldn't get rid of it no matter how many times I scrubbed the floors. We had a ragged old TV that only had two channels and the weather man kept saying a tornado was coming. Said it every day the first week we were here. And he was right, but I ain't see it. Couldn't see it. Couldn't see anything, not really. Was too busy missing my daddy. Ricky said it'd make me feel better if we were close like a man and wife supposed to be. I ain't think so but he was sure and he was my husband so...I let him love me. And he loved me every day sometimes twice a day. Loved me so much he gave me a fever. I took to the bed for a few weeks and by the time I got up I realized I'd missed something.

Nikki was born nine months later, ten months to the day my daddy died. The exact date. The thirteenth. Ricky ain't even notice what date it was. Was too busy being happy—proud even. Said something was wrong with me because I wasn't celebrating. That I ain't love our baby. Wasn't that. I loved her, I did! I did. But he ain't let up about it. Just kept right on picking at me like a day old scab. Until one day when I started acting happy. Started smiling real big. I was somebody's wife, somebody's mama. So what if I wasn't nobody's daughter no more. Right? It ain't matter. The past was gone, no use crying over it. Right?

It ain't happen right away, me realizing all the lies I'd told myself. Took me a while to see them but the signs were always there. We'd been living in Chicago about three years when things finally came clear to me. Ricky got up at the crack of dawn, as usual, and I got up to fix him and Nikki something to eat and make sure his clothes were ironed and ready. He kissed me goodbye and asked me if I loved him.

Should've told him the truth. That I ain't know enough about myself to love anybody. That I wasn't even sure I had it in me. Maybe folks were born with a specific reserve of love inside them and maybe mine was all used up. But instead of saying any of that I just said, "'Of course I do. I'm your wife." And Ricky ain't know the difference. He was like that back then. Not really knowing or caring about my lies as long as they were what he wanted to hear.

Then by the time noon came around a voice in my head was saying go...go...GO! Other folks might have asked the voice some questions but I ain't need to. By then I knew what I'd done. I'd lost years of my pretending to be who he wanted just so I wouldn't feel alone. And I couldn't be in that place, be that person no more. Had to go somewhere real and true. Had to be free from all those damn lies. Sometimes I think it was my daddy talking to me from way down deep inside.

So I packed up my baby and all the clean clothes I could find. Searched all around the apartment for enough bags to hold everything. Ended up with a bunch of old plastic bags we'd been saving from the grocers. I would've gone with trash bags but they were too big for me to carry along with Nikki. She came with more stuff than I did. Toys and things I got from church giveaways. It ain't matter if it was missing pieces or missing eyes, she still loved it. I had so many bags they hung around my waist, twisting and slapping against my legs like a skirt made of wrinkled up old plastic.

So there we were, bundled up, nothing but our eyes sticking out, standing on the street. Nikki could walk just fine on her own but there was no less than a hundred people marching up and down the block screaming about justice and murder, so I held her. The police had shot somebody named Hampton while he slept in his bed. I remember thinking that it sounded too crazy to be true. Nobody gets shot in their own bed. While they're sleeping? I told Nikki to hold on tight and huffed and puffed toward the train station. We'd gotten a few blocks away, the dull roar of the crowd was at my back, when I saw it. Ricky's '61 Cutlass, bright red, covered with snow, and cruising down the street towards us. Cars back then lasted forever, but Ricky never took care of his so you could hear it from a mile away. Nikki twisted around in my arms, pointed to it, and in her innocent way said, "Daddy!" I just about died and the bitter cold blew through me in a way I'll never forget. I was frozen, right to my bones. If I had been in the crowd, he wouldn't of seen me but I wasn't. His car door slammed shut and his footsteps tracked across the snow. The cold ain't bother Ricky none. He ain't have nothing but a leather coat and it wasn't even buttoned up all the way.

"Where y'all going?" he asked.

"No-Nowhere...we not...nowhere."

"Yeah? Nowhere, huh? Y'all going nowhere? Get in the car," he growled.

"But—"

"Get in the fucking car, Pecan."

I tried to tell him we were just going to the market—the grocer's, but he knew better. He just looked at me carrying a million bags and his only child and he knew. I told myself he grabbed me so hard to keep me from falling on the ice as we stepped down off the curb. Told myself he was just worried about me and our child. That was why he pretty much shoved me into the passenger seat.

I held Nikki still on my lap and Ricky slammed the door. All the bags crowded up around me, fighting for space in the passenger seat. Ricky kept on glaring at me all the way around the front of the car until he was back behind the wheel. He parked in his usual spot right in front of the building and nodded to the little old lady that lived on the first floor. She'd come out into the hall to see about all the ruckus on the street. I tried to explain some guy was shot in his bed.

"What?" she barked. She was hard of hearing.

"HE GOT SHOT IN HIS BED!"

"Oh." She nodded and went back inside her apartment, leaving me alone with Ricky.

Ricky looked at me like he ain't know whether to scream or sigh and I could feel the tears congregating in the back of my throat. I ain't have a good story. I'd never told a lie before in my life. Not one that I hadn't convinced myself was the truth first. But I could smile. Probably ain't look no kinda natural, but that's what I did. Smile. A train ran past our window as soon as my key went into the lock. Nikki was getting heavy and I wanted to drop the bags to give my arms a break, but I was afraid if I did that, Ricky would get a good view of how much I'd planned to take. So, I held on to everything.

"Where were you going, Pecan?"

The heater hissed in the corner, spewing lukewarm water into the air and I let it steal my attention. He yelled like a maniac for a good ten minutes and turned beet red. Sweating so hard it slicked down his hair over his forehead until it looked like he had a bang. I heard every one of his words but told myself he was just worrying about us. It was so cold out there he ain't want us to freeze.

"Answer me, Pecan! Put that girl down!"

Me and Nikki was both sweating by then too. Our snow gear still on—scarves and hats and mittens. I dropped the bags and felt his eyes follow them to the ground. They had fell like rocks. He knew. I knew he knew. He knew and I ain't even know. Not until that very moment did I know I wasn't coming back. I was gonna leave and never come back. No note, no reason, just gone. He wasn't a bad husband. He was funny and folks always liked him. They liked him before they liked me. But most of all he kept his promise to me. He took care of me and I wasn't never alone. But still, there I was about to leave him. Ricky picked up one of the bags and tore through it, tossing the clothes on the bed. Then he went for another one, and cans of fruit cocktail landed on top of the clothes.

"You leaving me? Huh? Where you gonna go? You ain't got nobody! Who gonna take you in? Huh?"

"I don't know."

"You don't know?"

I hadn't gotten that far. I hadn't even known that I needed to be taken in. I was just going.

"You ain't leaving me. You got it?"

And I really wasn't. Ricky looked friendly and talked real smooth, but if he wanted to, he could kill a man with his bare hands. So even though he'd never hit me before then I knew if I even looked at the door he'd make his move. So I stayed still. I tried to make Nikki stay still too. But she couldn't wait to get down. Kept on wiggling and fussing, and fighting with her scarf.

"Take that shit off of her. She ain't going nowhere. You ain't going nowhere."

So I did. And she bounded around the room, happy to be free. I was watching her so hard I ain't see him until he was right up on me. His fingers. Cold. Brushed up against my neck as he yanked and unwrapped my homemade scarf. His pretty eyes danced all over me— examining my face, my chest. Searching for something.

"Where you was going?"

"N-Nowhere."

Our apartment ain't never want for no heat. Was always plenty to go around so when he finished unwrapping my scarf I got a little more comfortable than I should have. Let the heat tell me things were gone be okay. Ain't matter that he was looking at me all crazy, like I was a lying cheating scandalous kind of woman. I ain't wanna see it. Ain't wanna see him stomping back and forth, thinking things I would never have imagined.

"How you gonna go nowhere? Tell me the truth, Pecan. You going to meet somebody?" He chewed on the last word, turning it into something dirty. Somebody. The thought was tearing him up inside; I could see it plain as day. "You...You got some nigga waiting for you somewhere? Why you looking at me like that? Huh?" He paced from one end of the room to the other. Glaring at the floor boards and kicking things out his way. "I...I do right by you. I take care of you, don't I? Pay the bills? Put food on the table? Huh? I gave you a baby! And this how you wanna repay me? You gonna sneak up outta here when my back's turned?"

"No..."

"No? You think I'm stupid?" Ricky stopped pacing long enough to put both his eyes on me. "Huh? Think you about to out-think me? That I can't see what's right up in my face! Who is he?"

"Who—he ain't nobody—I mean...ain't nobody."

"You fucking around on me?"

"No. I...I was just going to the store. I was...I was coming right back." First one hurt the most. The slap. Backhanded me like I was just a fly. But the second one hurt too. Ricky made it real clear he could send me flying in either direction with any one of his hands. Had me balled up on the bed, crying and pleading. Him on top of me. Screaming and holding me down. "Rick-ky, please..." That's all I could get out before he hit me again. And again. And again. I just couldn't believe it. Not me. Other girls might have that happen to them but not me. My man was not doing that to me.

"You ain't leaving me! You hear me, Pecan? I ain't gone live without you. You hear me? And you ain't living without me." I was too busy crying to say something but he acted like he ain't see that. Demanding an answer. Swearing and spitting on me until he got his way. "Hear me?"

"Yeah! I…I hear you!" It came out so hard I started shaking. And he backed up off of me real slow like I was the one who was hurting him. Like me crying held some power over him. Like me bleeding and swelling and bruising was something I was doing to him. Then he looked over at Nikki. She'd seen it all. I couldn't wait for no tissue, made use of my sleeves and wiped my face best I could. "Nikki! Come here, baby! Come to mama!" A good girl, she came and I wrapped her up in my arms. Thinking I could keep some part of me safe.

"Stop looking at me like that. Pecan."

"I ain't. I ain't looking at you no more. Never." Me and Nikki rocked back and forth at the foot of the bed, shutting him out best we could.

"You…You my wife. You supposed to love me, not…"

"I said I ain't looking at you!"

"It wasn't my fault! You did this—you made me…you did." Ricky scratched his head and wiped the sweat from his brow. "I ain't mean to…I…I just…a man got a right to know where his wife going, and if she don't tell him he gonna think something!"

Nikki was crying softly into my shirt, so that was where all my attention went. I ain't wanna think no more about this man that was supposed to love me. But he wasn't having it. More I tried to calm Nikki, louder he got. Demanding I see things his way. How it looked to him. What was he supposed to do? Of course he lost his temper. But it ain't mean nothing he said. I was lucky. I would've been out on the street if it wasn't for him. Would've been all alone. I was real lucky. Ricky knelt down on the floor and his pant leg got caught on one of the floorboards that was starting to stick up so he yanked it free. Yanked it so hard he tore a little hole right on his knee but he ain't give it much thought. Just went right on with what he wanted to say.

"I ain't never gone do that again. I promise. I know how sensitive you is and I ain't mean to hurt you. I just can't think of you with some other man...him putting his hands all over you." His hands found they way to my back, closing in around me and Nikki like they could make us feel better. "You cold, baby? Huh?" I shook my head even though I couldn't stop shivering. "Don't be like that. Look at you. Your face getting all puffy. I...I ain't gonna...again. You believe me right, Pecan?"

"Mmhmm."

"You know how much I love you. I just wanna protect you, keep you safe. This here a big city and you don't wanna end up like these girls be out here on the corner, begging for food and having to sleep up in alleys, do you? But if you wanna leave, go ahead. I ain't gonna stop you." He watched me, waiting for me to look over at the door.

I ain't need nobody to tell me it was a test. He was waiting for me to slip up. I knew how Ricky thought. If I was leaving him, it was because somebody else was waiting to take care of me. And wasn't no man going to take care of some woman and her chile if she wasn't giving it up.

"Pecan?"

"I ain't going anywhere."

"How I'm supposed to believe you? How I'm supposed to leave you alone tomorrow while I'm up at the gym? You think I wanna come home find my wife and kid gone?"

"...No."

"So, how I'm supposed to know? Unless...unless you say it was all a mistake. Maybe you was just overwhelmed with all the love you got for me. That it?"

I nodded at first but he needed to hear the words. "Yeah."

"Yeah?"

"Yeah. I just...I ain't know what to do with all the...the love I got for you."

Ricky planted a kiss on my forehead then threw a clean towel into the sink. The water came out in a rush so I knew it was cold. He brought it back to me dripping wet. Since Ricky ate and slept boxing he knew all about injuries and how to make things feel better. So, I told myself I was in good hands.

2

Best of It

"Mama, look."

My baby was always finding something to play with, didn't seem to matter to her that it wasn't a toy. Her baby hands slapped up against the fragile wall and it rewarded her with bits of plaster and flecks of paint. White layers on yellow on white. She watched it rain down like it was just for her. I prayed she wouldn't think to put any of it in her mouth but she started to squat and I forgot all about the blood-stained shirt. Cold water they say will take out anything if you soak it long enough. I was just going to have to wait and see.

"No, no, baby."

She was a bit on the chubby side, even for two years old, so I always felt bad that we ain't have money to get her more clothes as she grew. Her dresses came too short and shirts fell too high. It was a good thing she was too young to realize. Even my clothes were faded and outdated. I saw girls my age strutting down the street in bell bottoms and those shirts that barely came to their navels. Tried to imagine myself in one of those outfits, my hair kinky all the way to the end. Ricky said those girls were working their way around to being dikes. Said that girls like me, innocent and all from the South, new to the big city, said we had to be extra careful because they preyed on girls like us. I ain't tell him that I kinda liked most of the things they said. About doing for yourself and having a voice...yeah sounded real good to me right about then. But I ain't say anything.

I took Nikki on my lap and we sat on the window sill, looking down on the folks as they passed under the train tracks. I swear Nikki looked at me like I was wearing some scary kinda mask. Like I used to be her mama but had turned into something else. When she got a little excited and started banging on the window I was relieved. As long as she was focused on something else, we were good. Until one of the guys on the ground looked up. We were only on the second floor. He could see us, see me. My hands started to shake and by the time I looked back out the window he was gone. I told myself he didn't see anything, wasn't anything to see really. He was probably looking at the baby, not me. The only mirror we had came with the apartment. It was old and foggy, blurring most of what I didn't want to see anyway. The bruises and swelling. But the cut that ran straight down the middle of my bottom lip, damn near split it in two. Ricky said I ain't need stitches and I believed him because I didn't wanna explain it to no doctor. I'd promised myself I wasn't going to leave the apartment until my face went back to normal. But none of that stopped Ricky from having his fun.

I heard him singing before he was even at the door. Ricky was like that. One minute the world was his enemy, the next they were all his friends. He danced through the doorway, bringing at least three inches of snow with him. "Can you dig it? Guess what!" I didn't even get a chance to answer before..."I got a fight!" He shed everything in a matter of seconds and lifted Nikki above his head, teasing her until she giggled. "Daddy's got a fight!"

"What kind of fight?"

"The kind that's gone put me on the map, baby. Ain't you happy for me? Huh? Baby here's happy for me. Ain't you happy for daddy? No more living in this shit hole. We gonna have real food and a real roof over our heads. Pecan, why you ain't saying anything?"

"You doing all the talking. I thought I'd let the two of you work it out. You hungry?" I knew he was. He was always hungry. So I ain't need to wait for an answer before heading toward the cabinet that kept all our food.

"Hold on, hold on."

"I'll make you something."

"Hold on. Let me look at you." Ricky plopped Nikki down on the bed and she scooted around, kicking her feet against the bed covers. He had both hands against my face, kneading my cheeks with his thumbs. "You got such pretty skin. You know that?"

I did. Or at least I knew it the day before. When I looked like me. A piece of his hair was sticking up over the middle of his head and it kinda waved in the draft from the door. Stole my attention for just a second but then I was back to knowing him better than I wanted. Last thing I wanted was Ricky's hands on me.

"It'll heal," he said like it was no big deal.

"I know."

"You still pretty. Ain't nobody pretty like my girl. You hear me?"

"Yeah."

"You believe me?"

"Yeah."

"Good. Because I got a surprise for you." Ricky ducked out into the hall and came back with a flat white box stretched across his arms. He held it out level with his chest and refused to give it up until I sat down on the bed. "It's for the fight," he said.

I wanted to ask him which fight. The one between me and him or the one he was so excited about. But I ain't say none of that and he laid it gently on my lap.

"Open it."

It was a dress. Blue. With a turtleneck and long sleeves. I held it up and could tell right away that it was shorter than he probably thought.

"Put it on."

"Now?"

"Yeah, yeah, put it on. Come on, baby."

I took my time undressing, folding everything neatly on the bed, hoping he'd lose interest but those pretty eyes never left my body. A train rushed by and the entire apartment, walls and all, shook with it. The shades were still up since I was looking down on the folks below. Ricky marched over to the window and yanked the string until the shade fell to a good length. I started to relax a little after he did that. The dress zipped in the back so I stepped into it and waited for him to do the honors. He took his time.

"It's shorter than I thought it was gonna be," he said.

"All the girls are wearing their skirts here. It ain't that bad. It's fashionable."

"Hmmm. Turn around. Let me see the front." He could see I ain't want to, but that just made him impatient. "Come on now. What you think I'ma do? If it don't fit, I'll just take it back and get another size."

It wasn't that it ain't fit. I had always been a six, a perfect six. It was that the dress ain't fit the way I knew he'd want it to.

"Damn. That...that looks real sexy on you." Ricky scratched his head then wiggled his finger around inside his ear. "They had another one that...that had this V-shaped dip in the front. You know that kinda came together like...this."

"A V neck?"

"Yeah that makes sense. That what it's called? Anyway, I thought about that one. Good thing I ain't get it. That would've been too much! I'd be trying to knock this fool out and get all distracted!"

He laughed and I smiled. The cut on my lip stretched thin so I didn't hold the expression for too long. Just long enough to think that just maybe...things were starting to look up.

We had canned spaghetti for supper. Cold and slimy, it settled in my stomach and I swear I could feel it moving around in there. A few times, my fat lip got caught up in my hunger, standing between me and the noodles. I bit it once and that was all it took for me to lose my appetite. Ricky finished his meal no problem and started in on what was left of mine. Our bed was the supper table. He stretched out and half of him hung over the sides while he scraped the bottom of the can.

"When's the fight?"

"Two weeks. I got two weeks to get in shape. They say this dude went up against Ali back when he was Clay."

"Is that bad?"

"I look worried?"

"No."

"Then n'all it ain't bad. It just is."

Sleep wasn't too far off. I could feel it sneaking up on me. I eased

Nikki off so I could slip into my nightgown and caught Ricky giving
me that look. It was the second time I'd undressed in only an hour.
It was all stuff he'd seen before but still he gave me that look. Like I
was selling something he hadn't had in a long while. I wasn't. But as
soon as the lights went down, he got up...straight up. Ricky never was
one for no extras. He was an in-and-out kinda man, not that I knew
the difference back then. I just thought that all men climbed on and
worked theyselves into a tizzy before becoming sweaty pieces of dead
weight. It wasn't entirely uncomfortable. He ain't try to kiss me so that
was good. And my body responded the way he wanted so he was happy.

I know because he said, "Pecan, you make me happy. You know
that?"

I did. And two weeks later I found out I was pregnant...again.
I wanted to be happy about it. I did. But every time I thought about
what was growing inside me I kept thinking that it wasn't supposed to
be there. I was supposed to be free. But I wasn't. He had me. And he
was growing inside me. Tried to make it go away by just thinking that
maybe it was all a mistake. The test got it wrong. But that ain't last too
long since Ricky made me go up to the free clinic to get checked out.
Said his trainer told him about how women need to be checked out a
lot when they with chile.

He was so happy. That was the first thing he asked about when
he came through the door. He wanna know how his baby was doing.
He wasn't worried that we couldn't barely feed ourselves. Said it was a
sign his boxing career was about to jump off. So, he spent longer days
at the gym, training day and night for his big fight. My condition
seemed to give him twice as much energy but made me stay in bed.
By the time he'd get home the pillows would be soaked from my tears.
Ricky chalked it up to woman stuff. Said it was because the baby made
me delicate and it'd go away just like the morning sickness that never
actually came. I just ate, slept, and cried. But he acted like it was the

most normal thing in the world. Nikki would look at me all sad like. She wanted to play. She wanted me to talk to her, to do something anything, but all I could do was lie there. I'd lie there, thinking "How'd this happen to me?" I'd close my eyes, squeeze them real tight and try to go back in time. To the day I met Ricky. No, because then I wouldn't have had Nikki. Back to the day I almost got away. If I had left ten minutes earlier...If I had gone in the other direction...If Ricky had stayed at the gym like he was supposed to...but then other things would come to mind. Money. I had none. Had no place to go, no friends, no family. How was I going to take care of myself let alone a baby...or two? I wasn't going anywhere. I would've ended up right back where I started. Maybe a day, maybe an hour would pass but then I'd come to my senses. That was my life. I could've rolled over and died or I could've made the best of it. So, I made the best of it.

3
Good Neighbors

Ricky won his first few big fights and made a name for himself. Was like folks were just looking for somebody to make a big fuss over. And just like he promised, we moved outta that awful hole next to the train tracks. We moved clear across town to a halfway decent house. Ricky made sure I saw it was the biggest on the block. It looked much better on the outside than it did on the inside but I ain't give a plugged nickel! There was a huge wrap-around porch with a swing and tons of windows. The bedrooms were small but there was more of them than we had use for. And the yard. A bit wild, almost overgrown, but it was green and had what they call potential.

"You like it?"

I couldn't stop smiling. I was determined to make the best of it.

The next day I went on a baking spree before I had even unpacked everything. I fixed oatmeal cookies, a cheesecake, and of course some pecan pie. Ricky was real mad because I packed it all up before he had a chance to get any. Me and Nikki used it to introduce ourselves to our neighbors. It was the right thing to do as my daddy would say. By our third stop we were kinda getting tired. Everybody wanted to know what Ricky did, how long we had been together, and stuff like that. It was tiring so when we ended up at Anise Buckley's house, I sank into her sofa like a rock and had no plans to get up. She was a young girl, like me. She lived with her grandmama who looked so old she could've been a passenger on the Underground Railroad. Turns out she was Anise's mama's grandmama. She never left her wheelchair and every so often barked at Anise to change the channel on the TV.

"Mama, you want some of these here cookies?" Anise asked. She had already ate like five of them. She was moving on to the pieces of pecan pie. "Here try them. They real good." The old woman kinda grumbled but she bit off a small piece and then a bigger one. "She like it. She not gone say it, but she do."

Their living room was so dark I thought it was night the first few minutes I was there. The only light came from two places—a sliver where the curtains met and the TV screen. The curtains were drawn and the furniture was some dark print that might have been flowers years and years ago.

I recognized a few of the characters on the TV and realized it was my favorite soap opera. "You watch the stories on channel two? Me too."

"Mama, you hear her talking to you? I'm sorry. She don't hear too good. You made all this yourself?"

"Mmhmm."

Anise was making herself a nice pile of cookies and pie pieces in one hand, and sampling the cheesecake with the other. I don't know why I ain't pick up on it from the beginning. Anise was hungry. And not in that hungry for dessert way. She was hungry.

"You can have as much as you want."

"Don't you wanna take some of it to the other folks?" Her hand stopped in midair then snatched back to the pile on her lap, covering it to keep it safe. "I ain't mean to take so much."

"No, it's fine. You go ahead. I been all over the neighborhood already. I guess folks watching their figures. You see, I ain't got that problem. I'm already big as a house."

She smiled at me and took one more wedge of cheesecake. I felt bad I ain't bring no real food but figured sweets was better than nothing. I didn't know why she was so hungry or where their food was. I ain't ask. I just got up to go and accidentally left the basket of sweets on the floor near the sofa. Ricky wasn't too happy about that. Said the basket cost him two dollars. But that was it. Wasn't much he could say. And that's how I handled it. He wasn't too interested in the housekeeping and cooking and stuff. He just wanted supper on the table when he got home. Wanted food he liked to eat the way he liked it. So when I could I would fix a little extra and ask Anise to sample it for me. She must have thought I was the most forgetful girl on the block, because after she was done sampling, I always forgot to take the rest of it home. By that time I was so full of baby, folks let me get away with everything. Ricky had to carry me up the stairs every night. They were so steep that it was like climbing a mountain I suspect. It was almost romantic.

"Look at you, looking like a princess!" He'd cry as soon as we cleared the first step. "I got me a real live princess. What's your name, sweetness?"

"Elizabeth Taylor," I'd say in real dramatic fashion and throw my head back like I'd seen them do in the movies. He loved that.

"You cool?" he'd ask while turning the fan toward the bed.

We had a huge bed that reminded me of the little monsters that sit on top of castles on account of the ugly faces carved into the posts. I'd lie there, trying to figure out if they were human or animal, dog or cat.

A month or two had gone by since we moved in before he said, "I left word at the Sears on Madison so you can go on down there and pick out some furniture. On credit. Don't go all crazy now."

"What kinda furniture?"

"Whatever."

I actually got giddy at the idea. I had free rein to pick what I liked. Ricky never asked me what I liked. But this was even better than him asking. I started crying.

"There you go with that woman stuff again. What? You don't wanna go down there by yourself? Want me to find somebody to go with you?"

"N-N-No."

"Then what's the problem? Stop all that damn crying. What you got to be crying about? Huh? Got you this nice house...so...stop crying. You making me feel funny."

❦

I WANDERED FROM ONE living room set to the next. Leather...suede... plaid...I even saw a sofa in the shape of somebody's lips. And big flaming lamps with all sorts of things stuck to them. Then there was the rigid looking pieces, made of all white with a little gold thrown in around the edges. I was lost. Nikki thought they were all toys. The brighter it was, the more she wanted to touch it. The more something moved or had moving parts, the more she wanted to play with it.

"Need some help, girl?" Her name tag read Helen E. She ain't look like a Helen. She wore an electric blue miniskirt with bright green tights and her legs just kept on going from the floor up until they reached the green swatches across her eyes. I never saw anybody with green paint across they eyes before. "You look lost."

"I am I guess."

"Whatcha looking for, honey?"

"Furniture."

"That's good. Because we got a lot of that. What kinda furniture? You don't look like you into the latest and most fashionable."

I smiled even though I was embarrassed pretty tough. I had a new dress that would've changed her mind but I'd only worn it a few times before I'd outgrown it.

Helen leaned into me, taking my arm to apologize. "I'm sorry, honey. That ain't come out right. You see that couple over there?" She asked and pointed to a tall thin man with platforms and bell bottoms. Both him and his old lady had the same shoes on. There were little bitty fish swimming in them. "They wanted to snatch up every black light and lava lamp we got. Like they ain't never heard of going overboard. But anyway...who's this? She yours?"

Nikki wrapped herself around Helen's legs and looked up at us like she was sure to get some extra love or something.

"I'm sorry! Nikki, stop that."

"Oh it's fine."

"No, she can't just be running up to folks and grabbing them like that. Nikki, stop."

As it turned out Helen had family from the same corner of Mississippi that I was from. She had only gotten down there a few times but that was better than nothing. We wandered around the chairs and sofas, chatting about the way things were changing and she steered me away from the pieces folks came back in to complain about. Nikki helped us test out each piece, and by the end of it all, I'd told Helen all about Ricky and our life together. Well not everything, just the stuff you'd tell folks when you don't want them to pity you.

"What he look like? I've probably seen him walking up and down the street here."

"Um...about yay tall. Wide shoulders. He got real pretty eyes and that straight wavy kinda hair like he permed it only he didn't. Most folks think he mixed or something."

"I bet. You two must be something together."

"I guess."

"You should get the dining set over there. The one with the skinny legs. I had a customer come by once and say it looked sexy. You believe that? Sexy furniture. These people...I tell you. There's no less than a hundred types of crazy in this world. Now, we got some real nice dishes and stuff that'll go with it."

"I want red."

"Whatcha say, honey?"

"Red. You got red dishes? I always...kinda liked the color red. You think that's too much to eat off of?"

"N'all. I think that's hot. Come on, let me write all this stuff down."

"And um...maybe we could get a chandelier to go over the table. I see a lot of folks have them."

"Sure thing, sweetie. What else you want?"

It was like the flood gates opened. I couldn't stop. Matching chairs, un-matching chairs, I needed them both. Beds to go in all the bedrooms. Two sofas, well three if you count the one I got to go in my bedroom. But it was a real small one, just the tiniest cutest little thing I ever saw! Lamps, lights to go in the ceiling, rugs...by the time we'd finished Helen had invited me out for drinks. She said because of me she was going on vacation and the least she could do was take me out for a few drinks.

"I'll wait until you done with this here." She grinned and swirled her index finger in the general direction of my stomach. "But don't take too long."

And I didn't. Two days later Mya Ann Morrow made her appearance. Ricky was in the ring but he came right after. His face was puffy and bruised but not too bad. He said I should've seen the other guy. I ain't need to, I could imagine. He slumped down in a chair and yanked his sweater over his head. Said it was hot. That was the beginning. He complained about the heat, about the sheets, he complained that the nurses kept coming in and bothering me. Then he demanded a private room.

"Mr. Morrow, we don't have any other rooms available."

"Yeah you do! I know you do! You just don't wanna give it up! And how long it take for the doc to take a look at her anyway? Huh? What you doing to my baby?" Ricky got like that after a fight, especially when he thought he could've done better. Knocked the guy out in three rounds instead of four.

The poor nurse was quivering in her boring white shoes. "I'll go and s-s-see."

I felt bad for her but I wasn't about to get in it. I'd just pushed a human out of my body. I needed my rest. "Ricky, baby, calm down." He cut his eyes at me and then dragged himself to my bedside. "She just doing her job."

"I wanna see my kid. Don't you wanna see her? She yours too."

I did wanna see her but not with the same hardness that he

did. I got the feeling if he ain't see her in about ten minutes he would go on a rampage, checking each one of the hospital rooms for her. I don't know if he thought somebody had stolen her or what, but I just nodded. When they finally brought her to us silence filled the room. It was like watching some kinda miracle. He ain't wanna give her up. He wrapped his sweater around her like the blanket wasn't enough and grinned like a man gone insane.

"She look like me, don't she?"

"I don't know. I can't really see."

"She look like me. Look at her. She got my hair. My lips." He dug around in the blanket a bit and lifted his pointer finger to show me the tiny hands that clung to it. "And she got my hands. Fighting hands. She's a fighter, just like her daddy. Ain't that right, Mya? Open your eyes so I know you hear me."

"They don't do that right away."

"She gone do it. Come on, girl."

"Ricky, come on. Let me hold her."

"Not until she open her eyes. I'm gonna be the first person she sees. She'll do it. Watch."

Only I couldn't. All I could see was his sweater and some blankets. He walked toward me like he might just give her up but stopped when they were still outta reach. The nurse came back and gave me a sympathetic look. I'd get her soon enough, or least that's what I thought. As soon as she started crying he'd hand her over. He was like that with Nikki. Couldn't stand the sound of a baby crying. I yawned and suddenly the hospital bed felt just a bit more comfortable. I moved around until I found a good spot.

Next thing I knew the sunlight was tickling my eyelids. Ricky was in the chair, still holding her. I guess the nurses decided it was easier to give him his way and let him keep her.

"Hey, you awake. Look, look she opened her eyes. And she smiled at me. You believe that?"

4

Surprise

THE FIRST FEW WEEKS I tried real hard to be good to her, just like any mama would. Tried to get her to take my milk but she wouldn't. She'd fuss and fuss until we were both tired out. Doctor said she wasn't getting enough nutrition so he put her on formula. I remember standing in the examining room, watching him say it. She was still on the scale, crying so much Ricky finally picked her up. It should've been me to pick her up but I couldn't move. The doctor had this high voice that sounded like he was talking outta his nose. And he was saying it like it was something he said a hundred times a day.

"We will just put her on formula then. It's the same."

But it wasn't to me. What I have tits for if they weren't to feed my babies? I loved my babies. Loved them like I just knew my mama ain't love me. She probably never even thought to nurse me.

"I can do it. I wanna keep trying."

"Pecan, let it go. Now the doctor already done said it's the same."

So it was the same. I told myself that over and over, watching Ricky stick a bottle in her mouth. She took it every time. Took the bottle over me. On top of that wasn't nothing about her like me. She was a beautiful baby and smart too, everybody said it so I knew it was true. Other babies was just holding their heads up but not Mya. By six months she was scooting around and getting into everything, and I mean everything. When Nikki was a baby she always stayed close by, checking to make sure I was watching but Mya acted like I ain't even exist. If I put her down for a second she'd take off and end up somewhere we couldn't see her. But she was polite and all. She'd let me hold her, play with her a little, and then she'd take off again. I got to thinking maybe it was my fault since I'd tried to wish her away to begin with. Maybe she knew. By the time Ricky'd come home she'd be all pooped out so she'd just lie in his arms. I'd watch from a safe distance, hating him. She was my baby, or she was supposed to be anyway.

"Pecan, come on in here!"

Nikki'd already gone down but Ricky liked to stay up and watch TV with Mya. It was their alone time.

"Yeah?" I stood next to the television set, working a towel around a bowl to dry it. "Want me to put her to bed?"

"N'all I'll do it later. What's this here red mark on her foot?"

"I don't know."

He rested her tiny foot back onto his thigh and glared at me. Somehow I'd let something happen to his baby. I backed up through my day. What did I do? I baked a cake. Nikki had helped me with the batter.

"How you not know? What kinda mama don't know?"

I made a cake and then what? Then what? Ricky lifted her leg again and this time she stirred in his arms and for a second I thought he might get distracted but nothing could ever distract him from something like this. I wanted to get closer to get a better look, maybe get some clue as to what caused the mark, but my legs wouldn't move. My hands neither, they just held onto the towel and the bowl. I might as well have been a statue.

"Look like a splinter. Bring me some tweezers."

I did as I was told. I couldn't risk being still if he was going to give me a chance to redeem myself. I handed him my manicure set and watched real close as he eased the sliver of wood out. So gentle she ain't even wake up. I didn't know he could be that gentle.

"Where her socks? Why you ain't put no socks on her?"

"I…I did."

"Don't see them."

"She took them off."

He ain't believe me. If Mya could've talked he would've asked her if that was really what happened. Like I was making it up, lying just to cover up the fact that I was a bad mama. The sports announcer said something interesting so Ricky went back to watching the TV. I loved the TV. It gave me some peace and quiet. Ricky could sit in front of it for hours. Some nights that's all he did.

During the day I kept busy with chores and the girls and sometimes I'd run into other housewives at the grocer's and we'd chit-chat. Comparing notes on recipes and our kids. That's how I met Paula. She had two kids too and she was young like me. Paula and Helen, with her long legs and in your face make-up, were my only links to the outside world. If I ain't have them I don't know what I would've done. But Paula was more happy than the rest of us. Her husband worked at a bank and he was into backyard barbecues and stuff. Him and Ricky ain't really get along. But me and Paula's carts stood side by side and our kids giggled up and down the aisle as we caught up on what had happened in the last week. Mya was just about ten months by then and she started whining from her seat in the cart. I could tell she wanted to get down and run with the others. She was still too young but she kept at it until I took her out.

"So, I asked Harold about going dancing. You and Ricky should come with us this time. There's this real nice piano bar called Tuesday's."

"Tuesday's?"

"Yeah I know. It's kinda a weird name but they got live music. It'll be fun!"

"I'll ask him. Ricky like dancing and all but I don't know if he's gonna feel like it after training all day."

The sudden crack of bone against tile went through me something awful. I knew it was Mya before I even looked down the aisle. She was hollering up a storm and the other three kids stood around her in awe. Screaming bloody murder she was and the lump on her forehead grew with each passing second. The store manager came around and wanted to know why I wasn't watching her. I told him I was just right over there, that I was watching. He made a point to say that the floor wasn't wet and they weren't responsible and then asked me to make my purchases and leave.

"She just fall." Nikki said as we headed home. "Mama? She just fall."

I wasn't blaming her but she felt the need to defend herself. I'd explained to her that she was the big sister now, that she had to look out for the baby. I figured that way I could keep bad stuff from happening to Mya. But sometimes kids just fall.

I set the table for supper but ain't really expect Ricky to be home in time. I'd hoped I could get Mya down before he noticed the bump on her head. I was wrong. She ain't appear to be in any pain but he took one look at the red knot and chased me from the dining room to the kitchen to the living room.

"It was an accident! She just fell!" But he ain't wanna hear it. He'd made up his mind. I was a bad mama and I needed to be punished. "She's okay! Look at her, she's okay! Ricky, please—" I saw his fist pull back and I was desperate. So desperate that I told him the only thing I could think of. "I'm pregnant!" And I was.

A light might have went on somewhere behind his eyes but it wasn't enough to stop him. Twisting and turning to get out his reach, I landed right on the coffee table. Or right through it really. It was the type made of glass. The whole right side of my body was in hell and covered in tiny bleeding cuts. I tried to get up but my knee kept scraping on something sharp so finally I just gave up. I'm not sure how long I laid there before he got me up.

⁓

"You want another table? I just sold you one what...nine ten months ago!" Helen thought it was hilarious. "And what's with the shades, girl? There ain't no sun out. This is Chicago in November!"

I should've waited until she went on lunch and had someone else help me but I didn't. I strapped Mya into a stroller and told Nikki to stay close. I thought I could cover my limp by wearing pants but a few folks gave me curious looks already and now my best friend was. Maybe I wanted her to know.

"Can I get the same one?"

"Why you wanna get the same one? What's the point in that?"

"It broke."

"Oh well, girl, why you ain't just say so? You know they'll replace it or fix it or whatever. Just tell me what part broke."

"All of it."

"All of it? How you go and do that?"

I wanted to tell her I had help. That I had bruises and cuts that would never heal. But I didn't.

꙳

WHEN I GOT HOME Ricky was waiting and he wasn't alone. Aunt Clara was his daddy's sister. She was short and round but spoke her mind and spoke it clearly. She used to have a beauty shop back when she lived down South but it closed a few years before Ricky sent for her. She hugged the little ones first, making sure to comment on how much Mya looked like Ricky then came in to hug me.

"Pecan, don't like to be hugged, Auntie."

"Oh. Why not?"

"She just don't. She's going upstairs to lie down."

That was my cue. I took my time going up the stairs but tried not to wince too much. It was nice of Ricky to have his aunt come stay with us. I don't think that at the time he thought too much about what it would really mean. Aunt Clara never had kids, never got married. She said men were too much trouble. On top of all that, she wasn't the kinda woman to take no stuff neither. Thinking back on it, Ricky must have been real desperate to have an extra set of hands around the house.

Taking off my coat was such a chore I decided to lie down with my clothes on. I set my shades on the nightstand so they looked back at me. My left eye was swollen shut so I couldn't see outta it. Ricky had a way with the front door, a way of closing it and opening it that let me know it was him. And I knew he had to go to the gym so the sound of it clicking shut made sense. I lied there, listening to Aunt Clara playing with the girls and dozed off. When I woke up I smelt the most delicious smells.

"Hungry?" She stood at the door holding a tray of steaming food.

"Um..." I nearly broke my neck trying to get my shades back on.

Aunt Clara just set the tray on the foot of the bed and walked out. She came back when she was sure I was done, this time she brought a dishtowel soaked with ice cubes. "Let's take these off," she said, removing my shades. "What you really need is some meat but I'm gonna put this on your eye for a little bit. It's cold, now, so don't be shocked."

I didn't know what to say. I wanted to say something. "Thank you," squeaked out.

Aunt Clara was a gift from God. I'm sure she ain't know it but I did. I never missed having a mama, not really, not until I had Clara. The missing part ain't last too long, though, because I learned how to be a mama from watching her. Even though she didn't have kids she had a real mothering kinda way about her. Everybody around her couldn't help but feel loved. Folks in the neighborhood flocked to our kitchen door, asking for advice or just wanting somebody to pray with them. Clara would make them some coffee and light herself a cigarette at the kitchen table. Me and Nikki watched while she saved women from nosy neighbors and cheating husbands and bosses that treated them like they were made of steel. These women would come in crying or so angry they couldn't sit still. Clara had her way and they left just as calm as could be.

She had that effect on me and Ricky too. Over the next few months everything changed. Ricky ain't lay a hand on me except to be real loving. He made a point of taking me out a few times a month. Sometimes we'd go dancing. It was a real sight, me as big as I was. But he ain't seem to care so I ain't care. It was fun. Fun that we should've had before we got married. Yeah, only took a few months before Aunt Clara was a full-fledged member of our family and we were all loving on her. She had no plans to leave, not that we would've let her. She was teaching me to make butter beans the way Ricky's grandmama did and telling me all about the good old days when I came up with the name.

"Jackie."

"Jackie what, hun?" She always called me hun. Not honey, just hun. And sometimes she'd call me Pecan girl.

"I'ma name her Jackie."

She shuffled around the kitchen with a cigarette dangling from her lips, chuckling in the way that she did when she found something sorta funny, not all the way funny. "You done with them onions?"

"You don't like Jackie?"

"I likes it just fine. I see you done named Nikki, Nikki not Nicole. Jackie ain't a proper name. Jacqueline. Now that's what you put on the papers. Spell it real fancy like with a q."

I nodded. It was settled. I patted my belly, thinking about the little person that would soon be coming out. Wondering if she'd look like me or Ricky. I ain't really care I just wanted to be sure she would love me. I think I loved all my kids the same. Well I tried to anyway. But I'm pretty sure they didn't all love me the same. I just wanted one that I knew loved me. That ain't make me feel like I was inside out. I shut my eyes and tried to send all my love to my belly. If she felt it, maybe when she came out she'd be ready to give some of it back.

"Now how you gone finish chopping onions with your eyes closed?" Clara laughed at me and I felt warm all over. I was funny. I ain't know I was funny until Aunt Clara laughed at me. "Pecan girl, I tell you...God must have been feeling real good the day he made you." She exhaled a ring of smoke and her eyes danced all giddy like at me.

"Why you say that?"

"Because it's true. That's something my mama used to say when one of us did something particular that she found funny. I tell you about the time Ricky's daddy—my brotha—decided he was gone catch himself a chick-en?" I shook my head and waited for the story to begin. Nikki was sitting on my lap but she slid down to the floor, giggling at Clara's face, how she pronounced every syllable of the word. "Well, see, we lived on a farm. We had chick-ens but daddy said those was his chick-ens and he meant to sell them. Bobby Lee ain't like that. He got it in his head that he was going to have his own farm with his own chick-ens. Pass me them onions since you done with them." I met her at the stove and offered up my part a the meal. "Just go on and dump them in there."

"All of them?"

"Yeah, whatcha wanna save them for? Now Bobby Lee call himself sneaking into the chick-en coop to get an egg so he can have himself a chick-en. He got in there and all the chick-ens go crazy, flapping and quacking, feathers flying everywhere. They start attacking him with they sharp little beaks and he come out screaming, calling on Jesus to save him. Know what happened?"

"Nuh-uh."

"Daddy came outside, saw what he was up to, and he was about to get Bobby Lee good but he figured the chick-ens had already got him. The next day Bobby Lee went back to the chick-en coop. He said they were introduced now so there wasn't gone be no problems. Know what happened?"

"They attacked him."

"Yeah. Damn near put his eye out. My brotha wasn't too bright.

And he sure was hard-headed."

"He went back again?"

"Mama had to finally tell him, she say...Bobby Lee, you got to know when enough's enough. He couldn't ever tell when enough was enough. Did everything too much. Drank too much. Ate too much. Had too many women. Sung too damn loud. And he never hit the right keys!"

"Too bad Ricky never knew him."

"Who said he ain't never knew him?" She shook her head just once and flicked the stub of her cigarette into an empty soda can. "They ain't lived nothing but a few blocks from each other his whole life! Ricky mama and Bobby Lee was sweet on each other something terrible. Since they were real little. Hell, all of Biloxi knew that! Bobby Lee just ain't wanna sit still, if you know what I mean."

"Oh."

"He my brotha, the only one I got so you know I ain't gonna lie on him. He was the first one of us to...go on. Mama and daddy ain't know what to do. Ain't no parent supposed to bury their child."

"Guess not. Wish I could've met him."

"Yeah..." Clara gave me a firm kinda smile. "He would've liked you. You'd probably liked him. Wasn't many people that ain't like Bobby Lee."

"Ricky like that."

"N'all he not." Clara shook her head twice for good measure then went back to the beans. "They ain't nothing alike—Ricky and his daddy. For all his faults Bobby Lee was sweet."

Nikki stood on her tippy toes, demanding that I watch her be a ballerina. That's what they were teaching her in preschool. How to be a ballerina.

"Ricky's sweet, Auntie." Then as if to test my point Mya ran stumbling into the kitchen. My heart nearly stopped.

"Pecan girl, you okay? What is it? Is it the baby?"

"No, no, Auntie, I'm fine. I'm fine." I reminded myself that Ricky had changed. He hadn't even yelled at me in months. Things were good, perfect even.

≈

"Mmmm, Pecan, you feeling real good, baby." Ricky whispered in my ear. He told me that so much now that I was starting to feel it myself. "You hear me, baby?"

"Mmhmm." I sorta mumbled, afraid that Aunt Clara would wake up to the sounds of us making love.

Ricky ain't care. He'd do it with the door wide open. He'd get into bed butt-ass naked and wrap his leg over my hip. I'd seen two stray dogs do that once. If I was asleep he'd start off real slow and gentle like, moaning and groaning in my ear. Wanting me to remind him how he was my first and only. Sometimes he'd have me bend over the edge of the bed and he'd really go to town. At first I was worried about Jackie but the doctor said it shouldn't be a problem. I was kinda glad of that since I was starting to enjoy doing it a bit more. Paula said that was crazy, that she couldn't stand for her husband to touch her when she was pregnant. I agreed for the first two but something had changed. He was crazy about me, couldn't get enough, and I loved it. When we would finish he'd hold me close—squeezing my tit in one hand, the other hand planted firmly against my stomach.

"I been thinking. It's time for you to gimme a boy. You hear me, Pecan?"

"A boy?"

"Yeah, every man want himself a boy to carry on the family name. I think this one's my boy."

I hated to break it to him that I had my heart set in the other direction. That I had even named her already. "If it ain't...a boy, we could have one more. That one would most likely be a boy."

"N'all I want this one. This one right here is my boy."

5

New Woman

I WISH EVERY MAMA COULD know what it feels like to give life to somebody and watch them turn into the person you wanna be. That's what it was like for me with Jackie. I was never very outgoing or funny but she had it all. She was a one-person talent show! Sometimes we'd sit around and just watch her. Me most of all. I couldn't help it. I couldn't believe she came from me. From the time she was a baby she made the whole room about her. She'd cry and cry as soon as you looked away and giggle and wiggle as soon as you looked back. And she loved me. I could tell. She'd get so worked up at times and all she wanted was me. Even Clara couldn't calm her down and they were kindred spirits. I could tell that too from right off. She'd dress up in my clothes—purse and heels—and sing into a hairbrush until she was hoarse. And this was at four!

Clara would egg her on with "Ooo sing it, chile" and "Go on now, do it right." Clara loved soul music. Me and Ricky was more into what they call R&B but Clara was real specific. Not all R&B was soul music, she said. And not all blues was soul music neither. She'd put on her records as we were cleaning and Jackie'd get up on the sofa or a table and try to be heard over the vacuum. That's how her and Ricky got to be on opposite sides. He was watching the game one night, a playoff or series or something real important, and she got the itch to start singing.

I was in the kitchen with Clara and the baby. I'd had another one by that time. Another girl. Ricky was still mad at me about that. But I'd made up my mind not to have any more so the doctor gave me these pills. Ricky ain't know. It was best that way.

So, anyway the girls was running through the house the way they did on rainy days, playing some make-believe game when Jackie got it into her head that she felt like singing. She waited until a commercial but Ricky was never a very good audience. He'd sit there and listen, nodding along. Sometimes he'd tap his toes but that was about it. Jackie ain't care. She'd just sing louder. So when the commercial was over...she kept on singing. He probably told her to move, waving at my baby like she was a fly or something..."Move so I can see the TV!" he'd say. But Jackie was stubborn, just like him.

I ain't know it'd happened until afterward. Nikki came running in the kitchen all outta breath. "Daddy...daddy hit Jackie."

The walls started spinning and I swear I was moving in slow motion but they told me later I wasn't. It sure felt like it, though. When I got there...he couldn't even look at me. He sat on the edge of the sofa, his hands folded, and both eyes glued to the TV set. Jackie was lying on the floor next to it. She looked stunned more than anything. I ain't even see the blood dripping from the corner of her mouth until Clara picked her up.

"What'd you do?" I asked him. He was quiet. I moved closer and threw the dishtowel I was holding at him. "WHAT DID YOU DO?"

"She was in the way. I...I told her to move. I did. Tell your mama! Tell her how I warned you! Why she can't just sit down and be quiet? Huh? A man can't come home and just put his feet up and not be bothered by nobody?"

My breath ran straight out the room without so much as a word. My hands suddenly had a mind of they own. Went after him, they did. Screaming and scratching. I might have drawn blood, I ain't sure. I was crying so hard I got a headache right from the beginning. Then I heard the smack and felt the floor beneath me, brushing against my elbow. I wondered if that was what he did to my baby. He stood over me for what seemed like hours. Wanted to kick me I could read it all over him. But he stood there still, like a statue.

When I finally got up I understood why. Clara had run to the kitchen and returned holding the cast-iron skillet, still wet from the dishwater and each soapy drop took its time hanging off the skillet's rim. She was well into her fifties and with less strength than me so she had to hold it with both hands because it was that heavy. Swung it off to the side like she might let it rip against Ricky's head at any moment. Don't know what Ricky was expecting but he damn sure wasn't expecting that. Clara was his blood.

"Auntie?"

"Back on up, now." Was all she said to him.

For me, watching the two of them size each other up was like going to the zoo and seeing a tiger pause over its prey. Wasn't no reason for it. No natural reason. No physical reason. But Ricky did as she said, glaring at me as he walked around the coffee table and into the hallway. She may have been his blood but she was mine. My aunt

Clara.

That's how our truce came to an end. Me and Ricky's. Five years of peace gone. It scared me but not like before. Maybe because he looked at me like he ain't know me. Like I wasn't the same seventeen-year-old girl he'd married so I believed I wasn't. I was twenty-five years old by then. And I was mad.

⟪⟫

HELL, THE MORE I loved my baby, the more mad I got. She was so easy to love, Jackie was. And I ain't see no parts of Ricky in her. Made me think that I had some good in me. Especially when she'd look at me with those eyes like she was watching something important—everything I said or did it was all of a sudden important. And when she didn't understand it or just didn't agree she let me know.

"Mama, how come you always inside? You afraid of outside?" She asked when she should've been playing with the bubbles in the bathtub like Mya. "Mama, outside is fun."

I answered by cleaning her ears and saying something like, "I'm real glad you like it."

"You can come with me. I'll show you. We got a spot out back where we princesses. You can be one too."

Mya jerked around and the bathwater went in the opposite direction. She shushed Jackie, like it was a club that belonged to just them. But I ain't mind. My girls had each other. I had always wanted a sister. I was glad I'd had them so they could have each other. It was about this time that I figured something out. Nikki was always hanging around the outskirts of things. She watched me just as much as Jackie but for some reason I ain't notice it until right then. It was kinda like remembering something I used to know but over the years I just forgot.

Like a part of me shut down and some things just disappeared. Things that had to do with her. She was leaning against the doorway, looking all sad and I just knew I had to make it up to her.

⁂

"Why not?"

"Later, baby."

"Why you not wanna hear me sing?" Jackie pouted.

Clara rocked back and forth in her rocker, threading a needle. She was always knitting something. This time it looked like something for the baby. "See. Your baby went and got all up in my LPs. She been stuck on Ms. Aretha for a good hour. Got it down pretty good." Clara chuckled a bit, looking at Jackie jumping up and down just bursting with the new song.

"Two minutes, okay? I just wanna talk to Auntie for a second. Y'all go play."

They went but the only one that really wanted to go was Mya. She took off and ain't look back. I could feel Clara looking at me and looking at Nikki and wondering what was going on.

"Go on now. Tell your sisters to stay in the front yard." Clara said it since she could see I was having trouble finding the words. The screen door closed and she lowered the needle and thread.

"Auntie...?"

"Yeah."

"You think something wrong...with Nikki? Think she happy?" Happy suddenly seemed like a reach so I corrected myself. "Think she okay?"

"What you mean? She a kid."

I ain't see no other kids moping around the house, dragging they feet to and from school. And I couldn't remember the last time I'd seen my girl laugh.

"Oh, she fine chile. Don't go worrying about things you can't control. Nikki be just fine. She just gotta find her place is all."

I nodded. Clara knew stuff that I didn't. I guess because she'd seen more, lived more. So, I trusted her opinion about things and I felt a little better about it all. But it still came down to me messing up. I wasn't as good a mama as I should've been. Wasn't as good as Nikki needed. She'd always wanted more of me than I was able to give. That's what ran through my head while we were fixing supper. I started to say something to Clara, see what she thought of that. But I kept still instead.

See, Ricky never had to try too hard to convince me that it was all my fault. I just knew. Me and him was my fault. Anything that happened with the kids was my fault. I knew deep in my bones that was the way it was. That I made him mad, made him hit me. I was still making him hit me by not loving him...not being a good enough mama. Maybe I just wasn't built to be a good wife and mama. Maybe I was just like my own mama. I leaned down on the knife to make it slice through the carrot nicely and ended up choking back tears.

Clara started yelling and shoved my hand under running water. "What's wrong with you, girl? You trying to cut your finger off?" She bandaged me up real good like always and handed me the chopping knife again, this time real slow like. Her eyes burned caution into mine. We finished supper but it was all a blur to me.

"Pecan need a night out." Clara announced over supper that night. Ricky looked at me to see if he was being set up. But nobody was more surprised than me. "She need to go out with her girlfriends. Women need to have women time." Clara explained it like wasn't no choice in the matter. It was just a fact.

"What I'm supposed to do about that, Auntie? She wanna go out? I ain't stopping her."

"Good. Then you pick a night. A night when you ain't got a fight and you ain't gone be training. A night so you can be home with your babies while Pecan go out. I'll be here but I ain't gonna be around forever. You they daddy. You can act like it."

"I wanna go too." Jackie's legs swung so hard under the table that she almost fell right off her chair. I know she had no idea what going out meant but in her mind it was something exciting. "Can I? Can I go out too?"

"No, you can't go. I said her girlfriends. You not a girlfriend, you a chile."

"But my mama need me. How she gonna have fun if I'm not there?"

"She's gonna manage just fine."

Jackie looked so confused that I got tickled. She just couldn't wrap her mind around it. Like I never had any fun until she came around.

As I was getting myself together for bed I kept thinking about it. A night out with the girls. I hadn't had one in a long while. Helen had gotten married and divorced and I'd only met the man once. I was sure she'd be up for a night on the town. We'd go dancing for sure. Never could tell with Paula, though. She only had two kids but they ran her ragged. She ain't have an Aunt Clara.

"So I guess you real excited, huh?" Ricky came in and I could smell the toothpaste from the other side of the bed. "Going out with the girls..."

"Well, it'll be nice."

"Don't let me stop you." He yanked the covers up. "Just don't go thinking you gonna make a habit of it. If I wanted somebody that was gonna be running out to the clubs I wouldn'tve married you. And don't go thinking you like all them girls you see shaking they asses on the dance floor."

"Course not."

"What?" He snapped, sensing the tiniest bit of sarcasm in my voice. "What you say?"

I ain't answer fast enough because he pushed me so hard I rolled right off the bed and hit my head on the nightstand. Not hard enough to draw blood but the tears came anyway. I ain't want him to see so I tried to keep my head down.

"You crying? You ain't gotta be crying. You wouldn't be crying if you knew how to show a little bit of gratitude. Instead of trying to be smart."

"I'm not."

"You what? What you say?"

"I said I'm not!"

He ain't say anything else, just looked down at me over the edge of the bed. We'd gotten so good at it, he ain't even need to say nothing for me to get the warning. So, I got up. Careful to not look him in the eye because that usually got him more riled up.

"You done got Auntie all worried about you, poor Pecan. Ain't nothing wrong with you. But go on and go out with your friends, just don't go losing your mind." I nodded and took the covers in one hand. "What you doing? Ain't you got something to say?"

I was getting back in bed. I ain't think that needed explaining. But when he snatched the covers outta my hand and moved onto my side of the bed every bit of my body said to move back. Move back. Away. Move away. So, I stood against the closet and watched as he got comfortable. Real comfortable.

"Where I'm supposed to sleep?"

"Look like I care? Since you don't appreciate what I do for you, maybe you should sleep your ass outside."

My mouth dropped open. It was forty degrees outside so he couldn't of meant it, I told myself. He was just trying to make a point. "I'm sorry...sorry I ain't appreciate you."

"And don't you go running to Auntie, talking about I'm being mean to you. I don't wanna hear it! What's between a man and wife, stay between that man and that wife. Here." He tossed me a pillow. "Sleep on the floor. It's good for you."

The floor was cold and hard but it was better than outside. And knowing Ricky, he wanted me to think there was all kinds of things waiting in the dark outside. Wanted me to see the favor he was doing for me. To know that he loved me so much he gave me the floor.

6

Dancing Fool

I HAD EVERYTHING LAID OUT neatly on the bed. Stockings...my newest dress...my best shoes. I had gone back and forth a few times on the outfit. It was like I'd been waiting for this my whole life, like I hadn't been anywhere ever. It ain't make sense. One night. Just one night of freedom and I damn near lost my mind.

"Let me do it."

"No! You don't know what you're doing!" Nikki grabbed the make-up pencil right outta Jackie's hand, starting World War Three. "You too little!"

Three words I knew Jackie hated. But wasn't anything I could do about it. It was Nikki's brand new mantra when it came to her little sister. Clara said they couldn't help it. That they were destined to get on each other's nerves. Said most folks would've thought it would've been Jackie and Mya going at it all the time because they were so close in age, but Mya ain't like no parts of any kinda drama so that messed up the true order of things.

"LET ME DO IT! I'M GONNA MAKE MAMA PRETTY!"

Jackie ain't know anything about make-up. Hell she couldn't have because I'd just learned a little bit about it myself. I hadn't gotten as far as some girls with using a bunch of color. I ain't wanna over-do it and look like a fool. Anyway, just looking at my dress was enough to make me blush. Aunt Clara picked it out. She said I was letting all my God-given gifts go to waste. That there wasn't no shame in a girl being proud of being a girl. Then she marched right up to the salesgirl and made me buy it. Deep dark red like blood. Shorter than anything I ever had. I was wearing stockings with it because I felt so naked.

"Let-Let me go!" Nikki fell off the bed with Jackie clinging to her back like a chimpanzee or something. "Mama, get her off of me!"

"Nikki stop fighting with your sister. She just a little girl."

"She the one on top of me!"

They rolled one way then the other. I had to get out the way fast or they would've rolled right over my feet. Nikki was all outta breath but Jackie couldn't stop laughing. She was having the time of her life.

"Okay. I'm ready." I announced to the whole family a little while later. They were all crowded in front of the TV set.

"Oooo, chile. Turn around. Turn around." Clara demanded. I spun around in a circle, feeling like a princess. "Now that is a dress!"

"Yeah?"

"Girrrl."

"Mama, you look real pretty!"

And I did. I was sure I did. I found a picture of Diana Ross and copied her hair real good. Even went out and bought some cheap earrings that looked like hers. I could've passed for one of them girls who was always up to the latest fashions. Well...probably. Ricky looked me up and down with big snoopy dog eyes. He was eating a bowl of rice and a chicken leg. He stopped with the meat hanging just shy of his tongue.

"What time Helen coming to get you? She better hurry it up or else you gone be busy." Clara smirked, seeing exactly what I saw. "Ricky. Give Pecan some money so she can get herself something to drink."

He handed me a five dollar bill. He was just dying to ask if I was going to be drinking something other than a Shirley Temple but he was too set on giving me the silent treatment.

"Thanks."

"Mama, I'm gonna go with you."

Clara sighed and repositioned herself in her chair. She was getting real tired of Jackie's hard-headedness. But all I could think was nobody was going to tell my baby she couldn't have what she wanted. Nobody was ever gonna make her do something she ain't wanna do.

Helen's horn beeped and butterflies went up and down my arms before going to town in my belly.

"Ready?" Helen asked as I squeezed in the back seat of her itty bitty car. Paula was already snapped into the passenger seat.

"Ready."

<hr/>

THE SMOKE WEIGHED A ton. It pressed down on our chests, squeezing between us and our sweat. Everywhere I turned folks was just plain old having a good time. And the drinks just kept coming. They came outta nowhere. I'd blink and Helen was handing me another one. They were cold and sweet, the only salvation in the steamy hot club, so I sucked them all down, one by one. After a while Paula dragged me into the washroom. The door swung open and closed in one creaky, swift motion. The three stalls were already taken. The blue paint on their doors was in definite need of a touch up but it'd been long forgotten by somebody.

"Pecan! Girl, you hear me?"

I was sure I did. I think I nodded.

"Oooo, she done had enough!" Another voice said from somewheres up high. I know because I started looking for it and all I saw was the light flickering over my head.

"Pecan!"

The door to one of the stalls opened and I got to see just how tight it was. Got to see up close and personal like. Diana Ross was the last thing on my mind as I fell to my knees in front of the toilet. Paula helped me to my feet and somebody splashed some water in my face. About a minute later it all came clear. The voice from up high was Helen. She was wiping my face like I was a baby who'd just spit up. Don't know why but it was all of a sudden so funny. So funny I couldn't stand up straight.

"Girrl, what're we gonna do with you?"

Next thing I knew we were all laughing so hard girls was giving us the eye for taking up so much precious space in the washroom.

"You the only girl I know who wait until she married with four kids to go out and party!" Helen stood up against the door, holding it open so we could make our exit. "I guess we gotta keep an eye on you, huh?"

As soon as she said it some guy came over and swept her off to the dance floor. Helen wasn't the girl to turn any man down. She'd dance with anybody because of the idea that you never know who Prince Charming is gonna be. Me and Paula made our way to a part of the room that wasn't so crowded, a dark corner off of the dance floor. The air tasted a bit salty over there.

"I didn't think Ricky was gonna let you come out."

"Huh?"

"I didn't think Ricky was gonna let you come out!"

I pointed to my ear like I couldn't hear her and went back to sucking the life outta my Shirley Temple. Last thing I wanted to talk about on my night of freedom was him. I ain't even wanna talk about my kids. I was all set to pretend like I didn't even have them. That's when I saw him. Slender and graceful like a deer or something, he came through the crowd and I must have gasped because Paula looked at me then looked at him and back at me. "You know him?"

"No." I tried not to look directly at him but he was getting closer so it was getting harder not to see him.

"Well, he looking at you like he knows you."

The thought made me smile. Wasn't right but it did. Some man I ain't know wanted to get familiar with me. He stood in front of me saying nice things but I knew what he was really saying. I should've gotten mad, maybe I should've slapped him. But I danced with him instead. He wasn't a bad dancer but he wasn't a good one neither. Not that it mattered. He spent more time trying to strike up a conversation than he did trying to keeping on beat. But I ain't mind. He had real solid eyes, like rocks, like real solid rocks. He knew stuff. I could just tell he knew stuff. Stuff that I was dying to know. He asked me if I paid attention to politics and what I thought of this actor that thought he could be president. He must have been nervous because he ain't wait for me to answer before rattling on about some debate. His long bony fingers slid down my back and I forbid the smile that was just itching to show itself.

"You're a good dancer." The rock eyes said. "What's your name, dancing queen?" He grinned and I could see that one of his front teeth was shorter than the others, not that I cared enough to think on it too long.

"Pecan."

"Pecan? What kinda name is that? Your people named you after a nut?"

Smart and funny. It took me a second to wrap my head around that. "Belinda. Nobody really calls me that but...that's my name."

"People call me Heziah."

"Hezikiah? Like in the bible?"

"No, Heziah. Like...without the k."

The music slowed down and Heziah pulled me in. He held me soft like, like he was dancing with a loaf of bread and he ain't wanna squish it. Like I was precious. By the end of the second song, I ain't wanna leave. I was dying to be squished. I kept hoping that somebody would bump into us and close the gap but it never happened. Was probably best, though. What I need with some man treating me like that? Some gentle man who ain't know how to dance?

"What's wrong?"

"Nothing." Soon as I said it, I knew it was a lie. A straight out lie. That's when I saw him. Outta the corner of my eye. He was dancing like a grown man with nasty things on his mind. Dancing with some chick that wasn't his wife. I knew his wife.

"Who's that?" Heziah asked, looking where I was looking.

"My neighbor."

"Oh."

"He got a wife and that ain't her. Got a wife and two kids."

"That bothers you, huh? A married man dancing with a woman?" Heziah's grin came back, this time threatening to turn into fun for the both of us. "Guess you think married people aren't supposed to be dancing with people they're not married to, huh?" His hold on my hand shifted until he was mostly holding on to one of my fingers. The one with my wedding ring on it. "Is that right, Belinda?"

"I guess."

"Maybe it's innocent. Maybe she's just his friend."

I had friends. We ain't hump all over each other like they were doing. Like two dogs in heat, they were. Might as well got them a room somewhere and kept the rest of us outta it. Heziah was laughing at me by then so I tried not to stare at my nasty neighbor no more.

"You two know each other well?"

"Hmm?"

Heziah looked back over there but I kept on looking at him because my nasty neighbor wasn't getting no more of my attention. "They're gone," he said. "He took one look at you and took off running! Guess you really do know his wife, huh?"

"They live two houses over."

"What's she like?"

"His wife?"

"Yeah. I'm curious now. Sometimes people find the need to go looking for what they don't have at home. Sometimes...it's not so much a choice as it is a need. Everybody has needs, Belinda. Being married don't necessarily fill everything up."

"You married?"

"Me? No." Heziah shook his head and the fun that was on his lips left suddenly, leaving sadness behind. "I was...married. About two years ago. Now I'm divorced."

"You cheat on her?" I probably shouldn't of asked him that. But seeing as we probably wasn't gonna see each other again, I did.

One of the girls from the bar came around with a tray full of tiny glasses. Heziah took one and damn near swallowed it whole. "Want a shot?"

"No, thanks."

"You sure?" He folded a few bills on the tray and put the empty glass down on top of it. "My treat."

"You want me to get you something else, honey?" The girl asked, handing somebody behind her a few glasses. Whatever was in them swished so much she had to lick it from her fingers. "What you want? Rum? Vodka?"

I ain't want nothing. I shouldn't of had the few drinks I did. The girl looked from me to Heziah like she ain't believe me.

"Thank you, miss, but I think she's made up her mind. We'll let you know if things change."

She shrugged and went about her business. Heziah went back to looking at me. But wasn't no fun in his eyes. Looked the same as one of my kids did when they were about to get caught doing something they ain't have no business doing. Guilty. He looked guilty. I was right. He was a cheater. All men were probably cheaters.

"So where's your wife now?"

"She's not...not my wife anymore."

"Right..." I ain't have no right to be disappointed. So what if he was just a regular kinda man. Kind that cheated on his wife. That come up to a married woman, tell her how pretty she is and ask her to dance. I should've known.

"See somebody else you know?" Heziah asked, trying to see

where I was looking.

"Just looking for my girlfriends. We came together."

"Girls night out, huh?" When I ain't answer he started dancing in the other direction, turning us in a circle. Damn near knocked the couple next to us to the ground. "Oh! I'm sorry, man. Miss? I'm sorry," he said. I don't know if it was one of the colored lights that was shining out on the dance floor or if his face really was that red. They glared at him then moved out the way. "Guess I'm not too good at this."

"You fine."

"You're just being nice. Dancing's never been my thing. I just had to find a way to get you away from your girlfriend."

"Why's that?"

His eyes got real big and he swallowed so hard it looked like a ping pong ball just rolled down his throat. "Well...why does any man wanna dance with a pretty girl?" That wasn't nowhere near the right thing to say. He caught on a little bit after I did and started stuttering and stammering something awful. "I...I just mean that y'all run the world. Have us doing whatever you please if it means you'll give up one of them smiles. Make a man feel good about life to have the affection of a good-looking woman. But I apologize. I didn't know about your... um, that you're married."

"You apologize?"

"Yeah, I didn't mean any disrespect. If you want to go back to your friends, I understand."

Through the bodies on the dance floor I caught a glimpse of Paula standing exactly where I left her. She was smiling and doing her best to be polite to some man who was kind enough to ask her to dance. Let him down easy, she did. Not like me. No, I had to go and say yeah.

"Belinda?"

"I'm fine. With you. I'll just...stay here with you."

I ain't wanna believe it but there it was, the truth. In that dark smoky club, I'd found it. The one man that wasn't a horny devilish mess. Heziah Jenkins was what my daddy called an honorable man.

7
The Affair

"L EAVE YOUR MAMA ALONE!" Clara stood in the doorway, waiting for the girls to leave my bedside. "She ain't had nothing but a few hours of rest. How you feel if somebody come and wake you up after your head just hit the pillow? Now go on downstairs."

"It's okay. I'm up."

"N'all. Now go on back to sleep."

Clara disappeared and so did my little ones. All I needed was to hear her voice and the front door closing to know she got Nikki and Mya off to school. I yawned and stretched my body as far out as it could go. I still had on my dress from the night before but my earrings hadn't made it home with me. For the life of me I couldn't remember what happened to them. I remembered the trip to the washroom...the dance floor...and...Heziah.

Ricky was nowhere to be found but that was normal. He got up and out the door just before sunrise. He had a fight coming up in a few weeks that if he won would move him to the next division he said. It was the second time in his career he'd gotten close to it. Last time he choked against a weaker guy. That's how he'd put it. He just ain't wanna admit that somebody could beat him at something, could be more trained, more talented. He wouldn't even think it was possible.

"What you smiling about?" Clara came back, with a smile of her own at the sight of mine. "You have fun last night?"

"I think so."

"You think so? How you not gonna know, hun? You had that much fun? That you don't even remember?" I nodded and she kissed me on the head. A wet, brisk kiss. "It feel real good to live life, don't it? Instead of just letting it pass you by."

"Yeah."

I kept that feeling all the way through breakfast. We sat in the kitchen, sipping our coffee and keeping still. I gave Natalie her bottle even though she was getting to the age that she was more interested in what we were drinking than what I had for her.

"So you girls had yourselves a good time, huh?"

"Sure did, Auntie. We danced and drank..."

"Ooo, look at you! Guess you had a little more than them Shirley Temples you used to." Clara pushed her empty cup of coffee to the side, letting her bosom ease over the edge of the table. "You ain't buy all your own drinks did you?"

"No, Auntie."

"Good girl. You and Ricky been together so long you ain't have no chance to explore what life got to offer. Ain't nothing wrong with flirting with it every now and then."

I ain't know what to say to that, just nodded and tried to focus on Nat. The night before was over. I was back to being just a married woman. Good thing too. Wasn't no smoke trying to weigh me down and men trying to feel me up. Just me and my girls. Was better that way. What kinda mama would I be if I went looking for something outside my front door?

Jackie took up her usual spot in front of the TV set, explaining to her baby sister exactly what was happening on Sesame Street. She knew all the characters by name and thought that Nat should too. Nat wasn't yet a year but she was crawling and sitting up. If left alone, she'd crawl to wherever her sisters were and watch everything they did. I was lucky that Nat was a pretty easy baby. She ain't cry too much. She slept the right amount. The only thing was she looked nothing like Ricky. Ain't bother me none but I could tell it bothered him. She was darker than me, darker than anybody in his family, and when she was born he looked at her then looked at me. I thought he was gonna accuse me of stepping out on him. And on top of everything else, she was a girl. I guess I thought he'd get over it, get on to loving her like he should've. I was wrong. But he ain't have to love her. His love wasn't nothing to go calling home about no way. She was my baby and I loved her.

We had started cleaning the dishes when the phone rang. I didn't think much of it. Just kept rinsing and drying and humming to myself. Then Clara squinted at me and held out the phone. "It's for you."

From the second I heard his voice my heart went pitter patter in my chest. I nodded hello like he was standing in front of me, afraid that I'd give it all away by the sound of my voice. He asked me if I could talk and I muttered something that sounded like yeah. The phone cord stretched all the way across the kitchen so I went back to washing the dishes. Wasn't long before I ran outta dishes. Clara just stood there, watching me with that curious look she had. "I gotta go."

He wanted me to meet him for lunch. Said he couldn't stop

thinking about me, he wanted to see me, talk to me. But I couldn't do that. What would folks say? No good was gonna come outta meeting up with some man. He asked me again and I ain't say nothing. But he gave me his number anyway and I scribbled it on a piece of paper and hung up the phone.

"Mama." I damn near jumped outta my skin. Jackie stood at the table with both hands on her baby hips. "Next time you go out I'm going with you. Okay?"

I agreed. And two days later I told Aunt Clara I was taking Jackie and Nat out to lunch and to the park. Nat was still too little to get much use of slides and sandboxes but she liked the outside air alright. We went to the food counter at Woolworth's. Jackie loved it. She wanted a big milkshake and a plate full of fries. I ordered both for her just to see if she'd actually finish it. She sat up like a big girl and did me proud. All the ladies said how ladylike she was. I couldn't take the credit. I'd tried to tell her that her dress shoes shouldn't be worn to the park but she was so hard-headed. She wore them around the house same as I wore slippers. I even caught her wearing them to bed once or twice.

After lunch, we walked the few blocks to the park. I saw him before he saw me. I stopped dead in my tracks. What was I doing? Using my kids as chaperones? If Ricky ever found out ...

"Belinda!"

Too late to back out. He wore a tan corduroy suit that barely fit him. He took my hand and laid a quick kiss on my cheek before checking out our chaperones.

"Don't kiss my mama. She my mama."

"Well, I'm a friend of your mama's. Nice to meet you, little lady." Jackie shook his hand like she'd done it a million times before. "You can call me Heziah. Can you say that?"

"Yeah."

But she ain't try. Her mouth twisted to one side like she was thinking real hard on it. The laughter from the other kids drew her eye and off she went. We sat on a nearby bench, me and Heziah. I kept an eye on Jackie and a foot on the stroller, rocking Nat until I was sure she was asleep.

"She's cute. They both are."

"Thanks."

"I got kids." He gave it up like it was common knowledge and stretched one arm along the bench behind me. "They live with their mama in Cleveland. I don't get to see them much anymore."

"Oh." I couldn't think of anything else to say to that.

"A boy and a girl. Hazel and Louis, both teenagers. Folks say they look like me but I'm not sure I see it. Besides being lanky as all get-out, I mean. They definitely got that from me! They...um...well they're good kids. Smart. Good to people. What else can you ask for? Right?"

"I guess."

Heziah tugged lightly at the ends of my hair. It tickled a bit so I was squirming around trying to get out of it. That was real funny to him. "Why you always wiggling around like a worm on a hook? If you want me to stop, just say 'Heziah stop that.' And I'll stop. See." He showed me both his hands so I would know it wasn't a trick. "Speak up, Belinda. How are people gonna know you're there if you don't speak up."

"MAMA, WATCH ME!"

A giggling Jackie ran up the steps and flew down the slide. She made it to the bottom then surprise flooded her face when nobody was there to congratulate her. She ran to the edge, to the border of all the woodchips, and just looked at us. My baby that saw everything looked at me talking to this man and a chill ran down my arms.

"MAMA!"

"I see you! Go on back and play now!"

He just sorta chuckled at me and smiled at her. A real friendly sorta man, this Heziah was. Jackie waved and he waved back—proof that all this was a bad idea.

"What you want with me? I ain't some, some...I ain't one of them girls that's gonna..."

"Whoa. Belinda, did I do something wrong?"

"Just say it. What you want me for? Say it."

Heziah's forehead wrinkled up and I saw a flash of hardness settle in his eyes. I started to relax. I knew hardness. Hardness I could handle. But then I blinked and it all went away. He was looking at me like I was some dirty puppy trying my best to get up out of an old cardboard box. I wasn't. I was a grown woman and I ain't need nobody's pity. "Stop looking at me like that."

"Belinda—"

"Stop."

"Alright. You want the truth? Yeah, I'm attracted to you. And I had a good time dancing and talking with you. Doesn't mean I have any designs on you or anything. We can be friends...if you want."

"Friends?"

"That so hard to believe?"

"Uhh...yeah." I shook my head up and down, suddenly more gutsy than I'd ever been with any man. "You wanna be friends with me? Don't no man wanna be friends with a woman. What for?"

"If you don't believe that then why did you come?"

"This was your idea."

"But you came. I didn't make you come here, Belinda."

A gust of wind blew across the playground, taking his words up against me. Blowing through my hair and all over my stockings. His words started to sound like the truth. Jackie'd run off to play with some of the other kids but I wished she hadn't. Wished she'd stayed put to keep an eye on her mama. Make sure I ain't do something stupid.

"Belinda?"

"Guess I was looking for something."

LANKY WAS THE PERFECT word for Heziah. And those rock hard eyes had me but I ain't know it then. I just saw this man that wasn't nothing like what I was used to and he proved me right every time I saw him— once, sometimes twice a week, for about two years. He introduced me and my girls to art and animals and books and all sorts of stuff. The girls must have thought something but they never let on. Never was nothing but nice to him. And he'd buy them ice creams and treat them real good. Make them cry from laughing so hard. He had a way of teaching without making you feel dumb. He would always talk in riddles or what he called metaphors and stuff. That's where I learned it. His voice'd go up like it was soaring above a mountain or something then glide back down. I asked him where he got all that from. He said books. From then on he always had some old dusty book with him to prove it to us. Some had poems in them, others were just stories. He made reading fun, something none of my teachers had ever been able to do. I'd pack us some sandwiches or something that would keep and we'd meet Heziah under this great big old tree in the park near his apartment and flip one musty page after another. It got so that the girls would beg him to read something to them almost every time they saw him. Then we'd part ways and me and the girls would head back home. We never spoke of those afternoons with Heziah. It was a secret. We all knew. Knew that Heziah was what was missing from our lives.

I was tucking the girls in one night when they wanted me to read one of the books Heziah had given them. So we were all crowded in Nikki and Mya's beds. The younger ones shared the room across the hall. I was nodding off like I usually did when I was reading.

"Mama wake up!"

"What? I'm woke. I'm woke. Where was I?" It'd been a long day, so I began the awful task of getting them to agree to go to sleep. "Ain't y'all tired yet?"

"No."

But I thought I heard a few yawns. "We'll pick it up again tomorrow night." The book thudded shut and my toes went searching for my slippers. Natalie had already drifted off but the others were determined to win whatever hushed debate they were having. The three of them whispered back and forth then threw a few looks my way. "I'm tired. Come on, Jackie. Say goodnight." I swayed side to side to be sure to keep Nat asleep. "Come on now." She was big enough that the only time I needed to carry her was when she was asleep.

"Mama..." Jackie hopped down from the twin-sized bed and took a few steps to meet me at the door.

I should've known from the look on her face that whatever it was that was perplexing her was bad. I should've just told her to go to bed and not ask me no questions but I didn't. I said, "What?"

"Can Heziah be our daddy too?"

I couldn't believe it. Couldn't think, couldn't speak. I just stared at my chile. The older ones knew better and I knew they must have put Jackie up to it. She was just a baby. A seven-year-old baby, but still a baby. She ain't know what she was saying.

"Um..."

"You like him, don't you, Mama?"

Nikki and Mya looked at each other then back at me. "Go to bed. All...All of y'all gone get it in the morning! Now get!"

I ain't mean it but I suspect they all knew that. I hadn't seen it coming at all. Was just happy for the happiness they were having with Heziah. I ain't think it might lead to our lives changing beyond those Saturdays. The girls slipped into each of their beds real easy and I kissed them goodnight and put it all out my head.

Wasn't any point to even thinking Heziah's name when Ricky was around. He was like a vacuum that sucked up all things good. A snoring grumbling vacuum. Usually, he'd drift off right after supper but lately he was waiting a spell. Waiting for me to get into bed with him. Waiting...naked because he was determined to get a son outta me. Wasn't like we talked about it.

I just knew. I'd watched it build up inside of him ever since Jackie was born. He was about ready to bust. Heaving and growling up in my ear, saying all sorts a things but mostly that I was gone give him a boy. A boy that was just like him. It wasn't gone happen but I let him think it was possible. I had my pills tucked away in my secret place and every month got a whole new set. Wasn't no need for Ricky to know. Was easier that way. He climbed on to do his thing and when he was done I'd get to sleep, least that was how it usually went.

"Pecan..." Ricky's sweaty body whispered in my ear. He'd finished about five minutes ago but he was still on top of me.

"Yeah—Ricky, I can't breathe."

"How come you ain't telling me you love me?"

"Ricky..." He was everywhere. Couldn't roll nowhere, couldn't sit up without his say so. I was gasping for air but he was blocking it all. "I can't breathe!" Then as if by magic, I had all the air I could take.

And I took it all like a fat greedy little chile.

Ricky was standing over me. His bulging arms crossed over his hard chest and his thing hanging right in front of my face. "You acting different."

"No, I ain't."

"Yes you is. Now I don't know what it is and I let it go on for long enough but now I want it to stop. You hear me?" I nodded and waited for him to walk around to his side of the bed. But he just stood there, looking down at me. "You love me, Pecan?"

He was watching me so hard I wanted to crawl up in the covers and hide but wasn't no time. Wasn't a question that I was supposed to even think about. Was just supposed to answer, so I did. "I'm your wife. Course I do."

"Yeah?"

I nodded again and brought the sheets up to cover my chest. "You coming back to bed?"

Ricky knelt on the floor and raised one hand to brush my hair up off my face. Don't know what made him do it. Wasn't really Ricky's style. His idea of affection was sweating on top of me. But then I got a clue.

"You still my girl. My sweet little good girl. Ain't you? Hmm?"

"Yeah."

He tugged at the sheet, damn near ripping it off the bed. And his eyes got real big, watching me shivering in the night air. "I love you, girl. You know that?"

"Yeah—Ricky, I'm cold."

"I love you more than I love anybody. You know that, don't you?" Then he went about tucking me in like I was a chile. Pushed the edge of the sheet in under the mattress, pushed it so far in I was wrapped up in a cocoon. "You hear me, Pecan? You mine. Always been mine, always gonna be mine." He got in on the other side of me, giving me that hard look and pulling me back against him. "You know what I'd do if you ever left me?" He whispered in my ear.

"I ain't gonna...why you s-s-saying that?"

"Just feel like it gotta be said. Since you acting all different—"

"But I ain't. I ain't acting different."

His breath got real hot on me, smelling like leftovers as he went about exploring my body. When he wanted to, Ricky could have my body swooning to his drum. He wasn't clueless, when he ain't wanna be that is. It started off just as a little pat, then he started stroking it. He closed in on my womanness and gave it a real good squeeze. A chill ran through me and I was dying to blame it on the night.

"You like that, don't you? Hmm? I know what my girl like. Don't I?"

"Yeah."

"Yeah. That why you love me ain't it, Pecan? You ain't never gonna love nobody else. Just me. Only me."

Soon as he said it I knew it wasn't true. None of it was. Love a tricky thing. It don't just show up where you want it to and you can't keep it away neither. Love go where it want. It don't need nobody's permission, least of all mine.

8

Code of Honor

I'VE NEVER BEEN HERE before." Heziah looked around the room like he was searching for tiny enemies. "Didn't even know this motel was over here. Did you?"

Course I did. It was my idea. I'd seen it on the few trips I'd taken to Helen's house. But I ain't say that to Heziah. He kept on wringing his hat like it was soaked with water, he was so nervous. Like he ain't never been with a woman before. I was the one should've been nervous.

"How are the girls? You said something before about them being sick...?"

"They're okay."

I had the key even though Heziah'd paid for the room. The

wiry little guy in the office gave it to me because Heziah just stood there, staring at the receipt. So it was up to me. Take the key...find the room...unlock the door. Because Heziah was in another world.

"Is it a stomach flu? Or a fever? I heard that strep throat is going around. It's not that, is it?"

"It's just a cold. They fine."

"You know forty years ago they were worried about all sorts of sicknesses. Scarlet fever...polio...leprosy—did you know that was a real disease? It wasn't just made up for the Bible's sake."

The motel room smelt of rotten green tomatoes and bleach. The walls were covered in wallpaper that'd probably lived more life than I had. If I had asked the walls would've probably told me what to do to get Heziah to relax. They'd have known. Tell me to say something sexy. I was never no good at that sorta thing. Never had to be...

"Belinda?"

"Hmm?"

"You did take them to the doctor, didn't you? What if something happens? Maybe you should be with them."

"They not sick, Heziah. I just kinda said that so...um...so we could be alone."

"Oh."

"I lied."

"Yeah. I get that."

"I know. I just wanted to say it so...so it was said. I'm sorry."

All the jittery little coffee beans that was dancing under his skin must have got up and left at the same time. A mellow wave washed over Heziah and he sat on the edge of the bed. Disappointment written all over him. Disappointment in me.

"I ain't never lied to you before—it's just I ain't know how to... um...well I ain't never had to ask no man to...um..."

"Where do they think you are?"

"At my girlfriend's house. It be okay as long as I get back before Ricky. He don't take too kindly to changes in the schedule. He like to know exactly where I am."

"Belinda..."

"But he not gone care!"

"I find it hard to believe your husband won't care that you're alone with me in a motel room."

"I meant about my girlfriend. About me going to her house." I sat down next to him only because my legs were getting tired but soon as I did, Heziah looked up like he was being tested by what I was doing. "It's okay if I sit here with you?"

"We're friends, right? Belinda? We're friends?"

"Yeah."

"Then why are we here?"

"What you mean?"

"We've never discussed this. I didn't even know you thought about it. Have you been thinking about it?"

"You mean you ain't?"

"I didn't say that. I just don't want to come between you and your husband. Divorce isn't something to play around with." He sighed, looking to the ceiling for forgiveness. "It hurts everybody involved and I don't want that for you. Or the girls. I just don't want y'all to go through what my family did."

"Ricky and me ain't getting divorced."

"If he found out about this—"

"If he found out about this he'd just kill me and get it over with." It came out before I knew what to do with it but Heziah ain't give my words much thought. He just sorta nodded, rubbing his hands up and down the tops of his thighs. The coffee beans were coming back so I figured it was now or never. So, I kissed him. Until the sound of our lips puckering filled up the room.

"This ain't you."

"What you mean?" At first I thought he meant the kissing part. We'd kissed before—quick with more lip than anything and both of us pretending it was an accident, like we'd just missed each other's cheeks. I had never thought I would've just leaned over like I did. And I was starting to feel real raw about it, like I was on Candid Camera or something. "You don't wanna kiss me?"

"Belinda—"

"You don't want me at all."

"I didn't say that. You're putting words in my mouth."

"That's because you ain't saying nothing! You talking about what's right and folks getting hurt but you ain't saying nothing! You can't just take a girl up to a room a-a-and not want her nowhere near you!"

"You don't want to do this. A fling...it ain't...it ain't you. You're a good mother, a good person. You don't want to do this. Belinda? Say something."

"I ain't..."

"You ain't what?"

The yellow and green striped wallpaper curled up around me, laying me down on the bed. Wasn't the freshest bed I'd ever smelt—its tartness brought tears to my eyes. "You think I'm bigger than I am. I ain't nobody. Just a girl that married the first guy who asked her." Feeling Heziah's breath on my neck, I almost thought he was gone curl up behind me. Maybe even put his arms around me and hold me close. But he didn't. He just laid there. Close enough that I could hear him breathing but not close enough that he was touching me.

"You are most definitely not nobody. And I can't have you talking like that in front of me."

How he could say that and not wanna be with me I ain't get. Even when I turned around to look in his eyes, I ain't get it. I ain't claiming to be no expert on a man's love but I thought he had some of it for me. Then one by one he whisked each tear away from my cheeks. Telling them they ain't have no business in my life.

"Heziah, my life...it ain't what you think it is."

"What do I think it is?"

"Something good. Happy."

"You seem happy every time I see you."

"That's because I am. You make me happy. Ricky...he...he make me wanna die sometimes. Sometimes I wake up and I just think this is it, I can't take no more."

"Now wait a minute—"

"I ain't gonna kill myself or nothing. It's just what I think sometimes. I ain't gonna do nothing crazy! Don't worry." But even when I poked him in the arm he still looked at me the same way. Worried. "I got four kids! I ain't going nowhere. I promise."

"Why would you even think that?"

I shrugged, wishing I could take it back. I'd wanted to tell folks before but wasn't no reason to tell Heziah. He couldn't do nothing but make it worse. I knew that long time ago. That's why I got so good at hiding the bruises. I'd even cancel things with him if it was so bad I couldn't hide the marks Ricky's love left behind. I was a hiding fool.

"Belinda, there's something you're not telling me."

"It's nothing."

"You're lying to me again."

"Can you...can you just hold me?"

Heziah was a good man. An honorable man. So, he did as I asked. Let me hide in his chest. Still had on his suit jacket. The polyester rubbed against my cheek in its own scratchy way. Probably trying to keep us apart. It ain't work because after a while his body gave in to me and my womanness. I could feel it in his touch and in his breath. The air rose humid and sweaty between us and when he kissed me that just made it worse. Felt like I was dancing through a fog on my tippy toes with Heziah leading the way. He moaned and pulled me on top of him.

I ain't never had no loving the way Heziah gave it. Parts of me was thinking wasn't no honor in it but honor ain't all it's cracked up to be. I done had honor in my bed. Had it wrapped around my finger. Had it sewn into the length of my skirts. And kept it out front my house for all the world to see. Ain't none of that stop my man from loving me his way. With blood and guts and fear. Way I see it, honor be just like heaven or Santa. A real nice sounding word that don't mean a damn thing.

But my good honorable man, he did me good. Wound me up. Spun me around. He had me and my womanself. Loving me tight and secure. I ain't have to think about nothing but him and the feelings between us. The tingles running up and down my spine, promising joy and happiness. Promises I'd long ran out of. Promises that ain't rightly belong to me, but I took them anyway. Took them from my good honorable man. Because when I looked into his eyes I ain't see poor Pecan. I was a woman. In all her glory. Squeezing him inside me. Squeezing him tight until I had every last drop of his honor. He ain't fight me for it. Gave it up willing because I needed it. Gasping at the ceiling, sweat beating off my chest my stuff felt so good, like it should've all along. All because of my good...honorable...man.

Took my time putting my clothes back on. My stockings had a new run that must have happened when things got started. I rolled up one leg nice then sighed as the afternoon peeked through the blinds. We left the motel not long after. Heziah had to be at the carpet store by four for the last shift. I stood out on the concrete slab in front of the door watching as he looked for his wallet. Under the bed...on the dresser...the thing had just up and disappeared. The number six bus was making its way around the corner about twenty feet from the bus stop. If I ran I could've made it.

"Found it. Whew, that would've been...bad. What's wrong?"

"Nothing. I just missed my bus."

"I'll give you a ride."

He said it like it was no big deal, like he ain't know what it would mean. Even I wasn't that outta it. Ricky and me was pretty well known in our neighborhood. Black folks had a way of lifting folks up higher than they need to be. Wasn't nothing really special about us but they ain't wanna see that. They just saw the big house and Ricky on the TV every now and then. All I needed was my neighbors seeing some man drive me home. It would've got back to Ricky in no time.

"I'll wait for the next one."

"I'll wait with you."

"You don't have to."

"I'm not gonna just leave you sitting on the corner in front of this motel. We'll wait together." He sat down at the bus stop first and moved to an angle so he could see me real good. "We okay? I mean this was a big step...right?"

"Yeah. I guess."

He nodded but I could see he was disappointed. "I um...I'm a little older than you. You might have noticed. Probably not what you're used to."

Cars whizzed by, screeching to a stop at the light but I ain't even notice. It was true, Heziah was more than a few years older than me. And fifty pounds lighter than Ricky. Wasn't nobody in the whole state that would've paid to see that fight.

"You probably used to..."

"I only been with one other man before." He nodded. The disappointment hanging so heavy off the tip of his nose that he couldn't hold his head up. I ain't never seen no weakness in him until then. My Heziah was worried about how he'd compare. "Heziah?"

"Hmm?"

"You know the girls...they be asking about you. Asking what you'd think or say about something. Wanting to know where you is... they love you."

"Yeah?"

"Yeah. And...um..."

"Yeah?" He looked at me, already smiling.

"And me too."

He liked that. After I said that he pulled me close so both his hands were on me. Not in a sleazy way just more in a protective way. Like he was wrapping plastic wrap around me to keep me from spoiling. At least that's what it was at first. After a while his right hand got a little antsy and started rubbing my knee. My dress was making whosh-whosh noises against my stockings. I waited with my eyes closed for the kiss I knew was coming. Slow and dark like my favorite kinda chocolate. And then came this tingling feeling between my legs. I squeezed them together real tight and tried to hold on to it. I was so feeling that feeling that I ain't hear the car screech to a stop. I ain't hear the ones behind it blowing they horns. And I ain't hear the car window being rolled down.

"PECAN!"

Heziah snapped outta it before I did. I ain't wanna look. I ain't wanna know. I just wanted to keep right on kissing him.

"Belinda..."

"Pecan, girl, I know you hear me!" Helen was leaning all the way over to the passenger side. She wasn't more than five feet away from the curb.

"You know her?"

I did. Unfortunately, I did. Helen unlocked the passenger door and I got in. Her mouth dropped open like she had never seen me before then. I could tell even though I ain't see it. I was too busy looking at Heziah. I ain't get to say goodbye like I really wanted because the light changed and off we went. "Well? Ain't you got something to say to me?"

"Take me home?"

"Uhh yeah?" Helen could barely keep her eyes on the road; she kept studying me. "You wanna go home, huh? Sure you don't wanna stop by another part-time lover's house? Get a little extra loving?"

"He just a friend."

"Girrl, how you gonna pull that with me? That man was all over you. Hell, he had him some pecan pie, didn't he?"

"No."

"Look at you! You look like you in a damn daze!"

"No, I don't."

"You betta wipe that look off your face before Ricky catch wind of it. And you can't be sitting out on the street kissing the man neither. What if I was somebody else? Pecan, you listening to me?"

I was and I wasn't. I heard the words but they weren't making sense to me. I could still smell him all around me. He smelt like sweet sunshine. "He's just a friend."

"And where this friend come from?"

"Dancing."

"You went dancing with him? You trying to let the whole world know?"

"No. I went dancing with you. And Paula." It took her a while to remember that night. It had been about two years. If it wasn't for me having such a good time I wouldn't have remembered it either.

"You been seeing him all this time? And you ain't tell me?" She slammed on the brakes for a yellow light. She was more mad about the second part than anything. "Why didn't you tell me?"

"I don't know. I'm sorry." And I was. The light changed and we got moving again. Helen relaxed and I came down off my Heziah-high. "I think I ain't wanna believe it. But he's real nice."

"Mmhmm." She steered us through a turn.

"He works at a carpet store on State Street. He's a salesman. He reads a lot and he's got two kids but he's divorced...Don't be mad at me, okay?"

She took a deep breath and tapped her fingers along the steering wheel. "Well does he make you happy? I mean...really happy?"

"Yeah."

We kept still the rest of the ride. Still all the way to my house. Nikki saw us park and lifted Nat out of my rose garden like I wouldn't notice the dirt stains on my toddler's knees. Nikki was the oldest but the younger ones had more of their own opinions about things. Nikki was the easy-going one. Not really knowing what to do with herself if they weren't with her. It bothered me more than it bothered her I think.

Helen sighed and turned around in her seat, just looking at me. "Alright, Pecan. I ain't gonna say anything."

"I know, because you my friend."

"Mmhmm. Just don't do nothing stupid. Ricky ain't the type to be nobody's cuckold."

I ain't need her to tell me that. I got out the car and met the girls in the front yard. Mya was lodged on her favorite branch in the big tree in our front yard. So, I ain't see her right away. One of her legs swung free and she looked me right in the eye and waved. "Hi, Mama!" Her ponytails waved with her. At times she had more hair than I knew what to do with. It grew faster than I could keep it braided.

"Come down from there! And be careful!"

Last thing I needed was her to fall and break something. But she just kept right on smiling that bright kinda smile that looked like it ain't belong to her face. It wasn't her fault really. She couldn't help who she looked like. If I ain't know her I'd probably think she was more like her daddy than she was. It was mostly the outside stuff they had in common. She was real quiet on the inside, peaceful like. Maybe she was more like me than I wanted to see. Maybe that's what kept us from being real close. I ain't want no more of me to rub off on her.

"Mya, I mean it."

"Okay..." She wasn't happy about it.

Seemed like it took forever for her to reach the ground but once she made it in one piece I realized I could breathe again. "How many times I gotta tell you to stay outta the trees!"

"I'm careful."

"I don't wanna hear that."

Jackie and Nikki were into it over a game of hop-scotch. I was still in somewhat of a daze so I didn't get most of what they were arguing about but by that point all their arguments sounded the same. Gimme this…Do that…Let it go…all the same. I probably should've wondered why the kids were out but not too far away. I didn't. Later on I figured out that they were keeping watch. Aunt Clara had given them orders to stay outside while she had a talk with me and to make a serious racket when they saw their daddy coming.

I found her in the kitchen. And the kitchen was sparkling clean, like ain't nobody ever lived there. She'd been cleaning. That was her thing to do when she was real nervous. She even had a load of clean laundry sitting on the kitchen table that she must have been in the middle of folding when I came in.

"Where you go, Pecan?"

I went through the motions of starting supper and she just looked at me real hard like. "Just…around. Helen and me went for a drive." I tore the plastic from around the chicken and went looking for the meat cleaver.

"I ain't see her pick you up."

"I took the bus to her and then we…why?"

"That man called again this morning, didn't he? Who is he again?"

"Just a friend."

"Men and women can't be friends unless he funny. He funny?"

"No. I mean…maybe. How should I know, Auntie?"

Bits of chicken flesh flew up in the air and she waited until the racket of blade against bone calmed down and I'd shoved the pan of seasoned chicken parts into the oven. Then Clara snickered and followed me around the kitchen like a bloodhound that just caught his favorite scent. "I been keeping quiet around here for too long. Thinking maybe you'd see your way through this. But you in it deep now."

"In what, Auntie?"

"In this man. Running off to meet him...God knows where..."

"We just friends."

"Pecan girl, I reckon you better get to being a damn fine liar if you plan to keep this up."

"Keep what up, Auntie? How about chicken and gravy for supper?"

"Who is he, Pecan? What's his name? Hmm? Messiah? Tessiah?"

"Where you get that from?"

"Nikki. You know she love to talk. She talk all day about things that ain't none of her business. She talk just hoping that somebody listening. You know that, don't you?"

I washed my hands and started in on the laundry. I folded each piece until we had a couple of nice stacks. She followed me around the house as I put stuff away. Clara was determined to get something outta me. She hit me with one question after another. Eventually, I stopped trying to answer them and just shrugged my shoulders instead. It wasn't really a secret anymore. I didn't care who knew. Supper smelt so good, that's what I was worried about. I ain't want it to burn up.

"HAVE YOU LOST YO' MIND, PECAN? HAVE YOU?"

"No. Maybe. I don't think so."

"You got four babies out there that need they mama! And you got a man that's crazy."

"That ain't my fault. He'd be crazy no matter what I did. Why you don't talk to him about his craziness? Instead of putting it on me..."

"You a grown woman, Pecan. You know what you doing. You know. You gone mess around and get yourself killed!"

"Least I got to have some happiness before it happened."

She stumbled backwards into one of the kitchen chairs, clutching her chest like my words had hurt her. Never seen Clara hurt before. If anybody was invincible it was her. Fact was, I thought she'd be happy for me, proud of me even. In my way, I was living my life. Doing what I wanted to do. I was lying, sneaking, and hiding things but it was the most free I'd felt in a long time. Clara ain't see it like that.

"Don't be stupid, girl."

"I ain't stupid! Heziah...he loves me, Auntie. He really loves me. Ain't I got a right to that?"

She saw the tears in my eyes and swore sending specks of her spit flying across the room. "You wanna leave Ricky, leave him. Leave him but don't you dare leave him for another man. Some men big enough to handle that. But your husband, my nephew, he ain't one of them. You hear me?" She rose up from the chair and her hands dug into my shoulders not willing to accept anything other than a yes ma'am. "I can't take that. You hear me, girl? I can't take nothing happening to you."

"Auntie..."

"Now I know it ain't fair. Ricky act like a fool on a regular basis. I ain't gone lie about that but it is what it is. You can't do this, Pecan. You got too much to lose."

I watched Ricky that night. Watched him real close, just like folks watch the lion in the zoo, looking for some sign of the wild beast they know is in there but he ate in his own silence. The supper table was always full of giggles and the clanging of spoons and forks and plates. But he just sat there in the middle of it all, not saying a word, not looking at a soul. And Clara sat watching me watch him. He seemed smaller somehow. Not like the man I married. The man who loved to make me scared a him.

"Why you staring at me, Pecan?" His words jarred me back to

reality and shut down all other talk at the table. "Hmm?"

"Just wondered how your day was is all." The girls stared at us like they'd never seen us talk before. I guess it was pretty rare. "What'd you do?"

"What I always do. Train."

"Why?"

"What you mean why? Because. If I don't then how I'm gone win? What kinda question is why?"

"I just mean..." I felt real stupid but it had to be said. I couldn't just sit there and say nothing. So I rushed the words out my mouth like I might chicken out at any second and take them all back. "I justmean itdon't seem tomakeyou no happier."

"What you talking about, Pecan?"

"Being happy. I'm talking about being happy. You don't seem... happy."

"I'm happy enough." Was his reply.

I felt Aunt Clara take a deep breath, waiting for it. It was my opening. To let out my truth, tell him I wasn't. That I wanted out. Two words. All I had to say was two words and the rest would just come tumbling out. Two words. Two words. But I couldn't. I sat there, staring at my plate of cold food. But I wasn't about to give up on it. I just needed more time.

9

Love Me

Hᴏᴡ ʟᴏɴɢ ʏᴏᴜ'ʟʟ ʙᴇ having your woman's time?" Ricky asked. His hands were wrapped around me like my body ain't belong to just me. My nightgown was all bunched up between us and it was driving him crazy. "Huh, Pecan? How much longer?"

"Few days." I couldn't think of a better lie and just hoped that when my real time of the month came around he wouldn't notice.

"Two days, huh? Well that's it, okay? I can wait two days but then things gotta go back to normal. You messing with my training. Got me all distracted."

Ricky rolled over to his side of the bed and all the air I was holding in rushed out. I just couldn't be with him like that anymore. I ain't want no parts of him nowhere near me. It was all for Heziah now. Every minute it seemed like I was trying to get to him or planning to

get to him. I laid in bed just thinking about what I would say the next
time he called, what I would wear the next time he saw me, and all
the things I wanted to do with him. Nice things. Dirty things. Like
Helen told me once that there was this spot on a man's nether region
that would make him go crazy. That if you pressed it just right he'd
be yours forever. I wanted to find that spot on Heziah and see if she
was right.

"Pecan. Pecan." Ricky shook me until he was sure I was awake.
"You making noises."

"Sorry."

Heziah was even in my dreams. Nasty naughty dreams. I woke
up a few times a week all sweaty and outta breath. And it only got
worse as time went on. I couldn't wait for the morning to come because
I knew he'd call and I'd feel his voice all over me. Clara ran errands in
the morning and had folks to see. So, I'd sit down at the kitchen table
and twirl the phone cord around and around my finger. By then the
only one of my girls that was at home during the day was Natalie and
she wouldn't tell on me. She loved to run from one room to the other
taking things and moving them to where they ain't belong. She'd take
a pan or a plate and put one in the washroom then the other near the
door. And as long as she ain't break nothing I was fine with it. It made
her happy so I was happy.

Then one day the phone rang and it wasn't Heziah, wasn't even
for me. They were calling from down south for Clara. Wasn't until she
got home and returned the call that I was sure it was bad news. Could
tell just from the tone of her voice. When it was over she tried to scrub
down the kitchen counter but her hands were shaking too bad. I took
the rag from her and held her hand in mine.

"What is it? What happened?"

"My sister ain't doing too good." Clara said it with the toughness
anyone would've had if they already lost three of their four sisters.

"Doctors say she ain't in her right mind. That she probably been like that for a while and ain't nobody notice."

"Oh, Clara..."

"And her worthless no good son—my nephew...he don't give a damn."

"That can't be true."

"He wanna put her in a home." She looked toward the table so I pulled out a seat for her. "That ain't what we do. Family take care a family."

It was a verdict, confession, and apology all in one. I could see it in her eyes. "You leaving me."

"You don't need me, hun. You running things real good on your own. You done grown up since I first came here to stay with y'all. You be alright."

"No...no I won't. I need you. You can't go."

"Pecan girl—"

"No! You can't go! I mean..." A lump the size of a grapefruit was stuck in my throat. It had never occurred to me that Aunt Clara might one day leave. "You can't..."

"Now I'm a grown woman. I'm gone do what I'm gone do. Just like you. I can't make you do nothing just like you can't make me. Right now I need to be with my sister."

I couldn't see straight through all the tears and hurt feelings. I snatched my hand away from hers and took a little comfort from the hurt in her eyes. It ain't make sense but I told myself that she had tricked me. Got me to trust her, love her, depend on her, and then she wanted to disappear on me like I was nothing. I thought of all the things she'd done for me and it just made my heart hurt even more. She was mine. I lent her to other folks in the neighborhood every now and then but she belonged to me. My Aunt Clara.

"Fine! You wanna go, then go! I don't need you no way! So go!"

"Don't be like that."

But I ain't know no other way to be. I was no good at goodbyes. I stormed outta the kitchen, stomping and swearing like a chile. Grabbed the phone, locked myself in the hall closet, and dialed Heziah's number at the store where he worked. For the first whole minute all I did was cry. I couldn't even tell him what was wrong. He must have thought I was losing my mind. Once I calmed down he talked me into the idea of acting like I was a grown woman instead of a chile. It was the honorable thing to do, he said. That there was too much between me and Clara to let it go like that. Said that I could just pretend it if I ain't feel it but I should do it because I loved her and she loved me. So I picked my sad behind up off the floor and found Clara rocking back and forth in her chair with Natalie on her lap. They were both fixing for a nap.

"You got something to say?" she asked me.

"I'm sorry. I ain't mean it. I just..." The tears started to well up in my eyes again so I decided to keep it short and do my best not to look straight at her. "I'm sorry."

"I ain't leaving tomorrow. You act like I'm gone be gone forever. I been here for damn near seven—eight years."

"I know—"

"No, now you gone let me talk." Clara steadied herself with one foot and raised her chin toward me. "If I'd had a baby girl I'd of loved her just like I love you. And I love this here family and taking care of y'all but I ain't never want this. I likes my freedom. I like coming and going as I please. And I 'spect when it come time for it you the one that's gone be taking care of me. Now I know how you feeling. Like folks just keep leaving you. First your mama, then your daddy...now me."

"Clara—"

"But I ain't leaving you. You can't think of it like that. You gone call me up on the phone and we gone talk about these here kids and Ricky and this Messiah character. I'ma come up to visit when I can. Pecan...girl, you gotta stop crying. You making me feel bad."

Clara wanted to tell the girls in her own way so I tried to push it outta my mind and go on like normal. It was real hard the first few days but after that I just told myself it wasn't gone happen. Clara hadn't mentioned it again so I figured there was a chance she was gone change her mind. Folks did that. Make up their minds to do one thing then change it just as fast. It happened. Why couldn't it happen to Clara?

Then one night I got distracted from putting the girls to bed because Ricky wanted something from the kitchen—toast or crackers or something like that. When I got back to they door, Clara was in there telling them the news. They took it better than me. No blubbering or sobbing, they just looked real sad. But the same old feelings popped back up in me, and I couldn't stand it. I ended up hiding under my covers.

"What's wrong with you?" Ricky wasn't really interested in it but he asked anyway.

"N-N-Nothing."

"Then what's with all the boo-hooing?" He sank into the bed, brushing crumbs onto the floor for me to clean up later. "Pecan, I'm talking to you, least you could do is answer me."

"I don't want Clara to leave. Okay?"

"Oh," was all he had to say. Then he turned off the light.

Ricky had his first semi-championship fight coming up and that was all he thought about. He had enough time to buy Clara a train ticket and drive her down to the station but that was it. He never said

a word about Clara leaving other than to open the windows and enjoy
the fresh air now that wasn't no smoking in the house. Nothing about
missing her or anything. But we all knew he had his fight coming
up. It was a real special night. Ricky got nervous just before every
fight but we wasn't supposed to call it that. Nerves were for weak-
minded fighters, not Ricky. He knew he was gone win and that's how
we were supposed to think. Think like nothing bad could happen,
that was the rule. But the night Clara left everything reminded me of
her. Everything in my kitchen, in my house, everything reminded me
of her.

Ricky was sitting at the dining table all frowned up, smelling
the food that was resting on his fork. In fairness, nobody else was
excited about it either.

"What's this, Pecan?"

"Meatloaf."

"N'all this ain't. What's this crunchy stuff up in it?"

Nikki just couldn't wait for supper, so I made her a bowl of
cereal to tide her over and I'd accidentally knocked over the box of
frosted flakes when I was cooking. I called myself getting them all out
but I guess not. Ricky pushed his plate into the center of the table and
demanded something else.

"Like what?"

"I don't care! I ain't eating that! I know that. I'll tell you that.
So you go up in the kitchen and find me something to eat. I'm already
starving so..."

"You want me to cook something else?"

"I been at the gym all day. I'm training real hard—you know I
got this fight—what the fuck wrong with you? Huh? You trying to-to-
to mess me up? Huh? That what you doing?"

"No..."

"DON'T YELL AT MY MOMMY!"

"DON'T YOU START WITH ME!" Ricky pointed across the table at Jackie. "Your nappy head is just dying for a whooping!"

"Ricky..."

"I don't care! I'm not scared of you!"

"Oh, yeah? You not scared, huh?" He pulled at the tip of his belt.

"Ricky quit!"

"What? Your ass always letting them run wild. That why they don't respect nobody!"

"Okay, okay, fine. I'll...I'll make something else. Just calm down. Okay?"

My second try at supper that night wasn't much better. I threw some fish in a pan and, while it was sizzling, started daydreaming. Sat at the kitchen table just thinking about all the things Clara and me had talked about there. All the stuff she'd told me that I ain't know to pay attention to because I thought she'd always be there to tell me again. I was already crying by the time Ricky came into the kitchen.

"What the...?"

I shook the tears from my eyes in just enough time to see the look on his face as he turned the burner off.

"You can't do nothing right! Damn. How I'm supposed to eat this? This side burnt all up."

"I'm sorry...I'll scrape it off."

His feelings were all in his shoulders by then but I got up from the chair anyway. I wasn't thinking straight. Still thought I could fix it. But even if I could it wouldn't have made a difference. His feelings always came before reason, before anybody else's too. When he slapped me across the mouth I just stood there, holding my face. Couldn't cry.

Couldn't even look him in the eye.

"You can't be this stupid."

But I was. I was. Any other girl would've grabbed something and knocked him upside the head with it. Not me. I made him some pancakes. Not from scratch, the kind outta the box. I figured I couldn't screw that up. He sat in the kitchen, watching me just to be sure. When he'd had enough I made some more for the girls and myself and we sat alone in the kitchen, drowning them in warm sticky syrup. They smiled just for me and from then on it was me and them against everybody else. Me and my girls...

THE SATURDAY OF RICKY'S big fight I decided to make a real day of it. Take them someplace they hadn't been and stay there all day. Pretend like it was just us. Don't know why but I had it in my head that that was the point of the day. Guess I was wishing and hoping and praying, just like they were, that one day it'd be true. Heziah heard about my day of pretend and wanted to be in it. He came up with the idea of taking us to see some play, so we were meeting him at two o'clock. I ain't know what was proper to wear to a play so I just laid out the girls' best dresses and one of my new ones. I had to wait until Ricky left before we could go ourselves. I paced up and down the hall, peeking in our bedroom to see how far along he was in getting ready.

"Shit." Ricky's hands shook so bad that his watch slid right between them. "Shit."

"Want some help?" I picked it up and snapped it securely around his wrist. He almost said thank you.

"I got a lot on my mind."

I could see that but I acted shocked anyway. Ricky never

confessed anything to me. As if the mystery made him more of a man. The watch sparkled under the bedroom light as he rubbed it hard with a polishing cloth. He always wanted to show up looking good. Said it psyched the other guy out.

"Where you going?" he asked me, looking at my fancy shoes. I was wearing a ratty old bathrobe but I figured I'd save time by putting on my stockings and shoes. "You going somewhere?" He stopped polishing. "Where you going, Pecan?"

"No...nowhere."

"Shit. Don't be lying to me, woman! I got enough shit to deal with!" He brushed past me and slammed the door so hard I knew our next door neighbors heard it. "Where you going?"

His hands started flexing and curling and I started blaming myself. Why didn't I think this through? Why'd I think it would be easy? Why didn't I just stay downstairs and outta his way?

"PECAN!"

"Nowhere! I'm...I'm...we going to a play!"

"A play? Why you wanna do that for?"

"For...for the kids. It's religious. About how Jesus was born."

"Oh."

And he went back to getting ready. I watched him lace up his shoes, trying to catch my breath. "Why...why you do that?"

"Do what?" he asked.

I could tell he wasn't really paying attention. By then he was searching all the little boxes on our dresser for his best jewelry. I could have just kept still and he would've forgotten all about my question. But I didn't. One finger at a time, I relaxed enough to speak up.

"Why you hit me?"

"What? What you talking about, Pecan? I ain't hit you."

"No. I..I mean why you do it...at all. Not now. At all. It ain't right."

"What?" He chuckled, turning to look at me like I'd told a joke that wasn't funny enough to inspire a true laugh.

I don't know what I expected him to say. He'd stopped apologizing years ago and he wasn't the type to change just because I wanted it. Maybe I could've loved him if he was that type of man.

"You trying to fuck me up? You see I'm getting ready. About to put my life on the line for this family and here you go trying to guilt me about this."

"A real man don't..."

"A real man put food on the table and keep a roof over his family's head! You ain't had to work a day in your life because of me! How about a thank you?"

Living day in and day out with him was work. It was bone shattering, pride swallowing work that ain't pay me a nickle. But I kept still about it. Didn't tell nobody, didn't ask for help, didn't even admit it to myself.

He walked past me to the closet and pulled a blue and black dress from its hanger. "Put it on," he said.

I didn't make a fuss. Didn't ask why he cared what I was wearing. The dress didn't go with my shoes so I pulled out some other ones. I followed Ricky downstairs and watched as he asked for good luck from everybody. Nikki sat rocking to a slow rhythm like Clara used to and nudged Jackie with her foot. Jackie was spread out in her dress, pretending to be watching TV. I know she was pretending because it was the news. The weather ain't interesting to nobody at seven years old.

"Hey, girl! I know you hear me. You ain't gonna wish your daddy good luck?" Ricky grinned, somewhat tickled by her stubbornness. "Come on now."

"Jackie." Nikki nudged her more forcefully this time but she still ain't move.

And as usual Mya did it for her. "Good luck, Daddy. Knock him dead!"

"Sure thing, baby girl."

※

THE FIGHT CROWD WAS one of the biggest anybody had ever seen, or at least that's how it was told to me later on. Folks were bumping into each other, trying to get a good view of each blow. They were screaming and holding signs with Ricky's face on them. The signs went up and down and sometimes landed on the folks that were shouting for the other guy. Ricky's fans were loud and loyal. And there wasn't any shortage of women. Some of the womenfolk in the neighborhood couldn't wait to add that bit into the story because a good wife would've been at every fight to make sure her man got home alright.

Anyway, Ricky delivered a blow to the other guy, they called him Sanchez, to his gut and the ref blew his whistle. The two of them went back to their corners. Sweat was pouring down Ricky's face but he wasn't anywhere near tired. The ref blew again and the next round started.

I wasn't into boxing all that much, didn't know the rules or the moves but the way folks told it to me they could tell something was different. Ricky's eyes were rolling around in his head and about a minute after the second round started, he stopped landing any of his punches. He swung and damn near flung himself outta the ring. The other guy, Sanchez, he laid into Ricky real good. The old man standing in Ricky's corner was waving and shouting like crazy. Something was wrong. But the ref wasn't listening. Ricky's body went limp and leaned from one side to the other. He ain't go down right away. Not until Sanchez threw one last punch. Hit him right in the head. Ricky fell like a ton of bricks. The crowd went silent. The old man climbed the ropes and ran to the middle of the ring. Lord, forgive me, but the first thing that came to my mind was that I was finally free.

10

Stay

THE NEXT DAY FOLKS started popping over in groups of two. Like they knew I wouldn't be enough to keep just one of them entertained. Some of them I hadn't done more than nod to as I walked to and from the bus stop. They brought food but most of them just wanted to see the inside of my house. Wanted to ask me questions. Was Ricky in critical condition? Was he ever going to fight again? What did he look like? Was he a vegetable? Nikki was real helpful, keeping their glasses full. I ain't even ask her, she just did it.

"Mama, you want more?"

I shook my head no and went back to listening to Mrs. Banks and Mrs. Henderson tell me how a friend of their cousin died because the doctors and nurses didn't realize he had an infection.

"Oh, Pecan, listen to us just going on and on! We're not trying to scare you or anything."

"We just want you to be on the lookout for those sorts of things. Lord knows, nobody wants anything bad to happen to Ricky."

"He such a big strong guy, I bet he just bounces right back."

They looked to me to say something but the best I could do was kinda smile. I hoped they'd be the last of my neighbors to pop by but they went on for a few minutes more before Nikki came running in the living room all outta breath.

"They fighting!"

"Who fighting?" I suddenly found my voice.

"Mya and Jackie! Jackie said she hope daddy's dead and Mya hit her!"

I was so embarrassed I couldn't think straight for a minute. What a mess we were. Mrs. Banks and Mrs. Henderson looked at each other and then at me like they ain't know whether or not to take it as a joke.

"Mama, they fighting real bad!"

"Okay, Nikki. Would y'all please excuse...me? Um...thank you for the meatloaf. It looks real good." I followed Nikki down the hall before they could say anything. I could hear them mumbling to the door and peeking down the hall after me. It was gonna be all over the neighborhood that I had one crazy daughter, I was sure of it. What I wasn't too sure of was what Nikki was saying. Sometimes she would exaggerate things.

We had what they called an enclosed porch out back that we used to store stuff on. And both of my girls were rolling around, knocking into stuff, pulling hair and screaming, scratching each other. I had never seen them like that. Not so much as a bad word had ever passed between Jackie and Mya.

"Stop it! STOP IT!" But they kept right on until I got in the middle of them. Mya was all red and pieces of Jackie's hair was hanging on one of the nails that wasn't hammered all the way into the window sill. I couldn't believe it. "Wh-What's wrong with you? Both of you!"

"SHE STARTED IT!"

"SHE HIT ME FIRST!"

"SHE MADE ME DO IT!" Mya yelled and I swear I'd never seen her look more like her daddy.

"She can't make you do nothing. She...she can't make you hit her. You apologize."

"But she said—"

"I don't care what she said! You apologize! I ain't gonna have you hitting folks! Don't you ever hit nobody! You hear me, Mya?" I grabbed her by both arms and she went kinda limp but it was too late. I couldn't stop. "You ain't gonna turn out to be one of those people! You hear me? I ain't having it!" Before I knew it I was crying and shaking her. I was trying to parent her. Every mama wants her kids to grow up to be sweet and nice to folks. I was just being a mama. But I ain't mean to grab her so hard.

"Let me go! I want my daddy!" She took off running at the first inch of slack in my grasp.

"I'm sorry. Mya? I'm sorry."

I went after her but it was no use. She was faster than me. I got all the way to the front gate but by then she was on the next block. Folks were standing out on their porches, watching me. Their eyes cutting into me, without any mercy whatsoever. I ain't do that to them, why they had to do it to me?

Came back inside to find my girls waiting in the doorway of the kitchen, looking up at me. Those big sad eyes I knew too well.

"Want me to go find her?" Nikki volunteered like she was some kind of grownup. "I probably know where she went."

"I know too, Mama."

"N'all. Y'all go back and watch TV. Mya come home when she ready."

The kids sat in front of the TV and I went about getting supper ready. Was nothing anybody could've said to make me feel worse than I already did. But I had to believe that my girl would come home to me. She wouldn't just leave me like that. I cracked an egg on the side of a bowl to add to the cornbread and I ain't even notice the shells floating around in it until I went to pour it in the pan. I was just trying to parent her. I wasn't trying to hurt her. She had to know that. I just wanted her to understand it was wrong to hit folks.

"The street lights is on. Mama?"

I set the table, put all food out, and slapped any one of their hands that made a move to touch any of it. "We waiting for your sister. She'll be back soon."

"What if she not?" Nikki was a nervous wreck. "Huh? What we gonna do then? What if sh-she get hurt or if somebody kidnap her? Then what? I'm gonna go find her."

"Nobody is leaving. We will sit and wait. She'll show up."

"NO SHE WON'T 'CAUSE SHE GONNA BE DEAD!"

"Stop it! Ain't nobody gone die! You scaring your sisters. See."

Nat was a blubbering mess and Jackie wasn't too far behind. She tapped me on the arm and said, "I'm sorry, Mama. I ain't mean to make Mya go away."

"It ain't your fault."

It was Ricky's fault. He wasn't even there and he was still messing everything up.

We spent the rest of the night waiting for Mya to show up. Every time the phone rang, me and the kids jumped. The last time it was Clara just calling to check in.

"I ain't mean to...you think she gone ever forgive me?"

"Kids got a way of forgetting what grown folks don't. She be okay. You'll be okay. You just gotta go find her."

"I can't..."

"Hun, it gotta be done. You can't leave that chile out in the world by herself. Ricky gonna have a fit."

I ain't get around to telling her about Ricky's fight. Couldn't deal with that at the same time. All I could see was what was right in front of me. "What if she don't wanna come with me?" I whispered to keep the idea from hurting too much but when Clara ain't respond right away felt like somebody took a knife to my heart.

"You gotta go anyway. You hear me, Pecan?"

"Yeah."

A good mama would never let her chile go like that, so of course Clara believed me, anybody would've. Had been a while since I'd told a lie that folks believed and that one was too easy. Because I couldn't do it. My knees wouldn't work. My legs...kept me sitting at the kitchen table. Voice in my head kept saying all the things I knew—she could be in trouble, she could be hurt...but I was stuck, chained to the chair. I wasn't nobody's hero. Couldn't even save myself.

"Mama?" Jackie just appeared right in front of me. I ain't even hear her coming. "Why you crying?"

"Because I'm scared." I yanked her into my chest, holding her tight. "Promise me you ain't never gone run off."

"I promise."

"You and your sisters all I got. You hear me?"

"Yes, Mama."

We ate in silence. Everything was cold by then but it ain't matter. I ain't taste none of it. Nikki glared at me from her seat at the table like I'd sent away her best friend. And I let her. Wasn't a thing I could say. Nothing I wanted to say.

Next morning I woke up with a horrible pain in my stomach. I ain't never been that scared before. She wasn't nothing but eight years old. What did she know about the ways of the world? She couldn't take care of herself. I had slept in my clothes so I made up my mind to just go find her and be back before the others woke up. I had to build up the courage to put on my shoes so that took a minute but soon as I did I grabbed my purse and headed out the door. I ain't get no farther than the front stoop though. A tiny yelp came outta me and I thought I was gonna explode, I was so happy. She was curled up on the porch swing. She'd come home sometime in the night and was just too proud to ring the bell. Her clothes were all crumpled up and tired looking and she looked up at me like she ain't have no words. Like she'd gone mute overnight. She was freezing so I went and got some blankets and piled them on us and turned on the TV.

"I'm sorry, baby. Mama ain't mean to hurt you, okay? I want you to know that. I love you. I love you more than I love me." I waited for her to say something but that mute look wasn't going nowhere. She just stared at the TV. I held her tighter, thinking it'd bring us closer together. And she ain't fight me. She just went limp. "Mya? Ain't you gone say something, baby?"

"I'm not hurt."

"Okay." I checked her arms to be sure and there were no marks on her so I guess I believed her.

Then she said, "I don't hit people. I don't, Mama. I just got mad."

That didn't make me feel any better. That she got so mad she couldn't stop herself from attacking her sister. Mya must've seen it on my face cause then she said, "If somebody said that to you...said they wanted grandpa to be dead..."

I choked back tears and held her head to my chest. She was right. I would've wanted to cause them some serious pain. "But you can't go fighting with everybody that say something you don't like."

"Why not?"

"Because. You just can't."

That's when I made up my mind. For the second time, I made up my mind to leave Ricky no matter what the doctor said about his condition. What he had was contagious like the flu. So, I told the girls we were going to the hospital to visit. I thought that would be easier than telling them to say goodbye to their daddy. I put on one of my favorite skirts and a nice blouse. I ain't do it for him or nobody really. I did it for me. I wanted to look strong. And I put the girls in their best outfits too so they'd feel the same as me. Mya wanted to wear her play clothes so I had to promise that she would only be in her dress for an hour or two. She made me promise. And I saw her looking at the clock on the way out the door. We were a real sight, though, the five of us. When we got to Ricky's floor the nurses oooed and ahhed over the girls while I went on ahead. Hoping he'd be in a coma like folks in my stories. I'd tell him it was over and the little machine would whine until somebody came in and said in a sad voice, "He's gone." Least that's what I was hoping. It ain't go exactly like that.

"Pecan!" He pushed himself up and I could see he had all his normal strength. "I was wondering when you was gonna come see me. They ain't believe I was married."

I had no words. Just looked at him with my mouth hanging open. Folks had gassed the fight up so much I was expecting...well I wasn't expecting him to just look normal.

"So. Ain't you wanna know how I was doing?"

I found myself nodding at his question and when he took my hand I let him. Thirty seconds at his bedside and I'd turned into that girl I hated. It was so damn normal that it made me sick.

"I know things ain't been real good between us. And I'm sorry about that. I been thinking about it, about you and me. About what you said before my fight...you know what I'm talking about?"

I nodded. He couldn't say it because nurses and patients were walking down the hall behind me. But I knew.

"Going through this...thinking you about to die...it changes a man. I got to thinking about all the things I got and how lucky I am. I got you and the girls, a nice house, nice car, got something I'm real good at that makes me some good money. Lots of men would want what I got."

It was all true so far. In fact, I could think of one man in particular that might want all Ricky had.

"I could've been dead." He said it like he wanted me to be shocked by the words. Watched me so close like he was hoping I might break out into tears any minute. "Pecan, you hear me? I could've died but I didn't. You know why?" I had no freaking clue. "Who would take care of y'all if I wasn't around?"

"We would've managed."

"How? You ain't worked a day in your life. And Aunt Clara too old to be trying to send money this way. Don't you see? I realized something. That I'm here to take care of y'all. Make sure you happy." He started rubbing my hand real slow like and I ain't know what else to say. He was ruining my plan.

"Ricky I gotta t-t-tell you something."

"What, baby? What you gotta tell me?" He grinned and dropped his head back on the pillow like he was expecting something good.

"Hmm? Go on, I'm listening."

"I...um...well I think maybe—"

"What? You...you pregnant, ain't you? That's it, ain't it? That why you been pulling away from me? You feeling all delicate."

"No. Ricky—"

"That ain't it? You got some other reason?"

"I'm trying to say that um...I think maybe..."

"You think it's a boy!"

"Ricky, please!" His hands were getting all sweaty so I rubbed mine up against my shirt then folded them under my chest. Shouldn't of did that because then his eyes went straight there and lit up like a kid in the candy store. "I ain't pregnant."

"Yeah you is. I can tell."

"I ain't, so stop staring at me." I could hear the girls' voices getting closer and I knew I ain't have much time. I had to tell him before they got there. "I gotta go. I can't stay. We can't..."

"Pecan."

"Hmm?" I couldn't even look at him.

"What is it? You mad about before?"

"No."

"Yeah you is. I ain't gonna be like that no more. Okay? You hear me? You believe me, right?"

"Yeah, sure."

"Then everything's gonna be alright. We'll be okay."

I shook my head and glanced over my shoulder to the door. They were just down the hall. "I gotta go, Ricky."

"Wait—"

"I CAN'T DO IT NO MORE! I can't." My words sucked all the air out the room. But it ain't seem to affect Ricky none. He just kept right on staring at me. Then his eyes got real small and I backed up out of his reach.

"You leaving me? You come up in this here hospital to tell me that? Huh? I'm lying up here in a goddamn paper dress!"

"It ain't good for nobody. You and me."

"It because of how I was. I ain't gonna be that way no more. I ain't. Stay. Come on. Gimme a chance to prove it to you. I ain't always been like that. You know that."

"Mama?"

"I'm they daddy. Kids need they daddy."

I put on a fake smile for their benefit and Ricky looked at me as mad as ever. Mya and Nikki went up to him and gave him hugs but even that ain't wipe away the hard look on his face.

"Daddy, when you coming home?"

"Tomorrow. But your mama not gonna be around for too much longer."

"Ricky don't—"

"N'all, you wanna runaway? You go on and tell them! Tell them how you trying to break up our family! You wanna leave? Go ahead! See if I care. But you ain't going nowhere with my kids! They mine! They belong to me!"

"Come on y'all, time to go. Say bye-bye to your daddy." Another glance over my shoulder told me the nurse was standing in the doorway gawking at us. She must have thought I was a cruel sorta woman. Show up just to tell my sick husband I'm leaving him. But my girls ain't think that. They knew better. Half of them felt bad about it, I could see, but even they knew it was how things had to be. "Y'all say bye."

"Bye, daddy..." Mya wrapped her arms around his neck again and he whispered something in her ear until she nodded.

"Jackie. Nat. Say bye."

"Bye," Jackie waved from her position at my side. "We can go now?"

I nodded. The nurse looked horrified as we passed by her on the way to the elevators. Wasn't my fault I wanted to say. But the only way for her to understand was for me to spill my guts right there on the floor.

The elevator doors closed and Nikki pressed the button for the lobby. "You going somewhere?"

"No, baby. I just don't think your daddy should be living with us no more." Jackie opened her mouth to say something but I pinched her right quick so she'd think twice about it.

"Oww mama."

"Shh. You don't gotta say everything you think. It ain't a good thing. Daddies supposed to be good to they families and live with them. It ain't a good thing when they can't. You hear me?"

"Yes, Mama."

"Mya, what your daddy tell you?"

The doors opened up and a bunch of folks were waiting to get on so we had to hurry. But by the time we made it to the big glass doors, Mya turned to me and said, "What if daddy don't wanna go? What happens if he wanna stay?"

I ain't have an answer for that.

I was dreading the walk down our block something serious. I knew what I'd be getting before we even left the hospital. I was gonna feel folks eyes on me as we passed one house then another. Ricky's brand new Cadillac would be parked out front as a reminder of all that he owned. The car. The house. Everything. I had a good idea how the car worked but I'd never tested it. Ricky said was no point in me learning how to drive since I never went anywhere without him.

Before we could get to the bus stop the sky opened up and unleashed all this rain. I only had two coats, a winter one and another one I wore for most a the year. I was wearing the other one because it wasn't cold enough yet. The rain tore through my coat in a few minutes. Ten minutes later, my fine outfit was drenched too. What kinda justice was that? Ricky was healthy as an ox and I was drowning in rain. I ain't deserve that—rain clouds and thunder and puddles made of mud that just had to leap up to greet me. It wasn't fair. I ain't never did nothing to nobody. I stood there for a minute, glaring at the sky and cussing it in my head. Wherever Heziah was I bet it was shining. That's the way things went with him. I needed to be near him, to feel that sunshine.

"Where we going?" Nikki asked when we got on the thirty-nine bus instead of the fifteen. "Where we going?"

"Shh."

Heziah lived on the first floor of his building. I could see it from the street. The lights were on in the apartment on the right but his was pitch black. When we got to the door of the building people were coming and going so we just slipped in with them. I knocked on the door to his apartment and the woman across the hall opened hers, just to see what was going on. Nosy people. I knocked again. He wasn't at the carpet store. I'd called there already and they said he wasn't on the schedule. I knocked again, this time harder. Still no answer.

"Mama, where we is?"

"Shh! Let me think." A million things ran through my head. I'd just seen him two days before. It wasn't like Heziah to just disappear.

"Mama, who live here?"

"Heziah."

"Where he at?"

"I don't know—he'll be back soon, though. Okay? So..." The floor was made of diamond-shaped black and white tiles and they looked so friendly I just sat right down. Mya was first to do the same. Studying me like she was about learn something just from my face. "He'll be here soon. We just gone wait a little bit."

"But the floor dirty."

"Then keep standing, Nikki."

Whatever Nikki wanted to do, Jackie wanted to do the opposite so I wasn't surprised when she said, "I'll sit with you, Mama."

"Thank you, baby."

I just knew he'd see us and wanna know what was going on. I'd tell him and he'd listen real hard then tell me he loved me and that he wanted me and the girls to be with him. That we could start over, be a family. Heziah was a good man, the kind that would take care of us. I just knew it. Looking at them I figured they knew it too. So we waited. We waited a long time. So long, the sun had gone down and we were all dry and smelling like dew.

"I'm hungry. Can I get some money to go to the store? It's just across the street."

Searching through my pocketbook, the truth was staring me in the face. By the time Heziah came home somebody might have locked me up for being a crazy mama. My girls had to eat. I was crazy with a capital C. "We all gonna go. Y'all get a couple bags of chips to share because what I got might have to last us a while."

Walking across the street I thought I saw the curtains move in the apartment across the hall. The old woman was probably watching us the whole time. Maybe she'd done that before. Watch to see what happened at Heziah's apartment. Maybe she'd seen women come and go. Maybe she knew all their faces. I tried not to think about it. Just called Helen from the payphone at the corner to pick us up.

When she got to us, it was raining so hard that I got drenched again just running from the corner store to her car. She was just getting off work, or so I thought. She had on a brown and pink uniform that I'd never seen before.

"What happened?" she asked, not wasting time.

"Nothing."

"I heard about Ricky."

"He okay."

"So that's what you doing out here? Hmm? Celebrating?" She reached in the backseat and then wiped Nat's face with a towel before handing it over to Mya. "Girl, you sure making a mess of things."

"I'm leaving Ricky."

Helen's mouth dropped open and she looked from the girls to me. My mouth was growing drier by the second but I wasn't about to take it back. I had made up my mind. It was time. If Ricky really had changed then he couldn't be mad at me. He'd just have to deal with it.

"You okay with that?"

"I just gotta find Heziah. He disappeared."

"Oh, girl..." Helen shook her head like she was thinking something too awful for words but I wasn't trying to hear that.

"He got a sister up in Wisconsin. Will you take me up there?"

"Pecan—"

"Just take me up there! It gotta be tonight because Ricky's getting out tomorrow. Please, Helen!"

"I can't be going all the way to Wisconsin! I gotta work. And you can't be dragging these kids all over God's creation looking for this man!"

"You just got off work. We can be back before your shift starts tomorrow."

Her car sat parked in the lot, the windshield wipers swishing back and forth. Helen sighed and looked toward the stoplight that was changing colors for the cars that were actually going some place. "I got a second job at this diner. I'm supposed to be there in half an hour."

A second job. I hadn't heard of nobody needing more than one job. And Helen was single. She only had herself to worry about. It ain't make sense.

"Stop looking at me like that. Nobody's buying furniture in this economy. Folks worried about paying the electric bill, not buying a brand new sofa."

"Oh."

"What you gonna do, Pecan?"

"I'm gone be with Heziah. He loves me—loves us. He loves us."

"Yeah but that don't mean he wanna go from being a bachelor to having a wife and four kids. Girl, that's a lot."

"No, you don't know him. He loves me and he loves the girls. He better to them than their own daddy is!"

"Don't he have kids of his own?"

"Why don't you want me to be happy? If you don't wanna take me to Wisconsin then fine!" I threw open the car door and I yanked back the seat. "Get out. Come on, let's go."

"Pecan, it's raining! Don't make these kids walk in the rain!"

Least the rain ain't tell me what I was feeling was stupid. I heard Helen calling after me but I was already looking in my purse for bus fare.

"I got a quarter. I found it in the hospital."

"Thank you, baby."

We all had raindrops hanging off our eyelashes. Our best clothes were drenched but nobody said a peep about it. Nat let out a sneeze and I dug around my purse for tissues. Every mama supposed to have tissues and candy in her purse but I couldn't find one. It was like a dream. I was walking through my own dream. None of it was real. Ricky ain't get hurt. We ain't go to the hospital. We wasn't standing in the rain, waiting on the CTA. It wasn't real.

"Mama," Nat lifted both arms, reaching for me so I picked her up, hoping what was left of my body heat might warm her up.

"Mama?" Jackie whispered. "Heziah's our daddy now?"

"Yeah, baby. Heziah's gone be your daddy now. I just gotta find him and let him know."

11

Missing

M AMA, WHAT'S WRONG?" JACKIE climbed into bed next to me. Put her tiny hand on my forehead like I did to her when she was sick. "You got a fever?"

"No, I don't."

"Want me to sing it away?"

"Okay, baby. Go ahead and sing to me."

She sat cross-legged on Ricky's side of the bed, eyes closed, swaying from side to side. Was a song I'd heard before but couldn't name the singer. Must've come from one of Clara's records. When she'd worn it out real good, her eyes flew open, and she was smiling at me. "Feel better, Mama?"

"Yeah. I'm all better now."

Jackie fell back on his pillow and whispered, "I know what it is. You thinking Daddy gone show up before Heziah can get to us."

"No—"

"It's okay, Mama. I protect you." She was just a kid but she'd learned to read me just as good as anybody. I'd been held up in my bedroom since the night before, trying not to infect everybody else with what I was dealing with but I guess it ain't work.

"Mama. We could go away. Go to a great big island where it's pretty and it's just us. No boys."

"Jackie, ain't no place like that."

"Uh-huh." She nodded, determined to make me see it her way. "It be just you and me, and Auntie come back, and Mya and Nat and I guess Nikki could come. And Heziah!" She grinned so big I wanted to laugh. "He's not a girl but that's okay. We could make us a great big house made of cakes and we'd eat it all day long."

"That's sweet, baby."

"So come on. You gotta get up so we can go." She pulled at the sleeve of my robe and my arm stretched across the bed. "Come on, Mama."

The doorbell rang and the panic gripped my insides. But Ricky wouldn't be ringing no bell. He had a key. I heard voices downstairs, grown voices, polite and curious. And then I heard them asking how things were. A few minutes later, I heard feet rushing up the stairs. Nikki ran around to my side, her eyes all big and round.

"Them ladies back again. They say they wanna help get things ready for Daddy."

"What things?"

"I don't know. They say they gonna cook and clean so you don't have to. They say they're gonna come by every day and help out because you gone have to take care of Daddy and you not gone have time for nothing else."

"Nuh-uh!" Jackie sat right up. She ain't like that last part none. "We going to an island and it's gone be just us!"

"No we not. That don't make sense."

"Yeah we are!"

"Mama, tell her ain't no island."

"There is so a island!"

"No there's not and you just stupid to think so."

"Don't call your sister stupid. That's not nice."

"But she just making up stuff!"

"There is an island! Because I say so! And you just mad because I'm not letting you on it!"

"ENOUGH! The two of y'all is gone drive me crazy."

I settled on a sad looking brown dress and zipped myself up into it. My hair had gotten a tad wild from all the rain and could stand some attention from the hot comb but I ain't have the time or energy for that so I just pulled it back into a bun. The three of us went down the stairs in single file. My neighbors hadn't been there for more than five minutes and they were already at home in my house. There were three of them. Anise was wiping down the furniture. She looked up and smiled when I came into the room. The other two were banging around in the kitchen.

"Mrs. Banks and Ms. Hodgkins say they gone make you supper." Anise explained.

Christine Hodgkins was something of a black sheep in the neighborhood. She was a nice enough girl every time I saw her. I would run into Christine every now and then when I went up to the girls' school. She had three kids and no man to speak of. All three of her kids had different last names. We all assumed they were named after they daddies.

"Can we go outside?" Mya was already at the door. It wasn't so much a question as it was an announcement. "Can we?"

"Be back before it gets dark. And watch your baby sister!"

Nat never let them go anywhere without her. I think she learned to walk just so she could keep up. But it was good for them to get out. I picked up a rag and Anise pushed the jar of furniture polish across the floor to me. She'd done the television and most likely could've finished the room without any help from me but I didn't wanna be bothered with what was going on in my kitchen. Anise wasn't the real talkative type but the other two would have questions on top a questions. I got started shining things until I could see my face in them. Then the phone rang.

"PECAN!" A voice made of sterling silver rang out from the kitchen. Why she felt the need to answer my phone I don't know but I hurried in there and Mrs. Banks held it out for me. "It's some man looking for you." Audra Banks was probably a real pretty girl in her day but that was a long time ago. She mostly looked tired and proper. And she lifted one perfectly arched eyebrow, waiting for me to explain why some man who wasn't my husband was calling my house.

"Hey. Where you been?" The phone stretched all the way into the hall so I took it there and leaned against the wall. "I...I went to your place and you wasn't there."

"I went to see about a friend. My neighbor said somebody came by. A woman." Heziah let loose a chuckle. "A woman with a whole bunch of kids, she said. I figured it was you. Everything alright?" He hadn't heard. He was the only person in Chicago that hadn't heard about Ricky's fight. Just made me love him more.

"Pecan, y'all not allergic to nothing, are you?" Christine stuck her head into the hall. "Mrs. Banks was just saying I should ask to be sure."

"N'all we not."

"Okay." Her eyes danced up and down before she took them and herself back into the kitchen. "I'll just...get started then."

"What's wrong?" I could hear Heziah sitting up like there was something he could do from way over there. "Belinda?"

"I can't—can you hold on for a minute?"

I was grateful that folks wanted to help me so I did my best to be respectful of that. They ain't have to come over. They probably had their own stuff to tend. Still, I needed some space.

"Oh but, Pecan, you don't know how hard it's gonna be, taking care of a sick man and four kids!" Mrs. Banks let the fridge door close and started chopping stuff for a salad. "Trust me, you gonna need supper to already be prepared."

"Um...actually I'll be okay." I was still holding the phone and Christine looked like she was ready to run away but Mrs. Banks wasn't having it. She was going to do a good deed if it killed her. "Really. I'll just call you if I need something."

"No. Now, we'll have all this pulled together in no time. You just go on back to your little phone call. I bet folks—family just keep calling to find out about Ricky. How he doing by the way?"

"Fine."

"That's good. We been praying for him. They say prayer and family are all a person need to bring them home when they in the hospital. He got plenty of that."

I went back to the hall. The walls could've used another coat of paint. It was chipping right in front of me. Not enough to be too embarrassing but enough that I noticed. I could hear Heziah moving around, putting on his coat, rattling his keys. I hadn't even told him yet but he knew I needed him.

"I'm on my way, okay?"

"Okay." I nodded and hung up. Ricky was going to be out the hospital any minute and swore he'd never let me live without him. And now Heziah was on his way over.

"Everything alright?" Mrs. Banks mopped over my footsteps.

"My un-uncle. He's been missing."

"Oh, honey, that's too bad. Guess somebody's got it out for you. First Ricky gets hurt now this. Just hang in there now."

I needed to get out. I was scratching and clawing at the collar of my dress and my body felt hot all over. The locks on the front door were slippery and cold and then suddenly I felt the cool air rush over me. I couldn't swallow enough of it but I kept trying. Kept trying until I was huddled up on the porch steps, hugging the beams that held up the banister. I'd truly made a mess of things.

Heziah drove up just as they were taking supper out the oven. Lasagna. The girls had smelt it from wherever they were playing and came running. Mrs. Banks said it would keep well so we could keep eating off it for a few days. I just nodded, smiled, and waved to them from the porch steps. Heziah waited until they were a little ways down the block before he got out of his car. Just seeing him made this calm wash over me. Maybe all that other stuff wasn't real but he was real. Maybe Ricky ain't never exist and it was just me and Heziah from the start. He jogged up the steps but before he could say anything out came Jackie.

"Daddy!" Heziah froze. And she went crashing into his middle. His eyes got real big and he just sorta patted her on the back. It was a timid sorta hug. "You gonna be my daddy now. Right? Mama said—"

"Jackie, go on inside!" She looked at me like she had no clue what she did wrong. Just made it all the worse. "Please, baby."

Heziah smiled down at her and she backed away, looking back every so often to make sure we were still where she left us. "What's going on, Belinda?"

"I left Ricky."

"Okay..." he said real slow like.

"So now we can be together. For real."

"For real?"

"Yeah."

"That's why Jackie thinks I'm gonna be her daddy now? Because you told her we were getting married?"

"No—"

"No? You didn't tell her that? Because that ain't what it looks like."

"I just...I just said...what was I supposed to say? I mean you always so nice to her...she think what anybody'd think. I'm supposed to tell her that, what...maybe you don't want us?"

"I don't believe you. How could you do this?"

All he had to say was he'd been waiting for this. Waiting until we could be a family. But he ain't say nothing. He just paced back and forth across my porch with his hands in the pockets of his old worn out jacket.

"You wanna stay for supper? We got lasagna on the table."

"I can't do that."

"Why not?"

"Because you put me in an awful situation! I go in there and they're thinking it's because I'm gonna do something that ain't necessarily true!"

"Why not?"

"Why not? Why not?"

"You love us, don't you?"

"Belinda, I ain't tell you to leave your husband. And I never said anything about marrying you." He stopped pacing long enough to look me in the eye. "You can't just spring that on somebody. And you can't go promising that sorta thing to kids!"

"Okay! I'm sorry. I'm sorry."

"Stop. Stop crying."

"I...I can't." I fell into the warmth of his chest and half expected him to push me away. But he didn't. He just let me cry on his shoulder. Even unzipped his coat so I could get in it with him. My Heziah was a good man with a hard chest. The briskness of his sweater tickled my cheeks until they were dry and I felt strong enough to stand on my own.

"I do love you. I do. I just can't be...that to you right now. Things are too complicated."

"But, it's been two years. Two years and you been with us... taking us places...you and me we...we made love. Heziah..." His coat collar was turned down so I flipped it up and looked deep into his eyes. "You the best man I ever met. If you don't love me..."

"You what? You're gonna kill yourself? You gonna put that on me too?"

"No..."

"I gotta go, Belinda. I'll call you, okay?" And just like that my honorable man walked away.

12
The Test

"DADDY!" MYA SPRINTED FOR the front door. I'd never seen her so excited.

Ricky lifted her clear off the ground. It had been maybe three days since they'd seen each other. I guess that was a long time. He hugged the others but with less excitement. I stood back out the way, wondering how hard it would've been for him to love them all the same.

"Told you I'd be back. Didn't I tell you?"

"Yes, Daddy." Mya nodded, not knowing that he was really talking to me. Saying it for my benefit. I took my coat from the hook by the door and Ricky put his in its place. "Mama, where you going?"

"Yeah, Pecan, where you going? You ain't gotta leave because of me. We're family."

"I'm going to the store. I'll be back in a hour or so."

"I'm coming with you," Jackie said before I could get out the door. I couldn't argue with her. Why anybody would wanna stay there with Ricky was beyond me. But the problem was when she was putting on her coat, Nat was looking at me with big eyes. And so was Nikki. They didn't want to be left behind.

"Baby, you stay here."

"No, I'm coming with you!"

"Jackie. Please. Just stay here with your sisters." I knelt close to her ear and said, "Please, baby, you ain't gotta be next to him. Just keep your sisters company." She ain't like it. But she handled staying much better after I put it like that.

It was a cold bitter day. Even when I wrapped my scarf real tight around my neck I was still freezing. Chicago winters were like that. Fooling all of us into thinking they weren't coming then all of a sudden...there they were. The cars and trucks and buses had made dirty snowy tracks in the street. The slush slushed around the wheels of every car that went by. I thought about Heziah and wondered what he was doing. He ain't work on Sundays so he was probably sitting at home, reading the paper or something. And just maybe, he was thinking about me.

I got to the grocer's in good time and shook the snow from my boots. Plenty of folks came before me because I could see the same slush that was in the streets at the door. We needed laundry soap, eggs, bread, milk—all the usual stuff. We needed it about twice a month. The carts were freezing like they'd been banished to the outside for years and just let back in. I kept my gloves on as I went up and down the aisles and ignored all the stares I was getting from my neighbors. Since Ricky took to the hospital they made a habit of watching me real close like they were looking for something specific. I don't know why but that's what they did. In the freezer part...over near the fruit...at the butcher's counter. They'd whisper and watch. I wasn't the first woman to not want her man back but they acted like it was something special for me to do it. That's why I had to sneak down the women's aisle. Pretending to be looking for Tampax, in case one of them came by. Tampax was safe. Every girl need some of that. It wasn't nothing they'd go around telling folks they saw me buy. When I was about done and my cart had most everything I wanted I got in line. And one of them saw fit to come up to me.

"Hey, Pecan. How you doing? You doing okay?"

"I'm fine. How you doing, Carol Ann?" She looked at me like I was a sad little puppy and it just made me mad. I said I was fine. Wasn't no need for the puppy dog eyes.

"Oh I'm just fine. Just fine. My brotha's getting outta jail next week."

"That's nice."

"Mmhmm. He's a good boy. He just had a hard time of it. My daddy was never really around...growing up. You know how boys need their daddy to show them how to be men. You lucky you got girls. Ricky ain't want no boys?"

"It wasn't really up to him."

"Oh right." Her neck got all twisted around as she checked out the stuff in my cart. It came to me that I should've put it underneath something. "Pecan! Are you...you..."

"I'm minding my own business just like you should be." With my eyes squinting and hands on my hips, for a split second I was Clara Morrow.

After my neighbor slinked over to the other lane I felt real bad. I ain't mean to snap on her like that. It just came out. As I took the stuff out of my cart so the cashier could ring it up, I made up my mind to catch up to Carol Ann and apologize to her. Then I heard the cashier say the total.

"Fifty-five twenty-six."

"Fifty-five dollars?" All I wanted was eggs and bread! And a few other things...but I couldn't believe it. I had about thirty bucks in my wallet but I thought maybe more had fallen to the bottom of my purse.

"You got it or not?"

The line behind me was getting long and they were all looking at me. "I don't need...that. Or um...that."

She rolled her eyes and pressed a button then rescanned a few things and they disappeared under the cash register. "Forty-seven even."

"Okay um...I really just came for the eggs...the bread—"

"Look, you want me to un-scan everything?"

"No." I shouldn't have but I looked back at the end of the line and there was another one of my neighbors. "How much is the eggs, bread, laundry soap, and um...the cans of tuna and...the face cream, oh and...the fruit—the bag of apples? Please."

The girl huffed and puffed and tried to kill me with just her eyes. I felt bad enough but she must have thought I needed to feel it more. I'd never had to think twice about food. Even when we had nothing, Ricky just told me exactly what to get. Five cans of this...two jars of that...it wasn't something I was proud of but that's how it was.

"You still want the—?"

"Yeah. Please. Thank you."

Getting back to the house was more of a labor than it was getting to the store. I only had two bags but between them I couldn't see the two or three feet in front of me. I made it all the way to my block before my feet decided to go in different directions. Stuff went flying. And I landed face down on the icy sidewalk. Guess I was lucky the bags broke my fall. It ain't feel like that, though. Some kids were playing in the snow pile a little ways up and I heard them laughing at me. Guess I was funny. I took my time putting as much as I could into one bag then dragged myself up the porch steps. When I got in the TV was going so I didn't think much about what the kids were up to. Then I heard the slap. The paper bag slipped from my hands and I ain't even notice.

Nikki and the younger ones were watching the TV. The slap had come from Mya. Ricky was sitting at the very edge of the sofa, holding up both hands, his elbows were planted one on each knee.

"Turn your fist," he said. "Now pivot and go on and hit my hand. Right in the palm. Right there. Don't hold back, baby. You can't hurt Daddy."

"Ricky."

Mya froze in place. "Hi, Mama," she said and held both hands behind her back.

"What're you doing?"

"I'm passing on the family business!" Ricky grinned.

"I don't want them fighting. Mya knows that."

He sighed and fell back against the sofa cushions. Ricky wasn't used to defending himself to me. He just stared at me. Then the floor. I couldn't move fast enough to keep him from seeing it.

"What's that?"

"Nothing. Nothing. It ain't nothing." I scooted and scooped and knelt across the foyer, shoving things back into the bag. But it was too late. He was standing over me, looking down as I tried to pile other things on top of it. "Just stuff I got from the store."

Ricky's smile grew all big and I knew exactly what he was thinking. "You pregnant."

It was so quiet I thought I was going to suffocate from all the damn quiet.

"I ain't."

"Yeah you is that why you got that there test. I ain't stupid, Pecan. I can read."

"I said I ain't. Now leave it be." I didn't even bother to hang up my coat, just squeezed the bag to my chest and made a beeline for the kitchen. Trying to convince myself on the way that I was convincing enough that he'd leave it alone. Don't women just wanna have tests handy just in case? The bag rustled in agreement with me as I set it on the counter.

"Mama, you pregnant?"

"No, Nikki," I said. "Go play with your sisters." Ricky sauntered in behind her. I could see he was chewing on something that wasn't no good. "Nikki! Get in here and help me with supper."

"But I thought you just said—"

"I said...help me with supper. Okay? Here. Chop an onion." She did as I asked and I folded my coat over the nearest chair. Ricky sat in one of the others, staring at me, accusing me of something with his eyes. "Be careful, baby. Take your time. That knife's sharp."

"Pecan."

"Thought you wanted to see the girls."

"Nikki go on back up front with your sisters. I wanna talk to your mama alone."

"No." I held her by both shoulders so she stood right in front of me. Don't know what I was thinking. Just squeezing her itty bitty shoulders until I felt I had control of the situation I guess.

"Why you don't wanna just tell me the truth?"

"Because it ain't the truth."

Ricky's fist pounded against the table and we both jumped. "WHAT THAT 'POSED TO MEAN? HUH?"

"Nikki, go." She ain't need me to tell her twice. She took off running. But I stayed put. And looked Ricky in the eye. "You can't scare me..." Tiny little bumps rose up on my skin, calling me a liar. "I said I ain't pregnant because I'm not. I just got the test because you just wanna have one just in case you need it. That way you ain't gotta go looking for it."

"Uh-huh." Ricky bit his lip then spit the skin onto the floor. "So you just got it in case you need it in the future?"

"Right."

"Because you expecting me to come back home, right?"

"What?"

"How else you thinking you gone have use for it?"

"I...I don't know. I just thought—"

"N'all what you thought was that I was stupid enough to fall for that shit!" He flew across the kitchen like a crazy man and I ain't get no farther than the fridge before he pushed me up against it. "Either you pregnant and you lying about it. Or you trying to get pregnant by some mothafucka behind my back. Which one is it?"

"N-N-No one. I ain't doing nothing."

"You ain't doing nothing? Nothing, huh? Girls that ain't doing nothing don't need that there box. DON'T LIE TO ME!"

"I ain't lying! It was on sale. I just...I just thought I'd get one."

"You just thought you'd get one?"

I hated when Ricky repeated everything I said. Was like he just wanted to prove how stupid it sounded. I knew. I ain't need no extra help seeing it.

"Maybe I oughta ask the girls. Ask them if anybody been nosing around you since I been laid up in the hospital. Hmm? What you think of that?" Course he didn't really need my opinion. Just wanted me good and scared, which I was. "NIKKI! GET IN HERE!"

"Ricky..."

"What? You got something to say, Pecan?"

"She just a kid."

"Yes, Daddy?" Like all my girls, Nikki, got real good at acting innocent. But the nerves still showed up on her, twitching and pulling at her fingers. Plus, she couldn't hold eye contact for no long period of time. Was a good thing Mya came with her.

"You see anybody hanging around your mama when I ain't here?"

"She just a kid!"

"You. Shut up. I'm talking to my firstborn. My big girl. Come on over here. You ain't gotta be scared now. I just wanna know. Ain't nothing gone happen to you."

"Ricky—"

"SHUT UP! GODDMAN IT, WOMAN. What you afraid of if you ain't do nothing? Huh? HUH?"

"I'm afraid—I'm afraid you gone take whatever she say and twist it until it mean what you want it to! And then...then..."

"Ain't nobody been here, Daddy." The lie came as steady as it could. Gliding out her mouth and into the room like warm butter. I ain't even know Mya could lie like that. We were both so busy looking to Nikki when it came we had to readjust.

"No?" Ricky asked, turning his gaze to his favorite.

Mya shook her head side to side. Lying. Only her face ain't give it away. Not even a little. Maybe it was her youth. So sweet and gentle. Easy to make him believe her. Not like me. He'd have never believed me.

"Aight." Ricky backed up enough to grab the box in one hand and my arm in the other. "Then let's get this over with." We stumbled into the hall and I could hear the TV going but no voices. They always got real quiet whenever Ricky got into one of his moods. "Pecan, you go upstairs and pee on this here thing. Then we'll see if I'ma be a daddy again."

The stairs weren't big enough for us to walk up them side by side so Ricky pushed me ahead of him. Getting even more pissed when I fell forward on my hands. Dust and dirt and pebbles from the outside was ground up in the rug that ran down the stairs. Nineteen stairs. I counted each one. Around the sixteenth stair I got a little lightheaded, a little wobbly. Ricky's hands held on tight enough to my waist I actually thought he was searching me for some proof of his baby. Then was five more feet to the washroom. He sat on the edge of the tub and held out the box.

"I can't go with you looking at me."

He gave me that look, sighed real hard, and pointed his finger in my face. "You trying to get on my nerves."

"I—"

"You might as well go on and do it because I'm just about sure I'm right. Go on now. What? Huh? You still think you about to leave me? Think you gone have my baby and not tell me about it? Woman, you crazy."

Next thing I heard was a boom coming from downstairs. Then a sorta sizzling sound that made me think of grilled cheese. Ricky looked at me but wasn't no way he could blame me for it. I followed behind him a safe pace. Five feet then the nineteen stairs. The girls were all standing back in a half circle around the TV. Or what used to be the TV. At that moment it was no more than a broken screen with a mop sticking outta it.

"Which one of y'all did this? Huh? You know how much that thing cost? Huh? Answer me."

"It was a accident," Jackie said not looking one bit sorry.

"Yeah, I knew it had to be you. Always messing something up." His head whipped around to ask me, "Ain't you gone say something?"

"Accidents happen."

"That's it? That's all you gotta say? That's a hundred dollars right down the fucking drain! How the fuck you accidentally shove a mop into the TV? And why ain't none of y'all stop her? Huh? Nikki you the oldest."

"Ricky—"

"N'all you had your chance now it's my turn. I'm gone—"

"Jackie ain't do it. It was me. I did it, Daddy. They tried to stop me but I did it."

Ricky looked real hard at Mya then at Jackie. It ain't matter that Mya confessed with a straight face. It was the second time in only five minutes that she'd put her lying skills to the test but this time Ricky wasn't buying it. Still, wasn't nothing he could do about it. Short of beating the truth outta her. And that he wasn't about to do, not to her.

"And why you do it?"

"We were playing pretend. I was a knight."

"You were a knight? You don't even know what a knight is."

"Yeah I do. It's like a soldier and he rides around on a horse with a stick and knocks people down. I was a knight."

"Mmhmm."

"She...um...she been doing it a lot lately. You just ain't know because you ain't been here. She—they be pretending to be different things." Honestly, I ain't know where Mya got that knight stuff from but it ain't really matter. The hardness had gone outta Ricky's eyes.

"So y'all like to play pretend, huh? That's y'all new thing?"

"We always did," Jackie rolled her eyes.

"Well y'all about to get to do it a lot more because you ain't getting a new TV. Maybe if you good Santa'll bring you one for Christmas. Just like he's gonna bring something for me and your mama."

Test or no test, Ricky'd made up his mind that I was with chile. His chile to be exact. I ain't argue with him no more about it. Just let it be. My little trip to the grocer's showed me something. We needed things. Things I couldn't pay for. Every cent I had came from Ricky. So when he said he was staying for supper I just nodded. And when he said he was staying the night I kept quiet. But the next morning when I peed on the stick and it turned pink, I damn near cried.

13

Man Eating Dikes

I F IT DON'T WORK but ninety-five percent of the time, you supposed to tell folks that!"

"Look, miss. Your doctor was supposed to explain the risks to you. No method of birth control is perfect." The balding white man wasn't even looking at me. His peachy face and rosy head craned around to see the next person in line. "Next?"

"Hey! I paid good money for these here pills and they don't even work! I want...I want my money back." Nat was getting a little heavy but she refused to be put down so I held her on one side and searched my purse for the little white compact that had ruined my life. "Here! Take them back!"

"Ma'am, I can't take this back."

"Well I don't want them. I want my money. I need my money. You gone gimme my money."

"Ma'am, you need to leave." But I wasn't going anywhere, not without my money. He had little bins of chapstick and floss right by the pharmacy window and I accidentally knocked them over. "MA'AM!"

"Gimme my money. You can't just take folks' money and not give them what they've paid for! That was my money! You don't know what I had to do to get it!"

"Here! Fine! Take...money. There!" He crushed a handful of wrinkled ten dollar bills into my palm. "Now if you don't leave right now I'm calling the cops."

"Thank you."

Probably wasn't a lot to him but forty bucks was a lot to me. The way I figured it, I had eight months to scrape together enough to get far away from Chicago.

"Baby, you gotta get down now. You too big for Mama to be carrying you everywhere."

"No I not."

Natalie's third birthday had snuck up on me. Seemed like I blinked and there it was. She stuck out her chin so I could zip her little pink suit all the way up and out we went. It was snowing pretty good so I meant to take the bus as far as I could so we wouldn't have to walk. The bank I had picked out was somewhere I knew Ricky'd never go. Nobody I knew even lived in that part of town. Wasn't nothing but Pollocks and Jews. It was the perfect place to hide money from Ricky. The bus rolled up almost as soon as we got to the bus stop, making me think that my luck might be changing. We sat down near a window and watched as the world flew by in a blizzard. After a while we were the only black folks on the bus so I figured we were getting close.

"Can I help you, ma'am?"

"I wanna open an account," I said as I unwrapped and unzipped Nat then myself.

"Alright. Have a seat. What kind of account were you thinking of?"

"Um...the kind where I can keep money and can't nobody but me get to it."

"Alright. Would you like to earn interest?"

I nodded even though I wasn't real clear on what interest was. He went through some more questions, filling out a form at the same time. Then he gave me what he called a passbook. Said I should keep track of how much was in the account in it.

"We will send you statements from time to time and you can compare it to what you have in your passbook."

"Send me statements?"

"Yes ma'am."

"Like to my house?"

"Yes."

"I don't need that. No, I just...um...I just wanna put money in it."

"It's standard. Every account comes with a monthly statement. I assure you it is very easy to read."

"Right...sure."

"So, if you'll just sign right here...I'll take your first deposit."

The blue pen must have been used by everybody that came to his desk because it ain't wanna write. I shook it and pressed real hard but still couldn't get nothing outta it. He apologized more than I ever seen anybody apologize before then handed me another one.

"See...um...the thing is, Mister Silverman..." I had to lean in to be sure the other folks weren't listening to my business. "I don't want my husband to know about this account. That's why I came all the way over here. So, if you could not send anything to my house..."

"I see. Well, if you want to write a different address on this line we can send your statements there instead." I nodded and scribbled Helen's address on the line he pointed to. "Very good, ma'am. Is there anything else I can do for you?"

"I don't think so."

"Then let me give you my card." He pulled one from the little thing sitting on his desk then another from inside his drawer. "And... this is my brother's card. He has a family law practice. He's an attorney."

"Attorney?"

"Yes ma'am. One of the best...I think, but I suppose I'm prejudiced."

Joseph Silverman, attorney at law. His office wasn't but a few blocks from the bank so I thought I'd give it a shot. See if there was something he could do for me. But Nat whined the whole way. She wasn't nothing but sleepy but that ain't what she said. First she wanted candy then she wanted me to carry her and on and on and on...by the time we got to the door with Silverman spelled out in gold letters I was just plain wore out. The receptionist had a little basket of peppermints on her desk and she pushed it forward a few inches so Nat could get some.

"Say thank you."

"Thank you."

"Oh she's welcome. Mr. Silverman might be a while. He doesn't usually take walk-ins. But if you want to make an appointment..."

My watch said one twenty-two. The girls were gonna be outta school at three. I had time. And I was afraid to put it off. Afraid of what would happen between now and then. So, I shook my head. Nat fell asleep across my lap and I sat there, thinking about all the things he might ask me. And the one thing I ain't wanna say.

Joseph Silverman looked just like his name. His head was covered in silver hair but other than that you couldn't tell his age. He was about my height and looked like he was in a decent shape. I figured his wife was more or less happy.

"Mrs. Morrow, please have a seat."

"Your brother said I should see you."

"Oh? Which brother would that be?"

"Mr. Silverman..." I couldn't remember his first name. "He said you're the best."

"He's very generous. What can I do for you today?"

No matter where I put it my right hand just wouldn't relax. It'd curl up or just start shaking. I finally wrapped it up in my other one and held it flat against my lap. He was looking and smiling at me like he had all day to watch me fiddling with my hand. "I ain't really sure...I just thought I'd come by."

"Well, how about I tell you what I do here. Hmm? I'm a divorce lawyer for the most part. I help married people who decide they don't want to be married anymore. Sometimes this means dividing up assets, if there are children, settling custody questions, if there's a pre-nup involved, we might challenge that...any of this sound interesting to you?"

"Custody. How does that work?"

"It either goes to one parent or both. Usually the mother retains physical custody."

"But what if...what if I can't afford to—"

"It's called child support. Your husband would give you money to help take care of the children every month."

"So then he can't come around no more, right? If we divorced?"

"Well..." Mr. Silverman's chair squeaked a little as he leaned back, tapping his fingers against the arm of it. "If he wanted to go for visitation you would have to prove that he was a danger to your daughter."

"I can do that."

"You can?"

"Mmhmm. I mean you could ask them. They'd tell you." His eyes shot over to Nat who was yawning in the seat next to me. "She the youngest. I got three others. Nikki, she be twelve in January and Mya just made eight and Jackie seven. They good girls, won't say nothing to just anybody, but if I tell them to, they will. Not that they lie or nothing, not really...I just mean they'd tell the truth when I tell them to."

"And what is the truth?"

"That Ricky—my husband, he um...he a danger. To um...to anybody really. Anybody that get in his way."

"Well before I give you official advice, I should tell you that I operate on a fee schedule. I don't require a retainer or anything but there is an hourly rate of one hundred and fifty dollars."

"For an hour?"

"Yes ma'am. For every hour that I spend working on your case."

"How many hours will that take?"

"I'm not sure."

"Oh."

"I don't usually do this but...why don't we consider this a free consultation?"

"No, I can pay. I'll pay. Um...today?"

"Mrs. Morrow. Please. I've enjoyed meeting you. I hope that I can help you in the future."

"Yeah...yeah me too."

⋘

"WE WENT TO THE silver man!" Nat said loud enough that I could hear her in the kitchen.

Was a good thing Ricky wasn't home. Not that he listened too tough to the things the girls said anyway but I ain't wanna chance it. He hadn't said much to me since he got home other than all those looks he gave. Ricky said more with his eyes than anybody I ever knew. I could feel him itching for a fight. Eventually all that family stuff he kept talking about was gonna rub off and he'd go back to his regular self.

"So...how you doing, Pecan?"

"Fine."

Helen sighed and looked me up and down, sipping from my favorite mug. "Yeah? How's your part-time lover?"

"Why don't you just shout it out so the whole damn world can hear you?"

"Ooo, somebody's touchy."

"How I'm supposed to be?" I dusted another spoonful of sugar on the greens and stirred them up real good. "I'm married. And I ain't heard from him in a while."

"So that's why you and Ricky back together...because things ain't work out with Mr. Wonderful? Girl, you hop from one man to the other. Don't you know how to take a time-out?" She threw one leg over the other and laughed out loud like it was the funniest thing in the world. But I knew Helen ain't mean any harm. She was just saying what other folks would say.

"Yeah...I know." The greens were smelling good so I moved on to check on the roast. Wasn't that often we got to have it but since Ricky was back I made sure to get money from him for groceries. "I'm done with men!"

"Girl, don't even bother lying to me. I can't get enough my damn self!"

We were two cackling fools up in my kitchen. I even talked Helen into staying for supper. Figured more people to eat up Ricky's food the more money I could get him to gimme. And the girls loved their Aunt Helen. She said all sorts of things they thought were funny. Just Helen being Helen. But not everybody loved Helen as she was. Ricky sat at the head of the dining table, chewing all loud and glaring at us.

"I could put in a word for you with the store manager if you serious about working."

"Really? What kinda stuff would I do?"

She shrugged and sucked down a few inches from her beer bottle. "Could be in the office, could be on the floor. You know Sears is a big company, girl. What would you wanna do?"

"She don't wanna do nothing except what she doing." Ricky sliced through his meat like it did something to him personally. "Pecan, you ain't tell your friend about our little news."

"What news?"

"Nothing. He just joking."

Ricky swallowed real quick and went right back to slicing up another piece. "She busy. She got other things to be thinking about besides some nothing job."

"I don't mind—"

"What you wanna work for? I take care of you, don't I? Huh? Don't I give you whatever you want?"

"Yeah, Ricky. It's just an idea..."

I was real grateful when Nikki decided to ask Helen about her latest boyfriend. After a while everybody forgot about my bright idea. Helen went on explaining what he looked like and the way he talked. Had us all laughing with her.

"So, I told the man. You want all this? What you got for me? Girls, don't let none of these knuckleheads sell you half of what you deserve. Just keep on moving. Right, Pecan?"

"Yeah, they know." I was too busy grinning to see what was coming next.

"Y'all take y'all plates up in the front room."

"But ain't no TV daddy."

"Go on do as I say." But they stayed put, slow to follow his orders.

"Ricky—"

"I don't want them listening to all your man bashing! Turn them into man eating dikes."

Helen giggled and nudged me under the table. "I don't think dikes do that."

"Let me put it like this. I don't want my girls turning out like you. Can't keep a man to save your life."

"Ricky! She company!"

"I look like I care? She in my house. At my table, eating my food. You tell her or I will..."

I was so embarrassed I ain't know what to do or say. Just sat there holding on to my napkin and staring at the middle of the table. The girls were right there with me. But Helen was new to our table. She didn't know the rules.

"Well, I think there's a difference between not being able to keep a man and not taking no stuff. I can be miserable by my damn self. I don't need a man for that."

"Yeah..." Ricky took a gulp of his beer and got up from the table. "Pecan, come on upstairs when she gone."

Helen ain't even wait until Ricky was all the way upstairs before she turned to me with big eyes and said, "Ooo, girl, I ain't know that's what you was dealing with."

A quick nod and a smile was all I could manage. She kept on talking but I ain't hear much after that. Was too busy thinking about what was coming next. Ricky'd probably jump in the shower but then he would be expecting me. Expecting me to make him feel better, feel like the man he liked to think he was and was only two ways to do that.

"You want me to go?"

"What? No. No, stay. He just cranky because he got this fight coming up. It's okay. Girls, finish your supper."

"I don't remember him being like that. Was he always like that?"

"Yeah," Jackie piped up. "I ain't never getting married. Boys suck."

"I wanna get married," Nikki said dreamily.

Should've made me happy that she could still be so googly-eyed after all she'd seen but it didn't. Just wanted to shake her and make her see reason. Make her think more about protecting herself than whatever googly-eyed thoughts were rolling through her head. I had time to set her straight so I piled one plate on top of another and headed into the kitchen. Helen followed behind me, carrying as many glasses as she could.

"Look, I'm sorry if I was rude before. You know me. I get started talking and I can't really stop until I say the wrong thing."

"You ain't say the wrong thing. It ain't you."

"No. I should learn to just keep my big mouth shut."

Sudsy water washed over my fingers and the words were just sitting there on the tip of my tongue. Begging to be said. So I said them. "Ricky hits me sometimes."

"What?" She leaned against the counter not really paying attention.

I ain't blame her since it was barely loud as a whisper. "He hits me," I repeated. Then I waited. Seemed like forever. I washed a few plates, set them up to dry. And waited some more. "Helen?"

"Yeah, I heard you."

"When you leave...most likely that's what he's gonna do. You hear me?" She gulped down whatever she was wanting to say and nodded. I ain't never seen Helen speechless. Not until then. "Been going on for a while. Usually Clara could talk some sense into him but she gone now."

"How she do that?"

"Shouting mostly. Sometimes she use a skillet or a shoe or something. Anything to get his attention."

"Pecan, look at me." She squeezed both my arms until I thought she was fixing to ground me or something. My fingers dripped dishwater into little puddles all over the floor. "Why you ain't tell me?"

"I knew what you'd say. That I'm stupid or weak...I ain't saying you wrong..."

"I wouldn't ever say that!"

"PECAN!"

We both leaped up outta our skins then held so tight to each other I couldn't tell where she ended and I began. It was probably a good thing too. To have some of Helen rub off on me. Ricky kept on hollering, though. He hollered so much the girls came in the kitchen to see what I was doing. Helen just held me tighter. Then we heard his feet on the stairs. Tighter we held each other. And heard him coming down the hall. Tighter.

"Pecan, I know you hear me—oh, you still here?"

"Yeah," Helen finally let me go long enough to melt her hand into mine. "But I ain't leaving. Me and Pecan gonna have us an old-fashioned sleep over. What you girls think of that? Huh? Wanna have a sleepover?"

I never had a better friend than Helen. The next day she took me to work with her. Told her boss that if he ain't hire me they would miss out on the best saleswoman Chicago had ever seen. They put me on the schedule for the very next week. Said my paperwork should be processed by then. I was officially a working girl and hopefully one step closer to being one of them man eating dikes.

14

Focus

"Mama, don't leave." Nikki pleaded. "If she's sick..."

"She's not sick. It's just a cough. She'll be fine."

Nat was wrapped around me like one of them monkeys at the zoo. Coughing her short dry little cough on my neck. Putting her to bed wasn't too hard since she was barely awake. Nikki stood next to me, watching as I tucked her in.

"She gonna wake up."

"Not before I get back. She'll be fine. Okay? Just try to keep it down. Don't y'all go screaming through the halls or nothing. Your daddy'll be home in a few hours anyway."

"Why you gotta go?"

"I gotta work."

"Why?"

"Because, Nikki. I just do. Now you in charge until I get back. Y'all can go play in the snow once your daddy get home, okay? Just show him how to take her temperature and where the medicine is. Okay? You listening to me? It's my first day. I need you to help me out."

"Okay."

Soon as she said it I had second thoughts. Wasn't right leaving my baby alone when she was sick but I thought Nikki could handle things. The truth was I trusted her more than I trusted her daddy. But still...she wasn't nothing but eleven years old. When I was eleven I ain't have nobody to look out for but my dolls and stuffed animals. It was too much to put on her but she was all I had.

"Here, I wrote down the number to the store. And you know Anise right across the street if you need anything...and your Auntie Paula...I'll write down her number too. Okay?"

"Okay."

"Everything's gonna be fine, okay?"

"Okay, Mama."

On my way out the door I took a little detour across the street. Anise was always at home since her mama wasn't really able to go anywhere. She answered the door on the first ring.

"Hey, Pecan."

"Hey, can you go over and sit with my girls? Nat gotta little cold and I just feel better if somebody was with them. Or maybe they could come over here..."

"Mama can't have sick folk around her. Because of her immune system being so weak. You know she gotta have dialysis like four times a week now. They talking about just admitting her..."

"Oh. I ain't know."

"It's okay." Anise sighed and threw a quick glance over her shoulder. "Maybe I could go over for a little bit. When mama go down for her nap."

"Thanks."

"Um...Pecan?" She eased out the door damn near barefoot in her house slippers. It closed gently behind her and she rubbed her arms like she was trying to start a fire or something. "I ain't trying to um... start nothing but I heard something I thought—I thought maybe I should tell you because we friends and all and if it was me I'd wanna know..."

"Know what?" My watch said 3:15. I had thirty minutes to get to the store.

"It's just...you know how some folks like to shoot the messenger?"

"I ain't about to shoot you."

"It's about Ricky."

Maybe it was her tone. Maybe it was how she looked me straight in the eye. Anise never looked folks in the eye for more than a few seconds—but there she was standing out in the cold and looking me dead in the eye.

"What about Ricky?"

"I...I heard he got a woman up on Chestnut." I must have gasped something terrible because Anise started panicking and breathing all heavy, like the more air she took in the better off I'd be. "I'm sorry! Maybe it ain't true!"

Couldn't say nothing, just shook my head. It was true. I could tell it just by the way the wind was blowing down the street.

"Pecan? Say something."

"I gotta go to...to um...to work." In my head I'd made it down the porch steps to the sidewalk but in reality I was still standing in the same spot. Watching Anise look at me with those sad pitiful eyes. She was thinking poor, poor Pecan. "How? Where'd you hear...?"

"Mrs. Patton, she mama's nurse. She come by every few days now. She asked me about you and how come you don't never go to none of Ricky's fights...she say there be this big hip woman always hanging around. You know the kind that look like she asking for it. That she always sit right in the front and that they be leaving together after. She say everybody know. I ain't know so I figured you ain't know neither. Guess I was right."

"I gotta go."

My first day as a working girl was off to a great start. I got to the store just ten minutes before I was supposed to be there but it was enough for somebody to show me how to sign in and where my locker was. And then I hit the floor. The store manager had put me in the men's department, saying that men liked buying things from pretty girls. I started to argue with him, say I wasn't no pretty girl. I was a year away from being thirty and I had four kids. I may have started off as a pretty girl but I wasn't no more. Pretty girls had they pick of men. I had two that ain't really want me.

"So, how'd your first day go?" Johnathan Bryer was a tiny sorta guy with big speckled glasses that took over his face. He was mostly bald with peachy kinda skin, one of them white folks that ain't look real real white. And he ain't sound how he looked. He had a big voice that kinda reminded me of my daddy. "Mrs. Morrow?"

"I did alright, I guess. Sold two shirts. Took me a while to figure how to ring them up, though."

One side of his mouth went up in a grin and he stopped tapping numbers into the calculator on his desk. "Mrs. Morrow, don't you know you're supposed to lie to the man who signs your checks? When he asks you how things are going you just smile and say everything's great."

"Oh. Sorry."

"And?"

"And what?"

"Where's the smile?" I did my best. It couldn't of been that bad because he let out this laugh that made the pictures on the wall shake. "Well no one's going to accuse you of playing fast and loose with the facts. If you don't like the sales floor we can move you into the office."

"Okay."

"Okay. I'll see you tomorrow. Would you like security to walk you to your car?"

"Don't have one. I'm on the bus."

"That doesn't sound too safe. This time of night. Why don't you ask one of the other girls—"

"I'll be just fine. Thank you, Mr. Bryer."

Couldn't nothing else happen to me. If I could make it through a whole week living under Ricky's roof after trying to leave him a second time, I could make it to the bus stop. On the ride home I sat by the window and watched my life go by. When I was a little girl I used to like chasing butterflies. They'd fly all crazy like, had me running in squiggly circles. Seem like the very next day I was grown with a man and a baby, still running in crazy circles. Couldn't go back but I thought maybe I could go somewhere. Somewhere where nobody looked at me like poor Pecan. Where I ain't feel like her neither. Maybe I'd take the girls to go see Clara for a bit. They'd probably like the South. Then I saw it. Chestnut. Just hanging right there over the sidewalk like it was asking me to come for a visit. We rolled on past and I turned to watch it rock forward and back from the chain hanging off the stoplight. Wasn't like I knew where the woman lived exactly. Or even if Ricky was there. Didn't matter no way because when I got off the bus I knew something was wrong. Mya and Jackie was waiting for me at the bus stop.

"Nat sick, Mama! She real sick! Nikki say she got a fever of one oh five!"

"Um..." They took both my hands and led me down the block. Given how cold their hands felt they were probably waiting for a while. "How long...when her fever get that high?"

"I don't know."

"She awake?" The both shrugged and kept on moving. "What y'all doing out in the middle of the night? How come your daddy ain't—"

"Daddy not home yet."

The porch steps creaked underneath us but I ain't pay them no mind. He hadn't even seen fit to come home or at least call. Shouldn't of shocked me but it did. Some part of me still thought that deep down he probably loved the girls. I was a stupid, stupid woman. Nat was balled up on the sofa shivering and sweating buckets.

"I tried to put a blanket on her but she keep kicking it off, Mama. I don't know...I ain't know what to do."

"It's okay, Nikki. You done good. Okay?

"Mmmhmm."

Nat was just barely coming around. Her eyes opened enough to call out my name. Wasn't nobody else to save my kids, just me. They were all looking to me.

"Mama, what we gonna do?"

"Shh! Just let me think."

"She sick! Look!" Jackie pointed one finger just as Nat leaned over the side of the sofa to get rid of whatever they'd eaten for supper. "Mama, do something!"

"Okay, stop yelling at me!" I had to close my eyes to shut out the thoughts that were thundering up in my ears. For just a second, was like wasn't nobody in the room except for me. "Nikki, go get everybody's coats and stuff. Mya call your Auntie Helen—no Paula. She live closer. Call her up and tell her we need a ride to the hospital."

"Okay."

"Okay."

"What about me, Mama?"

"Come here, Jackie. Come sit right here and talk real nice to your sister. Tell her about something pretty."

I had a medicine cabinet full of stuff. Something had to work. Running up the stairs I went over the things in my head. Just because the kid stuff wasn't working didn't mean the real medicine wouldn't. Got halfway up before I got the scare of my life. The banister creaked and wobbled and leaned out, threatening to crash down to the hallway below if I ain't let it go. Was like some force shoved me to the wall, saved me before I could find out if the banister was gone break completely off.

"MAMA, HURRY!"

I found an ice pack and put that on my baby's head but wasn't much else I could do. Paula showed up like I knew she would and checked on us at every stoplight. Looking in the back seat to see how we were doing.

"Where's Ricky?"

Ricky wasn't like her regular old man. Her man was into playing catch and things in the yard. Having barbecues and things like that. She couldn't understand Ricky. I ain't understand Ricky. She pulled us up to the emergency room doors and we piled out, running. The nurses looked at me like I was crazy. A bad cold was all she most likely had. Wasn't no reason to go running and screaming into the ER where folks were battling gunshot wounds and knife fights. But I ain't hear none of that.

"She sick! See! Look at her!"

"Ma'am, please have a seat."

The dark red plastic chairs were all connected to this silver thing that gave them the proper support. But the arrangement had folks sitting right up on each other, back to back, waiting to get seen. All of them cutting their eyes at me, thinking I thought I was special. I wanted to say I didn't. I couldn't. I wanted to show them the old scars so they'd know for sure. Wasn't nothing about me special.

"Please...help her..."

"We will. We just need you to have a seat. Fill out some forms and we'll get to you as soon as we can." She lifted both eyebrows and walked me over to the nearest free seat. "Okay? Okay. Here. Just take this and fill it out best you can. When you're done just bring it up to the desk."

"Mama, what's that?"

"Nothing, baby. Here. Take your sister."

Took them ten minutes to get my insurance card back to me. Said they needed to make a copy. I ain't say nothing. Paula caught up to us but I sent her home. Wasn't no reason for her to be away from her own family just to sit in the waiting room. And after we were waiting for damn near two hours I got sick of doing as I was told.

"Ma'am, we are doing our very best—"

"Then your best ain't good enough! She just a little girl! She barely breathing! You supposed to do something!"

By then I wasn't much more than a thorn in her side. But she sucked it up and came around to look at Nat. She took her pulse then started shouting things to folks I hadn't even noticed was there. Before long my baby was up on one of them stretchers and I was doing my best to keep up and stay out they way at the same time. They took her into this room flooded with men in white coats. Talking and shouting and grabbing things...They knew what they were doing, I could see that, but the mama in me wasn't satisfied. I wanted to crawl up on that stretcher with her. Whatever it was that was doing this to my baby could have me if that would make it leave her alone.

"Ma'am? Ma'am, are you okay?"

The world got hard suddenly. And a blinding white light swung from side to side over my head. While feet covered by soft white shoes got closer and closer. They were so close I could've touched them. Then everything went black.

*

I see you're awake now, huh?" Her voice hovered somewhere over the machines, pulling at cords and flipping switches. They wasn't for me. Wasn't even turned on. "I'm just getting things ready for our next patient."

"My girls..." I was still dressed from head to toe and I ain't have to fight the hospital bed too much to sit up. "My baby, she okay?" The nurse put a hand to my head, studying my eyes. Made me think she had some bad news I ain't want, I ain't need.

"The doctor'll be in a little while to talk to you about it."

What it? Was it my baby? "Where is she? She gonna be okay?"

"I'll go get him."

"No! You tell me! Tell me where she is..."

"Mrs. Morrow, calm down. Alright?" She finally sat on the bed next to me, looking over her shoulder like there might be folks spying on us. "We pumped her stomach, gave her some antibiotics, and we're running some tests." The next part she said with a brittle kinda sadness hanging off her tongue. "Do you know how she could have gotten any toxic chemicals into her system?"

"Toxic chemicals? No. No—she just got a cold. A real bad cold. What toxic chemicals? Ain't no...we ain't got none of that!" We heard voices rounding the corner and the nurse turned around to stare at the curtain. It wasn't moving but I got the feeling that any second it would. "She's gonna be okay, though, right?"

"Ma'am, I can't say that." She swallowed real hard, her warm hands closing in on my frigid ones. "But you should really think about how she could have gotten anything harmful in her system. You seem like a good mother."

I was a good mama. But that ain't mean I knew what she was talking about. "Nat know better than to eat something ain't food. That what you talking about?"

"Just think about it."

The curtain rattled around the pole and a bunch more folks were standing at my bed. Man in a white coat, woman in a gray suit that was two sizes too big, and a security guard. They all had the same look on their faces. Same look Ricky'd gimme when Mya fell or something. Even the friendly nurse couldn't take it and ducked out before things started.

"Mrs. Morrow, I'm Dr. Levinsten. This is Mrs. Walker. She's a social worker. We'd like to talk to you about Natalie."

"What-What about her? She's okay, right?"

He was holding on to a file that couldn't of held more than a few pages in it but I couldn't stop staring at it. Wondering what was in it. What it said about me and my girls.

"Well, we're still waiting for the tests to come back to tell us exactly what she ingested but...I can say with absolute certainty that the compound included sodium benzene. Do you know what that is, Mrs. Morrow?"

"No."

"It is a common ingredient found in household cleaning products and is absolutely poisonous to adults and can cause lethal reactions in children."

"But she okay, right?" I was surrounded by sober faces full of unhelpful thoughts. "I wanna see my baby."

"She's resting comfortably in the pediatric ward with the rest of your children, whom my colleagues have already examined. Now, I'll leave you in Mrs. Walker's hands." He couldn't wait to get out of my presence, like I was making him dirty or something.

But the woman he called a social worker ain't have that reaction. She ain't really have no reaction. Her cool blue eyes looked me up and down and ain't move an inch. "Mrs. Morrow, your daughter...Mya has quite a few scars on her arms and legs. Why is that?"

"Mya? Because she...she like to climb trees and stuff like that. I try to get her to stop but she don't listen."

"Mmhmm." She glanced over her shoulder at the security guard like they were in it together. Them against me. "Did you try to stop Natalie from drinking bleach as well? I'd like to know how a three-year-old managed to ingest it without anyone noticing. Did she smell like bleach to you?"

"No."

"That causes some confusion. If it was in fact an accident...say she got into it by mistake, then her clothes or hands would smell like it. Now if someone gave it to her, perhaps fed it to her in her bottle then... do you understand what I'm saying?"

"I'm a good mama...I am."

"Mmhmm. Can you tell me what Natalie was doing all day?"

"She slept a lot. Threw up some. Was coughing. I gave her some cough medicine. The kind for kids."

"When did you first notice something wasn't right?"

"Um...last night? Maybe..."

"Maybe?"

"I was kinda distracted. I had to get ready for my first day of work. But I'm a good mama! I am! I love my girls. I'd...I'd die for them."

"Where's your husband, Mrs. Morrow?" She flipped open a pad of paper and pushed down on the top of a pen, making it click. "How can I reach him?"

"Why? Ricky ain't got nothing to do with this. You don't need to bother him none."

"His daughter is in the hospital. You don't think he would want to know?" She stopped writing. Her pretty little mouth opened up just a little to make an O. "Mrs. Morrow? What kind of relationship does he have with the girls?"

It was the perfect moment to let out my truth. Tell her what she wanted to hear. Ricky was a crazy man and he ain't give a damn about us. She'd want me to go into it more so I'd tell her about all the times he'd hit me or thrown me around. Tell her how I was planning to leave him and how much he scared the girls. Was so much I could've said but I just said, "He yell at them sometimes."

"Has he ever struck them? Did he give Mya those scars?"

I shook my head. I ain't want to but I couldn't lie on him. Couldn't say he'd do anything to Mya. He'd spank the others but I was always there to make sure it ain't go too far. And he wasn't about to poison nobody, just wasn't his way. Ricky liked to use his hands and see the look on folks' faces when he did what he did. Liked folks to know it was him that did stuff to them too. He wasn't gonna miss out on none of the credit that was due to him.

"Who has access to Natalie on a daily basis?"

"Can I see her?"

"Not right now. Please answer the question."

"Nobody. Just me and Ricky and the girls usually. Sometimes my friends come over or folks from the neighborhood. They all real nice. When can I see her?"

She threw another glance at the security guard who stood watch at the foot of the bed. When she looked back at me was when I heard it. Sound of a big angry man heading my way. The security guard disappeared first but he wasn't no match for my regular old man. Ricky probably just ran right over him.

"PECAN!"

The social worker looked at me anew. Like me sitting in the same spot was a surprise. "Is that your husband?"

"Pecan!" Ricky threw back what was left of the curtain and marched right up to me. Doctors and nurses stopped to watch as they hurried by. "You okay? Is it the baby?"

"No, no I'm fine. I just fainted is all."

"But my boy's okay? Right?"

I nodded. "Ricky this Mrs. Walker. She's a social...a social worker. She asking about the girls."

"What about the girls?" He frowned up real good. Was the first time I was happy about Ricky's rough outside. If anybody was gonna make the woman go away it was him.

"Mrs. Morrow, you're expecting?"

"Yeah she is. You ain't tell them? We finally having a boy."

"He don't know that. He just wishing."

"I know it." Ricky was already worked up. I should've just let it be. "How you gone tell me what I know? I know what I know. Where the girls? If you fine, then let's go."

"Mr. Morrow, your daughter Natalie has been admitted to the pediatric ward. We're waiting for the tox screen to come back but it looks like she's ingested a poisonous substance."

Ricky chuckled a bit then looked at me like it was a joke I must have been in on. "What she talking about?"

"They think somebody gave her bleach."

"Why somebody'd wanna do that? Don't make sense."

"Well, it is my job, Mr. Morrow, to investigate things like this and—"

"Investigate? Look, woman, ain't no need to do no investigating. Kids get into stuff. Right, Pecan? Ain't that the way it go? So, thanks but no thanks. We just gonna have to keep a closer eye on her. Come on, Pecan."

Ricky held back the curtain, waiting for me to slip on my shoes. She looked stunned to say the least. Guess she was expecting Ricky to take her side of things or at least listen to her.

"Mr. Morrow, I have to ask you to hold off on going up to Pediatrics until we have a better sense of what happened."

"N'all, I'm just gonna ask them what happened and they gonna tell me. I don't need you nosing around in my business."

"Mr. Morrow—"

"Look, I done already told you woman. Y'all can't be treating everybody that come up in here with a kid like this! What? You come after me because I'm a black man? Huh?"

"No—"

"Trying to take black babies from they families and put them with clean white folks. Huh? Y'all folks make me sick. Come on, Pecan."

And that was that. The security guard standing post outside of Nat's room looked a few years past retirement. He wasn't about to challenge Ricky. So Ricky scooped Nat up in his arms and led the rest of us to the elevators. Her little head rested against his big hard chest and I thought I was seeing things. It was the closest he ever got to showing her some type of affection.

15
Ghost

GOOD TO SEE YOU again, Mrs. Morrow."
I nodded and tucked my dress underneath me as I took a seat. "I got the money. Well, I got a job...so I'll have the money in a few weeks when I get paid."

"My secretary explained the details."

Mr. Silverman reminded me of all them rich folks I heard about. He ain't really care about money like most folks. His bills would still be paid even if he ain't get nothing from me but he wasn't about to let somebody think he was unprofessional.

"So, why don't we get started? Tell me why you want a divorce."

"I want Ricky to disappear."

He laughed and took a sip from a steaming paper cup. The sun shined bright through the window behind him, making him look like he had a halo around him. "Well, I will do my best. But what I mean is why."

I knew what he meant. The walls of his office were decorated with paintings that ain't look like more than splotches of color to me but he had them in big gold frames that screamed money. "How much that cost?"

"I'm sorry? Oh. I'm not sure. But the young lady who decorated my office assured me that they were from a very important artist. Do you like them?"

"Yeah...not that I know nothing about art."

"Well, I can look into who the artist is. That way maybe you can get one for yourself."

"Okay."

"Okay. So. Mrs. Morrow...how much do you know about your husband's property?"

"You mean the house?"

"Is that all? Just the house? What about stocks...bonds...anything that he might want to sell?"

"Nothing. Ricky don't talk about that sorta thing with me. I know he go to the bank around the corner from us to do his business. He say he like that they know his name. That every time he walk in somebody shouting hi to him. Make him feel like some kinda superstar or something. He don't say it exactly like that but I can tell."

It looked like Mr. Silverman was writing down everything I said. His hand scribbled real fast, pausing when I did, and finally he looked up at me. "I'll need an idea of your cash flow. How much money is coming into the house and how much is going out."

"Don't know that neither."

"Alright...I suppose I could subpoena the records after the initial filing. Do you think he's going to put up a fight?"

I ain't think it. I knew it. Ricky wasn't about to let nothing go down that wasn't his idea first. "How long until...um...until he know what we doing?"

"Well, I can get the papers drawn up in about a week. Give or take a few days for service...we're talking ten days, I suppose. Divorce is a difficult process and this is just the first step. Many people need to take some time to gather their thoughts and decide what they want out of all of this. So, don't feel like you need to rush through it. It can take a toll on you emotionally."

"That's not gonna happen. I just wanna be able to take care of me and my girls without him coming around."

"Right. You mentioned that before. Sole custody." He went back to scribbling. "Did I explain to you that it's rare for a judge not to at least award visitation? Especially if the husband wants it? Mrs. Morrow?" He looked up just as a cloud passed over the sun, blocking his halo.

"He got some woman a few blocks over."

"He's having an affair?"

"Mmhmm."

"How do you know this?"

"My girlfriend told me and I believe her. She wouldn't lie. Said she heard it around the way. And it ain't like Ricky too good for that. He think he better than he is. And..."

"Yes? And what?"

"And I ain't really been...doing like I used to...with him. He think it's because I'm pregnant but that ain't really got nothing to do with it. I just...can't."

"Wait, wait. Um...you're pregnant?" He sighed all heavy like soon as I nodded. "That makes things—well, it just..." His sigh came back on and pushed him to the back of his chair. His pen tapped uselessly across the pad of paper as he looked at me. "Why exactly do you want a divorce?"

"Because."

"Mrs. Morrow, I don't mean to seem insensitive here but most people, judges included, will find it difficult to believe that a young woman such as yourself with four kids and another on the way...has really thought this through. He's more likely to conclude that your husband needs to be involved. To help you raise these children."

"No. I don't need Ricky. He don't help none now."

He groaned and squeezed the arm of his chair with one hand, holding on to the pen with the other. "I'm trying to help you here, Mrs. Morrow. If there's something else that I don't know...is this about his affair?"

"Not really."

His glasses sat on his desk so he could rub the bridge of his nose. Guess I was a bit more trouble than he'd bargained for.

"Okay..."

"Ricky, he, um...he ain't no good. He don't—I mean he pay the bills and stuff and I'm real grateful for that, I am. But he still...he still ain't no good. He don't love me. Don't love my girls. He might love Mya but even that I ain't too sure about. He don't...he just ain't right."

"Okay well what would he say? What would your husband say about you?"

"What you mean?"

"Would he say that you were a good mother? Would he say that you were a lazy drunk? What?"

"He'd say...um...guess he'd say I was an okay mama. Sometimes the girls get into things and they get sick or hurt or something and he blame me. Like my youngest, Natalie, she was here last time. We had to take her to the hospital a few nights ago because she was sick. Turn out she got some bleach up in her system. My other youngest, Jackie. She call herself cleaning up after Nat because she'd had a little accident...in bed, you know? She poured half a bottle of bleach on the mattress. Don't know what she was thinking. But she ain't mean it. She get these things in her head and she just be trying to help...but um... Ricky was real mad. Not as mad as he could've been but still pretty mad. He say I just let them run wild."

"What about other people? Family? Friends? What would they say?"

Mr. Silverman'd started writing again so I figured I was on the right track. "They'd say everything was fine. Except for my girlfriend Helen probably. She um...she know the truth."

"Helen?" He underlined her name and then waited for me to explain. "What would she say?"

"That he ain't right." Before he could start sighing again I opened my mouth to keep going. I ain't know what was gone come out but figured I'd just keep going until I ain't have nothing else to say. Must've worked because when I finally took a breath Mr. Silverman's mouth was hanging open. In his world men like Ricky ain't exist. Just folks in suits and women in sparkling jewels. Maybe heaven for me would be something like his world.

❦

"MAMA!"

NIKKI CAME RUNNING TO the door before I'd even got a chance

to hang up my coat. First thought came to me was something was wrong with Nat. Doctors said she was fine but I kept waiting for something. I got up in the middle of the night just to look in on her. She'd be sleeping so quiet, like a little chocolate-covered angel, my baby was.

"Phone, Mama!"

"What?"

"It's Heziah!" Nikki grinned and took me by the hand. My coat was hanging off, dragging along the floor but she ain't think nothing of it. Heziah was on the phone. She snatched it outta Jackie's hand and held it out proudly. "Here, Mama."

"Hello?" It was what anybody would've said, that's what I figured so I said it.

"Tell him that I finished Moby Dicky!"

"And tell him I got an A on my spelling test."

"Shh!" I waved the girls outta the kitchen and straightened my dress so I'd look presentable as if he could see me. "How are you?"

Heziah only had one speed. He ain't say one thing when he meant another. Ain't use his words like weapons, aiming them at my heart. At least he ain't try to, that much hadn't changed. He told me that things were picking up at the carpet store and I told him about my new job. Made myself some tea and tried to pretend like things were normal. Same as they'd always been between us. We were friends. We talked about our days and I did most of the listening. After a while he got to the point.

"Belinda, I miss you. I wanna see you, if that's okay."

"I don't think so."

"Oh. Why not?"

"I'm real busy with work and stuff."

"Oh."

My fingernails tapped against the cracked vinyl of the kitchen table blind to the sadness in his voice. He'd left me standing in the cold. My honorable man as it turned out wasn't so different from all the regular folks that found they way into my heart. So I sat there listening to his silence. Listened so hard I ain't even hear the sun go down and the front door open.

"Belinda? You still there?"

"Yeah—" Soon as I said it I wanted to take it back. Ricky's voice boomed through the living room and into the hall. "I gotta go," I whispered covering the speaking end of the phone with both hands.

"You're upset. I can tell and I guess I don't blame you. We should have handled things differently. And I knew that. I just didn't follow my first mind."

"Mmhmm. I gotta go."

"But I'm trying to make up for it now. That is...if you'll still have me."

"I...I gotta go."

The floorboards were creaking up a storm just to let me know I had about a second or two before Ricky was standing in the doorway, looking down on me.

"Belinda?"

Should've just hung up on him. Don't know why I didn't. Just sat there holding the phone and waiting for what was coming next. Waiting to breathe. But Ricky had no idea I was on the phone with my honorable man because he kept on walking right past me to the stairs and up he went to turn on the shower.

"Belinda?"

"I'm here."

"Say something. I'm saying that...that I want to make this work. If you still want to that is..."

"I can't."

"You changed your mind about leaving your husband?"

My mouth filled up with cotton and I just sat there, staring at the table. Couldn't tell him my secret. Couldn't tell him what had been growing up inside me ever since he'd left. Didn't even matter if it was his because Ricky wasn't gonna have that. No. My honorable man wasn't no match for my regular old man. Ricky ain't need nothing but a minute to tear him limb from limb. My Heziah. My Heziah was a gentle man. He ain't deserve Ricky's rage.

"Belinda? Please. Just tell me. Have you changed your mind?"

"Yeah. Me and Ricky worked it out. We staying together."

"Okay. I understand." He got real quiet. "I hope y'all are real happy together. Hug the girls for me?"

"Yeah. Sure." The dial tone rang in my ear for about a minute before I got up the strength to walk over to the wall and hang up the phone. He ain't bother to say it but I knew what it was. Goodbye always sounded the same, no matter who said it.

"Mama, I'm hungry."

"Okay. What you want?"

"Pickles."

"Mya, pickles ain't a proper meal. Want me to make some potato salad?"

She nodded. "Extra pickles."

"Okay, baby."

I watched her skip back off to be with her sisters and wondered what it felt like to be free like that. To not have nothing weighing on you. Just then Ricky came down the stairs buttoning up a fresh shirt. It was already tucked into his slacks and his shoes were shined so bright I ain't need him to tell me he was going out for supper.

"Hey, Pecan."

"Hey."

"I'm going out. I'll be back later on tonight."

"Okay. I'll save you a plate."

"Yeah?" Ricky grinned that grin I hardly ever got to see, and kissed me on the cheek. "That's real nice. Make sure you feed my boy some protein. Make him some beef or something. So he come out strong like his daddy. You hear me?"

"Yeah. Oh, um, Ricky?" I hurried after him before he could get out the door. "The banister kinda loose. Maybe you could fix it?"

"Yeah sure. When I get back."

Ricky was always leaving the house smelling good and looking his best. Any other girl might have asked where he was going to begin with. Not me. His leaving wasn't what concerned me. It was the coming back. If I was lucky maybe one day whatever he was getting up on Chestnut Street would be enough to keep him there.

16

The God in Science

THE MEN'S DEPARTMENT WAS slow that day so they put me over in children's. I figured it was God trying to get my attention. Until that day I didn't have time to be thinking about this baby that wasn't even supposed to be there. But being surrounded by cute little clothes and things were making that harder than usual.

My first customer only wanted some cute little footies for Easter. She stood at the counter playing with the little barrettes we had in this big clear container while I rang them up for her. The registers weren't as hostile to me as they were when I first started. I'd seen enough go wrong with them that I ain't even need to call the manager to fix half the stuff. Just hit the right keys and put in the money. I was a working girl.

The fact that I wasn't all that familiar with the baby growing inside me wasn't all my fault. The baby had to take some of the blame because it was barely there. It ain't make me sick or tired or anything really. It was like it really ain't exist even though the damn test said something else. I told myself that most women wouldn't believe it either. They'd just go on about their lives, waiting for something to prove that damn test wrong.

The woman took her little bag and went on about her way, leaving me alone with my thoughts. What was this baby thinking about climbing up in my belly? It was probably flying around up there in heaven and looking down, trying to find a good mama to climb up in. There had to be better choices around here. Maybe I was the only woman around when it was looking down. Or maybe it was desperate.

As I was heading over to ask this man if he needed any help, I noticed something out the corner of my eye. Was a tiny little blue and brown suit. With a bowtie. I never paid much attention to boy stuff but something about it made me go over and touch it. Wasn't real soft but it was smooth, like if it was gonna get dirty it'd need to be dry cleaned. Wasn't practical. What baby would wear something that fancy? It ain't make sense but I kept right on touching it. I had to make myself stop. I was supposed to be working not shopping. So that's what I did for the next hour. But then I found myself back over in that section. I picked up the suit and put it carefully into a shopping cart then moved on to see what else I could find to go with it. Probably wasn't even gonna be a boy, I thought. Maybe it wasn't even a baby, just some kinda mix up. I started ringing things up when the other salesgirl took her break. She came back and I was still at it. I just wanted to know how much it all cost.

"Belinda?"

"Hmm?"

"Did somebody ask you to hold this stuff?"

I nodded. Wasn't about to tell her I just wanted to see the green numbers light up the register. That I wasn't about to buy anything.

"Who? You ain't write their name on it."

"I was about to." I scribbled Helen on a piece of paper and twisted a rubber band around the note and the hangers.

"Thought you was leaving early."

"Oh! Right. I am." I set the items I'd collected back in the cart. Was only a few minutes before two. "I guess I lost track a time."

"You better clock out. They get real picky about that stuff."

Half-running, I ran into the office and pushed my time card all the way into the little machine. Ricky hated to be kept waiting, especially for something like this. It was the day the doctor was supposed to tell him he was having a son. With the first three he ain't wanna know. He wanted to be surprised. But by the time Nat came along he was obsessed with knowing everything the doctors did. Pestering them about it every month until they told him. Nope. Another girl. He ain't take it so well. For about a week after that nothing I said or did was good enough. And every night he couldn't relax unless he'd hit me at least once. But then the week was over and things went back to normal. I had a sickening feeling I wasn't due to get off so easy this time.

"Where you been? I been sitting up in this parking lot forever!"

"Sorry. I got held up."

"I make time. You think I ain't got things to do today? Huh? I got a fight coming up next week—I need to be in the gym. What you up in there doing that's so important?"

"Nothing."

"That's what I thought."

Ricky jerked the stick thing toward the floor and backed outta the parking space. He wasn't even close to being a good driver. Half the time he ain't really look where he was going so I got in the habit of doing it for him. I watched to see which turning signal he put on then looked to make sure nobody was walking in the way.

"Ricky, watch out."

"I see them. They see me. They just think they ain't gotta move they asses. Move!" He hollered out the window.

"They just kids."

"'Posed to be in school." He spun the wheel hard to the right and sped off down the street. "I gotta be back at the gym by three."

"Okay. Girls get outta school about then too, so that's good for me. Anise said I can leave Nat with her for a few extra hours, though. I was thinking maybe I'd take Nikki, Mya, and Jackie to the park or something. Since the cold kinda breaking now. Maybe even take them to get ice cream or something."

"Mmhmm." He frowned at the road.

"Can I have a few dollars?"

"You got money. That why you got that job right? So you'd have money?"

"Yeah but I ain't get paid yet."

A red light popped up in front of us and Ricky leaned forward so the steering wheel was buried deep in his chest. He tossed his wallet from his back pocket to my lap. "Go on, Pecan. But when you get paid you gone pay me back. Since you a working girl now and everything."

I ain't say nothing. Just pulled a crisp brand new five dollar bill outta the leather folds of his wallet. At first I ain't see it. It was wrinkled and folded up like it'd been opened and closed a bunch of times. I counted. Seven numbers and a name. Connie. Connie on Chestnut Avenue maybe.

"What you looking at? Gimme my wallet."

"Nothing."

We got to the doctor's office about ten minutes late but I barely noticed. They made us wait another thirty minutes but I ain't notice that either. Ricky was pissed. Pissed at them. At traffic. And at me for not being pissed with him. I looked at my big strong regular man and just wished he was somebody else. Why he couldn't be somebody else? Somebody nice and gentle. Why'd it have to be him?

"Mrs. Morrow?"

"Yeah! She right here! Right here—come on, let's go."

It ain't take the doctor long to come in and put the sound thing on my stomach. Ricky stood by me, holding his breath. That's when I made up my mind that if I was having a boy, then he wasn't going to be like Ricky at all. I would make sure of it. Whatever happened to make Ricky like he was, wasn't gonna happen to my boy. He was gonna be sweet and nice and thoughtful. My baby boy was gone be a gentle and honorable man.

"So? What is it?"

"It looks like...a...a boy. Yep, most definitely a boy."

"WOOO!" Ricky let loose, punching at the air. "I knew it! Didn't I say it, baby? I said it was a boy!"

I nodded and tried to think happy thoughts. Only good thing about Ricky being on top of the world was he couldn't get mad no more at me or the traffic or the little old lady crossing the street when it clearly wasn't her turn. Ricky was just plain happy all the way home. He parked the car and turned to smile at me.

"I'm proud of you, Pecan. You a good woman, you know that? You always take good care of me. Gimme babies. I ain't even mad that it took this long to get a boy. You hear me? I ain't mad no more."

The clock on the dashboard said 2:57 but Ricky ain't seem to notice.

"We'll name him after me."

"Ricky Jr.?"

"Richard, baby. Ain't gonna call the boy—I mean when he's a boy—yeah we'll call him Ricky Jr. or maybe R.J. but we'll put my full name on his birth certificate. Richard Elijah Morrow. Junior. What you think? Sound good, don't it?"

"I guess."

Next thing I knew Ricky had turned off the car and was coming around to my side. Every bit of my body tensed up, waiting for that smile to turn upside down. Nothing good ever stayed with Ricky long. I'd accepted that about him.

"Come on, get out." He opened my door.

"Why?"

"Why what? Why get out? Because this where we live!" He laughed. "Pecan, you so funny. What, you wanna just stay in the car all night?"

"No, I mean why you opening the door for me. You ain't done that since we were teenagers."

"Can't a man wanna take care of his pregnant wife? Damn, woman." The car door slammed shut and the gate squeaked open. Ricky followed me up the stairs and into the foyer. Then he took off his coat.

"What you doing?"

"Hanging up my coat."

"I thought you had to get back to the gym."

"I do. I just wanna spend some time with my pretty wife first."

First I was his pregnant wife then his pretty wife. Next I was gonna be his sexy wife. When he was in the mood, Ricky wasn't too hard to figure out. He just smiled and said he wanted to go to bed with me. I ain't say nothing. Just let him push me toward the stairs. Undress me then him. I wrapped my arms around my stomach tighter and tighter but he just kept right on looking. Claiming me and my baby boy with his eyes and then his hands.

"You showing already."

"No, I'm not."

"How you gone lie? I'm looking right at you."

Ricky wasn't a man to be no kinda gentle. I knew that after having somebody else to compare him to so when his arm jutted out across my chest, pulling me into the bedcovers with him I just went limp, thinking it'd be over soon enough. But then he must have gotten something different into his head.

"Mmm, Pecan...come on now. Open your eyes." He was right over me, the sun shining against his skin until it was all golden and warm. "You love me, don't you?" His voice matched his skin and he pulled my hips to meet his. "Come on, baby."

Few minutes later he was hitting my spot. Stuff I ain't never said before came up outta me. About how good it was. And he ain't even flinch. Wheezing all heavy on top of me, felt like we were a couple of heathens in heat. My regular old man had a way with my body that made me turn red from the inside out. Burning hot red and wasn't nothing I could do about it.

"See. You missed me."

I curled up on the bed, listening to the sound of his pants zipping, his belt buckling. He bumped up against my feet when he sat to tie his shoes so I pulled my knees closer to my chest.

"I'm gone be late to the gym, but I think we needed that. Get us back on track. Ain't no reason for a man not to be intimate with his wife. Mess up things. Mess up how it's supposed to be between them. But it's gonna be alright now. I know it. You hear me, Pecan? I know I ain't always been the easiest man to be with but things gonna be different," he said patting my hip to make sure I was awake. "You hear me? I ain't even hit you in...I don't even know how long. Ain't you gonna say something?"

The clock said 3:25. The girls should've been home from school already. He ain't like it but that was about all I could let myself think about. My girls. All the panic I had built up inside me went straight to worrying about where they were.

"What—What you doing? You going somewhere?" Ricky asked. "I ain't never seen you get dressed that fast."

"The girls should've been home by now."

I couldn't find the shoes I was wearing so I just grabbed the first pair I could find. They were pink with a little bow across the toes. Ricky'd picked them out, said they looked like they were made for me—sweet and innocent. Wasn't no sign of the girls on the first floor but I could hear voices coming from somewhere. Ricky followed behind me, looking where I was, saying stuff like I shouldn't worry, they were big girls. I threw open the front door and there they were, looking up at me from the lawn. Their bookbags laid up against the porch, just waiting for the chance to come inside.

"What y'all doing out here?"

"Waiting," Jackie mumbled, kicking up grass with the toe of her shoe.

"Waiting for what? Nikki where's your key?"

"I got it. We...We just thought we'd sit out here for a little while."

"Oh." I was a horrible mama. It was plain as day. I kept making them promise after promise that I couldn't keep. Now this.

"Aight, baby, I gotta go. Gotta put in a few more hours." Ricky pulled me close and pressed his lips to mine, sucking on my mouth for the whole world to see. "Mmm, now that's what I'm talking about!

Y'all be good."

"Bye, Daddy."

We watched as Ricky started up his car and took off toward the sunset. Could've been a real happy family moment if we ain't know he was coming back. "Y'all go on inside. I gotta go get Nat." I hurried into the street, thinking so hard I ain't even see the car until whoever was behind the wheel slammed on their brakes.

"Mama!"

I was shaking something good. But I was still standing. I was fine. The driver hopped on out, asking if I was okay, my girls ran toward me too. I was fine, I told them. Just fine.

"You supposed to look both ways," Mya was more annoyed than worried. "Don't you know that? Even we know that."

"I did look."

"No, you didn't. I was watching."

"Just go on in the house! You a chile. I don't need you telling me what I did or what I ain't do. I'm the mama. If I say I looked then I looked. Now go."

After I got Nat we went about things as usual—me in the kitchen, fixing supper and the girls running about doing one thing or another. My dress was the kind that buttoned up the front, what they were calling a shirt dress. It came with a matching belt that I'd been using to hide my condition from folks. The chicken pieces fell against the plate of flour, dusting a cloud of whiteness into the air and I was fidgeting with the belt, wishing I'd put it in a bigger hole. Then I felt a little hand tap me on the back.

"What is it, Jackie?"

"We having fried chicken?"

"Yeah."

"Ricky like fried chicken."

"I know."

"That why we having it?"

"You do your homework already? Y'all just be running around here like you ain't got nothing better to do. I guess maybe it's time for me to give y'all some chores. When I was your age your granddaddy gave me all sorts of things to do."

"Like what?" Jackie hopped up on one of the kitchen chairs, looking all attentive like she did whenever I talked about my daddy.

"Like...washing things."

"Like clothes?"

"Yeah. And floors and windows and beating the dust outta the rugs and blankets. Sometimes he let me help him fix stuff too."

"I wish he ain't die." Her sweet voice carried the words like they ain't weigh no more than the wind, like it was just a simple sorta fact. "Did grandpa like Ricky?"

"Why you thinking on that?"

"Because. Grandpa was a big strong man, right? I bet he would've beat Ricky up real good." She grinned from ear to ear.

"Don't say that."

"But it's true, right?"

"Maybe."

"I think he would've." She nodded and then went about twirling the salt and pepper shakers that had been minding their own business on the table. "Mama, it's okay to fight when somebody's messing with you, right? It ain't the same as if you started it."

"Who told you that?"

"Nobody. I just know it. Because if you just give in all the time they gonna keep doing it. Right?"

"Maybe. Don't you wanna go play with your sisters?"

She shook her head. I'd braided her hair into three braids that morning but only two of them was in good condition. Jackie had a bad habit of playing with the ends until they undid themselves. Drove Ricky crazy, said she looked like some hopeless chile that ain't nobody care enough for. Once the chicken was all seasoned and floured I sat down next to her to give her my full attention. Most of the time it ain't bother me what she did to her hair. It was just how she was.

"Mama?"

"Yeah, baby."

"Where Heziah? When we get see him?" She must have seen how much I ain't wanna answer that because she kept right on talking. "Because he mean to us what grandpa mean to you—he the one that talk to us and play with us and he listen...he like us. Like me. I decided he gonna be my daddy. Ricky just gonna be Ricky."

It wasn't how things worked. Lil' girls ain't get to pick their daddies but Jackie wasn't the easiest child to convince. Her eyes stared back at me, looking just like mine. "So, when we get to see Heziah?"

"No, baby, I don't think so."

"Why not? Because he don't wanna marry you?" She might as well have punched me right in the gut. The grease cracked over the chicken, calling me to it so I got up to check on it. "Mama? Daddy wanted to marry you right? Maybe it ain't such a big deal to get married."

"Jackie—"

"We could still be a family."

"STOP!"

It was a bad day. First Ricky wanting to celebrate and Mya thinking I'm stupid, and then Jackie telling me the last thing I wanted to hear. Wasn't no point in even thinking about what wasn't possible. Heziah was gone. It was what was best. Him and me—couldn't no good come from us, only pain, and possibly death. That was what I thought about when I thought of Heziah. But wasn't no words nice enough to make her see that. She was just a kid. A kid that ain't think her daddy liked her. Wasn't nothing I could do about that neither. So I made up my mind to at least give her somebody to blame.

"He not coming back because I won't let him. It ain't him. It's me. He love y'all. He told me himself but that don't mean that we supposed to be together—us and him. Sometimes folks come into our lives just to give us something we need then they leave. That's what Heziah did."

"But—"

"But nothing. That's what it is. Now go on and play."

"I don't wanna play! I want my daddy back! And…And you j-j-just scared of Ricky! But I ain't scared and the next time my daddy call I'm gonna talk to him and I'm gonna tell him everything!"

She took off running and I was right with her. I ain't have no plan, just knew I couldn't leave it like that. She was halfway up the stairs when I got to the first step. I wasn't never no runner so my legs were ready to give out by the fifth or sixth stair. My arms pumped at my sides, making me fight for a good-sized breath. But that peaceful hot air just wasn't enough. Then a shoe went flying through the air, whizzing by my head and I couldn't believe it. My baby would never do that to me. Never wanna cause me no harm. Just the thought tripped me up so bad I stumbled on a stair and finally grabbed the banister for balance. I was almost to the top. I actually thought it was a good thing. Thought "I'm almost there." Thought I was safe with the banister. What a stupid woman I was, leaning up against the tired old thing.

Before I knew it, it started to crack. The wood split right down to the base of the stairs, with me still clinging to the top of it like a damn fool. On the way down I remember thinking back on the days when Ricky used to carry me up the stairs because they were so steep. I'd forgotten how steep they actually were but it all came crashing back to me. All the way down.

❦

"I'M SORRY, MAMA." JACKIE cried from some corner of the hallway. "I sorry, I sorry, I sorry."

I couldn't see her through all the pain that was running through my body. The smell of burnt fried chicken was lying just outta my grasp. It was all a fog. A painful mess of a fog. Couldn't even tell where it was coming from, the pain. One minute it was my back then it was my arm, just...everywhere. And even though the floor was hard like I'd never felt hard before, I ain't wanna leave it. Ain't wanna move an inch.

"Mama?" Nikki was crying over me like it was my funeral or something. "Mama?"

"I'm okay. You gotta call..."

"Daddy? Should I call daddy?"

"No. No..." The fog was getting deeper and so dark. Blinking ain't do no good but I kept at it anyway. Until it got so that my eyelids were too heavy for all that.

From then on I couldn't see nothing, just hear their voices. Nikki telling Nat to keep away from me. "Don't touch" she said. And then voices of folks I ain't know, fussing over me. Then a blinding light, too white to be the sun.

17

Just Dessert

Y EAH...I'M UP AT THE hospital now. Not tonight. Probably
tomorrow. Yeah...Alright. Bye."

He ain't look like his usual self. Ricky hung up the phone and
rocked himself back and forth on the edge of the chair with his hands
clasped together just under his chin. He looked some sorta sad or
worried, maybe both. But he was quiet. So quiet I almost ain't believe
it was really him. Then he looked at me.

"You awake? I mean you awake. I'll go and...And get somebody."
Then he was gone.

His shoes squeaked all the way down the hall like he'd been
jumping around in puddles and the plastic was soaked through.
Squeaking against the shiny white floor of the hospital. I remembered
what happened like it'd just happened but the pain was almost gone.

Vanished. Almost. And I felt...alone like I never felt before.

"Mrs. Morrow, I'm Dr. Sares. Do you mind if I take a look at you?"

Ricky was leaning up against the doorway, both hands in his pockets, staring out into the hall. He couldn't even look at me. Why he'd want to? I was stupid and weak and I ain't need no doctor to tell me nothing. I knew.

"Mrs. Morrow, you had a pretty bad fall. Do you remember?" He sighed softly, touching my shoulder as the first few tears slid down my cheeks. "We did everything we could but the baby didn't make it. Your body can naturally dispose of...um...or we can help it along. How would you like to proceed?"

Dispose. Like my baby was trash. The words were right there, right on the tip of my tongue but I couldn't. I just couldn't make them sound like anything. The doctor ain't seem to mind, though, like he expected as much.

"Shh, there there now. You can still have other children. You're very lucky that you weren't badly injured yourself. That kind of a fall... Well you could've had more than just a dislocated shoulder. Now, we gave you some painkillers so you shouldn't be in too much pain, but I'm going to write you a prescription anyway."

Ricky turned at the sound of him ripping some paper from a pad but he ain't move from the doorway. He hated me that much, I could tell.

"Do you have any questions?" He glanced over his shoulder at Ricky but neither one of us said a word. "Well, if you change your minds..."

Once the doctor was gone, Ricky finally came over to me. Put his hand on my bad shoulder, softly tracing the edge of the sling they'd put me in.

"I'm sorry," came out before anything else could even be thought up. "Ricky?"

"Yeah."

"I'm...I'm so sorry."

He nodded. "What happened, Pecan?"

"I fell."

"No shit. You don't think I can see that? What the fuck? I ain't asking you—I'm asking how did you fall? You knew the banister was loose. Everybody did. You couldn't be no more careful than this?"

"I tried..."

"You tried?"

"I wasn't thinking."

"What that mean? Hmm? What, you decided to take a rest as you was walking up the stairs?"

"No."

"No? Then what? Tell me. I gotta know." Ricky stood over me, that crazy look in his eye, but this time he was damn close to crying. I had never seen Ricky cry. "You gonna tell me or what?"

"It was...it was just an accident."

"Pecan—" His fist flexed in my face just as a nurse walked by the room. As angry and hurt as he was, he got it under control right then. Breathing all heavy, he tried to make his face look like a normal man's. "Look, just tell me. I ain't gonna get mad. Just tell me. I got a right to know. He...he my son, you know? He my boy."

"He my boy too." The words ain't sound right coming out my mouth but it was true. I'd finally gotten around to claiming him and he wasn't there no more.

"Fine. Have it your way." Ricky's eyes flinched a little then he backed away. "I be by tomorrow to pick you up."

My body relaxed inch by inch as Ricky walked out the room until I almost felt like me again. Thought about giving the girls a call but I ain't know what to say. Figured I'd see them soon enough and by then I'd know what to say. Know how honest to be. Know if I should come up with some kinda fairy tale that'd make sense to the younger ones. Mya's teachers were always sending notes home with her saying that the stories she made up and the pictures she drew, that they ain't from the mind of a little girl. Ricky said it was because she too smart for them other kids in her class, that she was mature. But that ain't what her teachers were getting at. For four years her teachers'd been telling me I was a bad mama. That somehow I let my little girl grow up too soon. It wasn't fair to her, they said. That a pretty girl like her should've been thinking about candy and fun and things like that. The nurse came around to check on me and I pretended to be asleep until all was quiet around me.

⫸

"YO' MAMA'S HOME!" THE front door closed behind us and Ricky threw the lock.

They came running from all sorts of directions and stopped to look at my arm, all except one. Jackie was nowhere to be seen.

"Well? Y'all not gonna give me a hug?"

"We don't wanna hurt you."

"You ain't gonna hurt me. Now get over here."

One by one they walked on over, all serious and careful like. Wasn't natural. Nobody supposed to hug they mama that way. So I made sure to smile real big for them. Ain't want them thinking I was nothing but fine.

"Aight, Pecan, I'm gonna head back to the gym. Y'all be aright?"

If we weren't it wouldn't have been because he wasn't there. Ricky's presence never fixed a thing. But I just nodded.

Looking around my living room, the hallway, none of it fit any more. It was all old stuff. Most of it had cracks or rough edges that I'd spent ten years pretending ain't exist. Up until then they hadn't posed no kinda threat but suddenly I felt like a fool for letting them near me.

"How about we get started on supper? Where's Jackie?" They looked around at each other and nobody said a word. "What? Cat got your tongue?"

"She upstairs."

"She sleeping," Mya added.

"Okay. Nikki, wanna help me in the kitchen?"

"I'll help too."

"Me too!"

It was nice having Mya with me. Most of the time she was like her daddy about the kitchen, wasn't no reason for her to be there unless she was getting food, but something about that day was different. The four of us mixed and grated and chopped up things then threw them all in the pot to cook. We were having what I called leftover stew.

"How come I don't have a apron like Nikki?"

"I ain't think you wanted one. I'll get you one, baby. Next time we go shopping. Okay? Remind me." Mya nodded and saw fit to give me a little smile. Sometimes my girls were a complete mystery to me. They just sorta sprung up outta the ground with no help from anybody it seemed. And I was left trying to keep up with who they were turning into.

"Where baby?" Nat climbed up on a kitchen chair and leaned her head against my stomach like she'd started doing. "Huh?"

The others just sorta froze. It was getting back to being flat so she was confused. Wasn't her fault she ain't know the game we were playing where we just pretended like things were normal. Natalie was a sweet peaceful chile, more than the others. She could ask the most painful questions with that bubbly damn grin of hers that was still full of baby teeth.

"Mama, where baby?"

"Baby gone."

"Gone?"

"Yeah. Now let's add some rice. What y'all think of that?"

"Okay, Mama."

"Then we'll go upstairs and wake Jackie up and the five of us go outside for a bit to get some fresh air. What you think?"

They should've been excited but not one of them looked it. The lid on the pot snapped shut, started whistling right away, and I couldn't help but wonder what I was missing.

"Let's go get Jackie."

"She sleeping," Mya reminded me.

"Well, how long she been sleeping?"

"I don't know."

"You don't know? She been sleep since y'all got home from school? Well, she can't sleep much longer or she not gonna wanna go to bed when it's time. School day tomorrow. Why don't y'all go get whatever toys or dolls or whatever you wanna take outside." I meant to do the waking myself. Got all the way to the stairs and couldn't go any further. Not one step.

"Mama?"

"Oh, y'all go on ahead. I'll be up in a minute."

"Daddy fixed the banister."

"I know. I see it."

"You not gonna fall."

"Yes, Mya, I see it. I'm coming. You go on ahead."

Just pieces of wood, wasn't no need to be scared of pieces of wood. They couldn't hurt nobody. But I cursed them, threatening to do them some harm with every step I took. The girls were piled up in Jackie and Nat's room, all of them giving me the same big-eyed look. Couldn't even see Jackie, just Mya sitting on Jackie's bed like she ain't know she in the way.

"She up?"

"She say she wanna keep on sleeping."

"Mya, go on and sit over there. Let me talk to her." The two of them was inseparable but not so much that couldn't nobody else be with them. And I was they mama. So I took Mya's place on the edge of the bed. Jackie was stretched out on her stomach with her head resting on her hands. She blinked a few times. That was all, though, no words. "You feeling okay, baby? Hmm? You got a fever?"

"She just wanna sleep. We could go down by ourselves..."

"You don't feel hot. Your tummy hurt? Hmm?"

Jackie shook her head back and forth, shook it so dainty and gentle that I would've missed it if I had a blinked right then. "I'm okay."

"Well, it's time to get up. Your daddy be home in a few hours and we're gonna eat supper. So up-see daisy."

I should've seen it. Seen the look that passed between them. Should've seen how she swallowed nervous and all at the thought of moving. She probably hadn't moved in hours. But she tried. For my sake, she tried. Her tiny little arms shaking under the pressure of holding her body up...But it wasn't until she started to draw her knees in, rounding her back that I saw it. Saw it, heard it, felt it. My baby was in such pain that it shined bright and bold from all over her body. Lit up every corner of her bedroom, shining so hard that she couldn't move no more.

"What...what..." I couldn't even get it out. Tears ran down her face, but still not a word. "What is it?"

Nikki was already crying buckets on the other side of the room, rocking back and forth with Nat on her lap. If it wasn't for the way she was moving I'd think it was her that was in real pain. She ain't have the way that I did to hold things in. I was good at that. I could take damn near any kinda pain and smother it so I ain't even remember it was there. Nikki ain't have that.

"I'm okay, Mama."

It was a lie just like the one I'd told downstairs about being fine. "Mama?" She sniffled, panicking a bit as I tore the covers from her bed. She was still in her school clothes, except for her socks. They were nowhere to be seen.

"I'm okay. I just sleepy."

"Come here." I was standing over her but felt like we were miles apart. I watched her sit up because I couldn't do nothing to help with just one arm, but once she was up it was easy to pull up her shirt and see. They stretched across her back, criss-crossing even, and they were damn near swelling before my eyes. "How...how your back get like this?"

⁂

I HAD FALLEN ON my right arm, and wasn't much I could do with the left, being right-handed and all, but I ain't let that stop me. I'd talked myself into believing I could use my left hand just as good as if I'd been using it my whole life. I talked myself into it then I put myself on a bus headed for Ricky's gym. Folks around me must have looked at me something strange because of how I was looking. I probably looked like any other woman except in the face. In the face I was different. Every other stop or so I had to put my hand in my purse to make sure it was still there. I wasn't worried about it slicing off one of my fingers but I should've been. Clara had always got on me about keeping the knives sharp. She said if I was gonna use them I'd better respect them. I was real grateful at that moment that I'd followed Clara's advice. I'd picked the longest, biggest, sharpest one I could find. I'd seen it slice through a twenty-pound turkey without breaking a sweat. It was gonna handle Ricky just fine.

The gym got real busy after work. Lotta men came by for a few hours just to keep in shape or keep up for fights they had with other gyms, not like Ricky. Ricky was always there. Training was his job but none of his people knew me and I ain't know them. I walked up in there and was covered in they sweat in about a minute. It just hung in the air, like raindrops waiting for the thunder to announce them.

"Hey sweet thing, you looking for somebody?"

"Ricky."

"What you want with him when you got me right here?" The black lips spread to show off two rows of messed up teeth. "Hmm? Ricky ain't—"

"I want Ricky."

"You ain't even gonna give a brotha a chance?"

"Where is he? He here?" We were starting to draw a crowd but my hand closed in on my friend anyway.

"How about this? You tell me your name and I'll take you to Ricky myself?"

I kept moving. His lips kept on talking but I wasn't trying to hear a word he had to say. I wanted my husband. The gym was nothing but a bunch of men sweating all over themselves while a few of them bounced off each other in the ring. I recognized his legs before I could make out his face. Ricky was one of the fools bouncing around the ring. Just made me mad, seeing him move like he did. He was free. He ain't deserve it but his body went where he wanted, did what he wanted but not mine. Not my babies'. We were all paying for his freedom. And I was done.

"RICKY!" My purse slipped from my shoulder to the floor and I snatched the knife outta it. The light made it look all shiny and new even though I'd had it for a decade. "RICKYYY!"

He mumbled something and folks stopped what they were doing to look at me. I was crying by then but they weren't sad pathetic tears, they were the kind I'd never had before. The kind that made me just as free as him.

"Pecan?" He looked around at all his friends and sorta smiled. "What the...you done lost your mind?"

"Shit man!"

"N'all it's okay." Ricky tossed the mask he was wearing to the mat and spit something out his mouth before starting to work on his gloves. "She just...she just going through a tough time. Come on, baby, put the knife down. What you gonna do with that?"

"I'm gonna kill you."

"Man, you want me to call the cops?"

"N'all she okay. Right? Pecan? You don't want folks to think you crazy, do you? Come on now...put it down." He squeezed between the ropes and dropped to the floor, sweaty and taunt. "Pecan."

"No. I gotta Ricky. I gotta kill you because...because of what you did. You ain't have to do that! She just a little girl. You ain't have to do that. She my baby."

"Your baby killed my boy."

"Ain't nobody—it was an accident!"

"Let's go in the back. Come on, we go on in the back and talk about this."

Don't know what I thought was gonna happen or how I thought it was gonna happen. Guess I ain't think about it too hard, just about making him disappear forever. But when Ricky started moving toward me something in me said to move back, so I did. And kept moving until I was right in the middle of folks, all of them staring at me like I was gonna explode at any minute.

"Don't...Don't come no closer!"

"I ain't gonna let you come up in here embarrassing me in front of my friends."

"Your friends! Your friends know how you beat your kids?"

"Pecan—"

"How you beat me?"

"I don't know what you talking about. You the one come up in here waving around a knife."

"YOU BEAT ME!"

"I ain't..."

"You...beat me. You know I ain't have nobody...nowhere to go... you..."

Something heavy clanged against the floor and I turned to see. Was a weight falling to the floor, sounded like it weighed a ton. That was all Ricky needed. I only had one good hand and before I knew it he had that. Squeezing it high above my head until the knife fell from my fingers. Even with all those men standing around I still felt raw, exposed. If he wanted to and I knew he did, he could've killed me. Just would've taken one good hit, just one and I'd a fallen on something hard and heavy and that would've been the end of me.

"Ricky? Man, why don't you back up a bit. Give the woman some space."

I don't even think he heard his friend trying to talk some sense into him. His eyes ain't waver from mine.

"No! Let me go! Let me go. You ain't no man! What kinda man gotta go beating up on little kids?"

He yanked me forward and I fell to my knees with him basically dragging me across the floor. A breeze blew in from outside and I thought maybe he was just gonna put me out the gym but then I heard a door slam shut. The back, as he'd put it, wasn't nothing but some lockers and a row of benches.

"Woman, you done lost your mind." The lockers were a dirty tan and one exploded with noise as Ricky's fist slammed into it. "I been doing my best to be good to you but you don't even care, do you? Huh? You see me trying? Huh? See me trying not to lose my temper with you? Now I could. After what you did...how stupid are you? Huh? All you had to do was be careful!"

"I w-w-was!"

"You think I wasn't gonna find out how it happened? Nikki told me. And If I left it up to you that girl wouldn't have no kind of punishment! And somebody gotta pay!"

From the look on his face I knew he believed that. I sometimes found myself wondering what made Ricky like that. Was his step daddy like that? He never talked about the man so I ain't know and I ain't really care enough to ask. I just wanted out.

"I'm done with you. You hear me? We done! You come near my kids again and I swear...it'll be the last thing you do."

18
His and Hers

I'D ALREADY CRIED so much I was running on empty but I felt like crying some more. Cry to celebrate that there wasn't gonna be more tears. And when they ain't come I just smiled and went about the business of being a mama.

I took Jackie to bed with me so I could watch her sleep. We laid there just looking at each other for the longest time before she drifted off. Mr. Silverman was real clear about the fact that Ricky couldn't come around no more because of what he did to her. I wasn't sure if I believed in what folks said about heaven but I'd made up my mind that divorce must be something designed by God. After so many years living in hell, we were finally getting what we deserved. Happy.

The next day I took them to school like Mr. Silverman told me. Explained things to the folks in the office and signed some papers so they'd know not to let Ricky get his hands on my girls. They were real sympathetic, looking at me with my arm in a sling and Nat hooked around my waist. Nat just pointed at them and whispered things in my ear. She thought they were weird. I wasn't sure if she even realized what was going on. Soon enough, I figured she'd ask where Ricky was but so far she wasn't interested. On the way out the school I had to stop by the sixth grade class. Just to look through the little square of a window to see what they were doing. Nikki wasn't taking things so well. I thought it would've been Mya but it was Nikki. She was afraid of everything—of going outside, of staying in, afraid of her own damn shadow even. She was sitting in the back of the class, staring out the window. Wasn't nothing to see but some weeds and a chain-link fence but she kept on staring.

"What wrong with Nikki, Mama?"

"Nothing, baby. She'll be fine."

It wasn't that cold but spring didn't always mean that the weather couldn't go back to bitter shivering cold. Nat and me hurried down the street, trying to beat the wind that was reminding us of the weather that was supposed to be gone. But when we got to the last block before our house I had to stop cold. His car. It was parked right at the curb.

A man I'd never seen before walked out onto the porch with a box full of my clothes. I just stood there, a gaping hole where my mouth used to be, while he walked down the porch steps. Wasn't long before two more men, one I recognized from Ricky's gym, walked out onto the porch too. They were carrying my mattress.

"Hey!"

"Pecan," a voice behind them said.

"What is this, Ricky? You can't just...just take my stuff!"

"Your stuff?" He laughed. He was holding on to an old dusty box that held our china set. "When you pay for all this?"

"I..."

"This my stuff! Your ass is lucky I let you use it this long. And now I'm taking it back. Besides I like my mattress. It's real good for my back."

"You-You can't just take my stuff." I don't know what was wrong with me to step to him like that. I grabbed Nat by the hand and ran into the house thinking I could stop the rest of my stuff from leaving. The two fellas strolled back in careful not to look me in the eye then asked Ricky what he wanted to do with the clothes upstairs.

"The ones in the big room. I'm taking those." He grinned at me. "My girl might like some of them dresses."

"My clothes? You gonna give her...You can't do that!"

Ricky set the box of china gently on a chair then backed me into a corner without a word. "You mean to say my clothes. I paid for them. So they mine."

"What you want with women's clothes?" I snapped. The curtains swayed in the cold air that was blowing through the front door. They swayed up against my back. Telling me to get out the way, so I did, tripping over one of the side tables and dragging Nat with me. "Your friends know you come up in here to get some pretty dishes and women's clothes? Huh? They know down at the gym how you taken such a strong liking to them?"

"Keep talking, here."

"Maybe you funny like that."

Ricky turned hot red, burning at me like a raging bull. If his friends hadn't come down the stairs right then he would've came charging at me just like a bull too.

"Hey, man. Anything else?"

"N'all. That's it. Gimme a minute." They looked at him and

ain't even bother looking my way. I was the one wanted them to stay so of course they left. They were his friends, on his side. "You started this, Pecan. You wanna sick that Jew lawyer on me—well I got news for you! I got a lawyer too and he say a man like me got certain rights. I done provided for you and this family and now you wanna take my stuff and my kids? N'all. It ain't even gone happen like that. My lawyer say that women like you always get they come up-ins."

"LIKE ME? BUT I AIN'T DO NOTHIN'! WHAT I DO TO YOU? I AIN'T DO NOTHIN'!"

"You took what's mine so I'm gone take what's yours. Just you wait."

I ain't have to wait too long before they had everything they wanted piled up in their cars and trucks. And I couldn't do nothing but stare from my porch. Folks were walking down the street just looking...looking at the stuff, probably thinking some of it was for sale, then looking at me. They'd wave at Ricky, a few of them even stopped to chat, talking him up about his next fight, just smiling away. But when they got around to looking at me, there was something else on their minds. I was an ungrateful wife, giving up all the nice things I had. And for what?

After Ricky left I still hadn't seen my way through none of it. Couldn't believe that he could just walk in my house and take what he wanted.

I sat at the kitchen table twirling the phone cord around my finger waiting for Paula to come to the phone. She'd never thought much of Ricky but once I told her what had just happened she got real quiet.

"What?"

"Nothing."

"What? I hear you thinking."

She sighed and asked me if what Ricky had said was true. Had he paid for everything?

"Don't make it his. Paying for it don't mean…it's still mine. I'm the one picked it out. Cleaned it. All he did was lay his behind on it."

"Okay Pecan." But she wasn't convinced.

"Mama, where the comfy?"

One of Ricky's friends had a pick-up truck. They'd slid the sofa into it. Leaving the broken TV for us.

"We're gonna sit on the floor from now on because…just because."

Nat ran from one room to another, calling out what was missing, like it was a game. She never paid too much mind to me being on the phone. When she got upstairs she called down to tell me that her Mr. Fluffy was gone too. I figured it was just somewhere it wasn't supposed to be like under her bed. What Ricky want with some old stuffed animal? It only had one eye to begin with. Wasn't until we got hungry that I realized he'd taken stuff from the kitchen too. Wasn't no food in the house. Fridge looked so empty it whistled when you opened it. Plates were gone. Forks and spoons too. And he ain't stop there. Most of the towels were gone, only sheets that were left were the ones on our beds.

"Mr. Fluffy need me!"

"Paula, I gotta go."

"Mama he need me. Gotta find him! He lost!" She whined and whined, making the headache grow bigger and wider across my forehead. "MAMA!"

"Okay baby."

So, I put it on the list of things to get. List was so long I needed two sheets of paper. Most of the stuff I could get at work, and with my discount, I was thinking it might have been better that way, maybe Ricky did me a favor. He'd robbed me of plenty but maybe it was a blessing in disguise. I was about to buy my own stuff for the first time in my life. And wasn't like there was anything else for him to take.

***

THAT WAS THE NIGHT my dreams about Ricky started. He'd come in from the windows, doors, outta my closet even. Sometimes I'd wake up and he'd be standing over me in the dark. Just standing there. Then came the part where I'd run outta my bedroom too scared to scream, run into one of the girls' rooms but their beds would be empty. I'd run across the hall and that room would be empty too. Always took a few seconds before I realized it was a dream. I'd wake up all outta breath and sweating up the sheets something terrible. Course wasn't anybody for me to tell about this. I had it in my head that it was some weakness in me that made Ricky have that affect on me. If folks knew, how was they gone love me? They'd just think I was stupid for staying with him long as I did. That I should've been stronger from the get-go. So, I kept quiet about it and made sure I always had some coffee and cigarettes on hand.

"Can I have some?" Jackie wiggled her way into my lap. "Can I, Mama? What is it?"

"It's bitter. You ain't gone like it."

But she watched me sip at it, taking in the strong scent of my French roast. "Please. I'll like it. I will."

"N'all you won't. Get some Kool-Aid out the ice box."

"But I want what you got."

"Fine. Take a little sip." I held the cup for her but wasn't long before I had to give it up. "Slow down now. Guess you like it, huh?"

"Mmhmm. But can I put more sugar in it?"

"Yeah. Guess I'll make me some more." I moved the tiny sugar bowl from the counter to the table and watched her dump half of it into her cup.

"Mama, this what grown folks do? Sit up in the kitchen drinking coffee?" It was funny watching her sitting at the table, her legs swinging like always and her back straight as a board, trying her best to look grown. "Like you used to do with Auntie Clara?"

"Yeah, guess that's about right. Me and Clara used to sit up in here and talk until y'all came home from school. We'd talk until y'all was ready for dinner and get right back to it when we were cleaning up after."

"Whatcha talk about?"

"Grown folks stuff."

"Did you talk about me?"

"Sometimes."

"What'd you say?" Jackie must have been imagining something good because she couldn't stop grinning.

"We'd say...Let's see...We'd say how you was an awful awful chile. And how we couldn't wait to get rid of you!"

"No you didn't!"

"Yeah we did. All the time."

"I miss Auntie."

"I know you do, baby. Me too."

"I miss...I miss how she tell us stories—like the one about how she grabbed the guy by his collar and told him a thing or two! That one's my favorite."

"Yeah I know. She'd tell it over and over just because you liked to hear it." Made me smile just talking about Clara, even though it reminded me of how long it had been since she'd been gone.

"Mama, whatcha doing?"

"Locking the back door."

"How come you gotta do it a million, ca-jillion times?"

The deadbolt snapped to one side, unlocking the door just so I could lock it again. Had to unlock it just to be sure it'd locked, otherwise I'd be wondering about it all night. I still had to check on the downstairs windows one more time but I decided to wait until Jackie went off to bed since it bothered her.

"Baby, what happened to your hair? Hmm?"

"Nothing." She shrugged and slurped down the last of her coffee.

She had four braids when the day started but by the time bedtime came around they were just a few loose gatherings of hair. The colorful little balls that wrapped around each one was two seconds from the floor. I got to fixing me another cup of coffee and me and Jackie sat down and talked about all sorts of things. About school...her teachers... kids in the neighborhood...wasn't until Nat came stumbling into the kitchen with a big old yawn that I realized what time it was. Nikki'd already gotten them in their bed clothes so I just had to tuck them in.

"But I ain't sleepy, Mama."

Was all the damn coffee. Jackie sat right up in bed, looking bright as the day is long. Wasn't like I could make her sleep so me and her sneaked across the hall and got into my bed. Snuggling up good so we were like two peas in a pod, nose to nose. Was all good, until my little pea had to go and ask me about Heziah.

"I think the time done come for you to let that go."

"But he's my daddy. I gotta love him. If I don't, then who will?"

Her little girl lashes fluttered with innocent belief and I knew she couldn't see the difference between the lie and the truth. Jackie had said it so much she'd actually talked herself into believing it was true.

"Jackie...baby..."

"You love him too, right, Mama? You just gotta have faith. That what Auntie used to say. She say when God got to feeling real good, he was gonna set things right like they supposed to be. He'll bring Heziah back to us so we can be a family. Heziah'll come like the-the man on the white horse—the man in the story that save the princess. Then you won't have to lock the doors a bunch of times every night."

"Jackie—"

"It's gonna happen, Mama. You'll see. It's gonna be like this." She bounced up outta bed and stretched both arms out in front of her then started running in slow motion. "That's the way it goes in the movies."

⫸

THE VERY NEXT DAY, it seemed, Mr. Silverman was sending me a letter saying Ricky wasn't going to fight me on the divorce but that he wanted sole custody of the girls. He had to get on the phone to explain it to me because my brain just wasn't getting it. Wasn't no way Ricky could've wanted them, not really. Wasn't no way he was going to get them after what he did. Mr. Silverman told me to be real calm and not let it get me upset. He said it was most likely some stunt that Ricky's lawyer was pulling to get out of paying child support. But he ain't know Ricky like I did. Money wasn't enough. My stuff wasn't enough. Not even my body. Ricky had set his mind to breaking my spirit too.

19

Mr. Boss Man

I WENT TO WORK, THINKING myself lucky that Ricky's friends ain't take all of my clothes. Wanted to wear something bright and fun to celebrate my freedom so I picked out this red and black dress with black tights and Mary Janes. It was one of them outfits that Ricky ain't never want me to wear unless he was taking me somewhere special. I was wearing it anyway and it felt good! By then it was all outta style but I acted like I ain't know it and pranced around the store like a peacock until it was quitting time.

Mr. Bryer came outta the woodwork, fitting his hands into brown gloves that probably cost more than my whole outfit. He smiled and I couldn't help but wonder what he was doing with suede gloves this time of year. They ain't keep him warm, ain't even keep him dry. Just ain't make sense. I figured Mr. Bryer was a smart man, at least he looked that way.

He offered to drive me home but it just ain't feel right. The last of the night shift was slipping past us, a few of them looking at me sideways. They were his employees too. Going home same time as me, on the same bus as me, and he ain't ask none of them if they needed a ride.

I ain't have no long history of getting special treatment so my first thoughts were to suspect him of something. But what did that say about me? Didn't I deserve someone wanting to protect me from the late night hours? Somebody to ask me how my day is going? Ricky was gone and still messing up my head. So, I let all that suspicion go and just accepted Mr. Bryer for what he was—a nice boss. To me, any ways.

❊

"Oh come on, Belinda—I can call you Belinda, can't I?"

"Yeah, sure, Mr. Bryer."

"I'm gonna let you in on a little secret about men." He was sitting on top of his desk and he leaned over and dropped his voice so nobody'd hear the secret but me. "There's three ways to a man's heart—food, sports, and well...the last one I'm sure you can guess. You should know this if you want to get remarried any time soon. You're thinking about it right? You're still young. Got your looks. You follow my advice and you'll snatch up another husband, like that." He grinned and snapped his fingers.

He was so sure of it, I couldn't help but smile, even though I wasn't too keen on the idea of another husband. Wasn't like I had any good record of picking them. All I needed was to end up with another Ricky.

"I know what you're thinking." He eased off the desk and poked his head out his office to ask his secretary for another cup of coffee. "You want one?"

"No—my lunch break just started."

"Now hold on here. Let me just make this one point then I'll let you go. Go on now. Sit back down." He took the seat next to me and crossed his legs. "I have a niece, got divorced around your age. Smart girl. Not so pretty. Or motivated but don't tell her I said that. Anyway... she's divorced. Couldn't find another man to save her life because, you see, her best years were already behind her. She kept putting it off and putting it off. By the time she hit forty, men her age were looking at women your age! And now...now she doesn't have any options. Her kids are going off to college and she's going to be all alone. It's really quite sad. I don't want that to happen to you." He sighed real heavy like and squeezed the top of my shoulder.

Mr. Bryer's secretary knocked at the door, carrying his coffee. She wasn't what most people'd call good looking but she dressed like she ain't know. "Black with two sugars. Just like you like it, Mr. Bryer."

"Oh, thank you. You can set it right on my desk."

"Um, Mr. Bryer, I really gotta get to lunch."

"Oh! Sure, sure, sure. Don't let me keep you."

I got up to go and made it all the way to the outer office where a few ladies had their desks pushed together, whispering. All of them stopped soon as they saw me. Everything in me wanted to run back to the sales floor but I suddenly remembered what I'd gone to see Mr. Bryer for in the first place.

"Back so soon?" He looked up from the pile of work he was sorting through on his desk.

"I forgot to ask you...um I was wondering if I could get the afternoon shift. Well really the morning shift. I just can't be here to open because I gotta get my kids off to school but I do kinda wanna be home when they get there because they not really old enough to be alone all night."

Clearing his throat in a raspy sorta gargle, he pulled off his glasses, holding them by one side until they dangled over his papers. "I'll see what I can do, Belinda."

And he did. From then on I was never on the night shift. Which made me the enemy of every other salesgirl on the floor but it made my girls happy. First few days they were real surprised to see me when they got home even though I told them I'd be there. I think it made me work harder too. I was just so grateful to have something work out the way I wanted, and I was grateful that I had a boss that was understanding.

⊰⊱

THE CAFETERIA WAS BUZZING with secret conversations and busy little eyes. Outside of Helen none of them girls were any kind of friendly towards me. I wouldn't have put it past any of them to run back telling Ricky everything I did.

Helen parked herself right across from me and crossed her legs, waiting for a answer to an unspoken question. "I'm your friend. I'm trying to be your friend. Now, I know this the first job you done had so maybe you just don't know—"

"Know what?"

"How it goes. Maybe you just don't know how hard it is for us... for women to get respect around here. Respect, Pecan. That's all any of us got."

I'd brought my lunch as usual and was finishing up my third cup of coffee. The clocks said I had about four minutes to get back to my station but Helen ain't notice. All she saw was me.

"Pecan, you listening to me?" Helen reached under the table and took my hand like it was a secret. "I know you. This ain't how you are. There's women like this and then...then there's women like us. We not like this." She looked over her shoulder at the other ladies crowded around the main tables. They'd sent her over to talk some sense into me, either that or they wanted to know if all the rumors were true. "They say you was up in his office for damn near an hour."

"So."

"So? So, what was you doing in there? Huh? I mean you gotta know how that looks. You only been here a few months and you get whatever hours you want—and you up in his office all the time doing God knows...You not thinking clearly. What with Ricky and the divorce and all."

"I think just fine. Ain't nothing wrong with how I think!"

"I'm sorry. That came out wrong."

I'd been right about my co-worker's assumptions about me. Was just the kind of stuff Ricky would throw at me in court. Say I wasn't a fit mama. I took a deep breath and forgave Helen. I needed as many folks on my side as possible.

"It ain't like that. Okay? He just like talking to me. He think of me like a daughter. It...It ain't like that."

⋘

I'D MENTIONED TO MR. BRYER about not having a bed and next thing I knew there was a Sears delivery truck outside my house and two real nice men came in and set it up for me. He said it was a loan and that someday I could pay him back. It was a nice enough bed. Not as big as the one I'd picked out but big enough. And every night that week I went to sleep, thinking maybe, just maybe, that would be the night I stayed asleep. But then just like always the clock would strike 2:00 or 2:15 or 2:47 and I'd jerk up outta bed like it was on fire. Only one thing on my mind. I'd sit there in the dark, listening to my house move, thinking about if I'd locked this door or locked that window. Of course none of that mattered because Ricky ain't need an invitation to come up into my house. He had a key and I didn't have the money to change the locks.

⋙

I HEARD MY NAME over the loudspeaker, asking me to come to the office.

"So...how are things?" He asked and reached out to rub my shoulder. "How do you like your new bed? Does it feel good to you?"

"It's nice."

"I'm glad. I'm really glad, Belinda." And he was. It was so obvious I ain't have to think twice about it.

I'd been working there for three months and made fifteen hundred dollars. I hadn't saved a penny. Child support was slow coming.

"Yeah, um...I was thinking about—um actually I kinda wanted to talk to you about getting more hours?"

"More hours? I thought you wanted to spend as much time with your kids as you could?"

"I did—I do. I just need more money."

"Hmm." Mr. Bryer stood up, yanking his waistband to a higher more comfortable position and walked around behind me. His short sweaty fingers went to work massaging my shoulders. "More hours...I'm not sure if that's something we can accommodate. If I give you more hours then I have to take them away from somebody else."

"Oh. I ain't mean—"

"No, now just let me think." He sighed, leaning more so into my skin.

I ain't mind letting him think. The harder he thought the more relaxed I got. I ain't even care that his hands were a little wet because they were so warm, kneading my shoulders, neck, and back like they were made of flour and butter. Ain't even come to me that it wasn't natural for nobody's boss to be doing that.

"I have been considering promoting a few girls...but...it would mean more responsibility. Do you think you could handle that?" The massage stopped suddenly. "Belinda?"

"I don't know. Maybe."

"You'd be in charge of a few of the sales associates. Just making sure they don't stay on break too long, that they don't have any problems with the customers...that sort of thing. How do you feel about that?"

Wasn't much I felt good about. I'd just about got used to doing stuff just because it was necessary. Necessary to protect my girls. Put food on the table. That had to be enough for me.

"Belinda?"

His fingers stretched down as far as they could until they were just above the round softness of my chest. He ain't really touch them. Not really, just kinda hovered over them. His wedding ring glinted against my skin but I tried not to notice. He was my friend. Most days it felt like he was my only friend. Took me to lunch when I needed it. Gave me a place to sleep. And now he was about to give me a promotion. I was lucky to have him.

"Mr. Bryer?" His secretary poked her head into the office.

I couldn't see her from where I was sitting but he jerked halfway around and his left hand slipped down the front of my blouse, resting against my boring beige bra. It wasn't an accident I was sure. His clammy fingers wiggled against my skin, squeezing my tit like he expected to get some juice from it. I wished I could make myself disappear. Click my heels three times and be sitting some place else. How could I have been so stupid? I'd been wrong about Ricky. Wrong about Heziah. And I was wrong about Mr. Bryer. All that affection he had for me…wasn't no parts of it in the family way. Men ain't do the things he'd done for me without getting a little something in return. Everybody had seen it before I did. The girls in his office. Helen. I swallowed hard and glared at his desk until my tears knew better than to come pouring out.

"What is it, Mrs. Holfstein?" He answered quickly then raised his hand back to my shoulder.

"You have a phone call on line two."

20
The Gray Woman

THE DEPARTMENT OF CHILDREN and Family Services sent a new woman to check up on us. She was younger than the one I'd met at the hospital but she was wearing a gray suit, just the same. She sat at my kitchen table questioning me from a list she probably used with every family she came across.

"So, you were recently promoted. That sounds promising but explain to me again, Mrs. Morrow, how your youngest daughter ended up in the emergency room a few weeks back."

I'd already spun the damn story too many times but she sat there, asking to hear it one more time like I was suddenly about to break down and tell the truth or something. It'd only been twenty minutes or so but I was on my second fantasy. Fantasy about knocking her head clean off so she'd stop asking me all those damn questions.

"Mrs. Morrow?"

"Stop calling me that."

Should've been enough I'd done the right thing and offered the woman my last cup a coffee. Had to sit back and watch as she took two little dainty sips then put it back on its saucer. Watch it get cold while she came up with one stupid question after another. She'd told me her name but I ain't make no effort to remember it. To me she was just the gray woman, because she was covered from head to toe in it. The gray woman from DCFS come to take my kids.

"Why you here?"

"I'm here to make sure this is a safe environment for your kids," she said without even bothering to look up from her ratty old notebook. "Now back to the hospital. You decided to leave, taking your daughter with you because..."

"She mine. Why I'm not gone take her with me? Where she supposed to go?"

"Well. You were supposed to wait until the hospital's social worker had assessed the situation. You didn't do that." Her beady little eyes were just as tired as they were hard and if it wasn't for the things coming out her mouth I would've felt sorry for her. "Mrs. Morrow?"

"It was an accident. I told you already. She slept in it and it got up in her skin."

"And you didn't notice?"

"You got kids? You notice everything they do? It was an accident!"

"I see. And the beating your other daughter received—"

"Ricky did that. Wasn't me. Why you don't go asking him about what he done?"

She stopped writing long enough to tip the corner of her mouth up at me. Wasn't no kinda happiness in that smile, was more like she was laughing at me. Making fun of me. I wanted to lean across the table and slap it right off her mouth. Got to thinking so hard on it that I ain't even hear her next question.

"Mrs. Morrow?"

"What?"

"This would go a lot smoother if you would cooperate."

"Your coffee gotta be cold by now. You gone drink it?" I asked just as I poured it down the drain. She ain't want it to begin with. I ain't know why folks ain't just say what they mean. She could've just said no thank you and I'd of let it be but n'all she had to go wasting my last cup of coffee.

Just then Nat came up in the kitchen. Wasn't nothing special about that but it was something in the way she was walking. Kinda slow and bouncy-like, and in her Easter dress that was a year too small for her. She skipped in, smiling at the DCFS woman then at me. "Pick me up," she said, throwing both hands up over her head. Ain't matter that I was entertaining company. But that wasn't special neither because she was the baby. It was what happened once I did that drove the social worker crazy. Nat squeezed my neck real tight, looking all peaceful in the face then said real loud, "I LOVES YOU, MAMA. YOU THE BESTEST MAMA."

The others had put her up to it and it would've been cute if it wasn't for the sinking feeling I was getting in my gut. My company wasn't charmed by my baby. Her lips got real thin and she started scribbling real fast on a fresh page in her notebook.

"I'll need to speak with the children now."

"Why? I answered all your questions already. I did."

"I need to speak with them. Alone. Would you please call them down?"

"What you gonna ask them? Stuff about...about me? Or about their daddy?"

"Mrs. Morrow—"

"I said don't call me that."

"Belinda—"

"Don't call me that neither. You ain't my friend. You can't go around calling folks by they first name then trying to take their kids!"

That smile came back and it was probably a nervous tick or something but I ain't wanna see it like that. Was better if she was making fun of me. That way I could let out some of the anger that lived inside me.

"Ma'am?"

"I ain't old enough to be nobody's ma'am."

"I will need to take a look around the house anyway so I guess I could just go on up to them."

"They not gonna talk to you about their daddy unless I say it's okay. And even then...it ain't a guarantee."

"Fine."

So, we both went upstairs. I took a slow drag on a fresh cigarette while she looked around, asking me if I had any weapons. I didn't. Then she asked me why I ain't cover the outlets.

"Because my girls know better."

She sighed and went back to writing in her pitiful looking notebook. I wondered how many families she'd ruined with that notebook.

They were waiting for us by the time she got done looking around. The three of them sitting up, looking all unnatural and proper. Their feet hung down over the sides of their beds, not moving at all.

Mya and Jackie on one. Nikki on the other.

"Hello, girls. My name is Mrs. Gibson. I'm a social worker. I'm going to ask you a few questions if that's alright." She sat down next to Nikki, which was a pretty good move since she was the most talkative one. But wasn't no way the woman could've known that. "Can you tell me what it's been like since your daddy moved out?"

Wasn't supposed to be a hard question I suppose but they all looked up at me like they weren't sure what to make of it.

"Y'all go head and answer her questions. It's okay."

"Do you miss him?" she asked, her pen just waiting for something to write down.

"Daddy?"

"Yeah. Do you miss him?" Silence. Not a word. They just sorta looked at each other and shrugged. "I'll bet he misses you. It's okay if you miss him...or if you don't. You can say either way." Still nothing. "Nikki?" The gray woman turned more to the side like she was real interested. "What would you say is the biggest difference between now and before, when your daddy used to live here?"

"We got more food."

"More food?"

"Yeah, because he ain't here to eat it all up. Daddy always wanna take two, sometimes three, scoops of everything, then he usually go back for seconds."

"Okay. What about you two? What do you think? Your mama says it's been a little while since you've seen your daddy. How do you feel about that? Mya?"

I held my breath, waiting to hear her say how much she missed her daddy and how much he loved her but Mya just shrugged, keeping the same steady expression that was hers and hers alone.

The gray woman ain't get to ask her next question because Jackie jumped in. My baby ain't take too well to too much talk about Ricky.

"My daddy, he take us places and we get to go far far away to where there is pink unicorns and tigers and bears and waterfalls and ain't no vegetables just ice cream."

"Okay. I'm not really sure I understand..."

"My daddy, he love us. And he-he gonna come get us soon. And he gone marry mama so we be a family. And live happily ever after."

"Um..."

"She just playing around. Jackie stop trying to confuse the woman now! She asking about your real daddy."

"He is my real daddy."

The gray woman just sorta smiled. "So, tell me more about your daddy. What does he look like?"

"He brown, like me. Tall. Nice. And he real smart."

"That's nice. What would your daddy say about what happened to your back?"

"Ain't nothing happen to my back."

"No? Are you sure?"

"Yeah. I'm fine." Her little feet started swinging just above the floor. She was a better liar than me but still not good enough to convince nobody.

"Well...I bet that it probably hurt a lot. Can you tell me how it happened?"

Jackie shrugged and flopped back onto the bed so all we could see was her legs shooting out from behind Mya. Wasn't that she was trying to protect Ricky none, she just ain't wanna talk about it. I ain't blame her. I shouldn't of blamed none of them but soon as Nikki opened her mouth ants started running up and down my arms, rushing me to blame somebody.

"She okay now. It was an accident but um..." Nikki's eyes went up to mine then her voice turned to a whisper. "But Daddy blamed her anyway."

"Your daddy? He blamed Jackie? For what?"

"Because...because of what happened to mama and to the baby—it wasn't really her fault. She was just being like she is. She can't help it. She a kid."

"I ain't a kid. You a kid!"

Nikki rolled her eyes and went right back to telling it. When she got started wasn't no stopping her. Nobody'd ever asked her opinion about things that happened before. Was like a great, big old spotlight came shining down on her. The more she talked the more the gray woman wrote down. If I could've found my voice I would've stopped her but I was speechless. I knew the story—knew what it was like living with Ricky just as good, maybe better, than they did, but listening to it. Listening to it come out my girl, my oldest...it was different. It ain't feel like I knew it was supposed to, the truth. Truth supposed to be familiar, like knowing your body but this truth wasn't like that. Was like looking in the back of a restaurant that has delicious food and finding out that the kitchen is nasty. Make you wonder about the food. About what you done ate thinking it was good. Nikki kept going until the gray woman had filled up the back of the page and had to turn to a new one. Her fingers were scribbling like mad and there my girl was soaking up the spotlight.

"And then there was the time he—"

"Nikki, that's enough. She ain't ask for all that."

It got real quiet, except for the sound of the gray woman's writing. Then she stood up and walked out into the hall. I figured I was supposed to follow so I put Nat down and did just that.

"Why didn't you file a report with the Chicago PD?" Her eyes were shooting daggers at me, and on top of that, the girls were so quiet I knew they were listening too. "Mrs. Morrow? Why didn't you try to get help for yourself and your children?" She sighed, squeezing her notebook to her chest. "He's been beating you for how many years?"

"Beating...that ain't how I'd put it."

"And how would you put it?"

"I don't...I don't know. He hit me sometimes."

"Fine. He hit you and he beats your kids—"

"He only hit her once—twice! And I got on him about that both times!"

"It didn't occur to you to go to the police? Or if you couldn't do it yourself, to ask a friend to? What exactly did you do to protect your kids?"

"I..."

"Because from where I'm standing it doesn't sound like you did anything at all. Sounds like you thought it was fine to raise them in a house where all they saw was you being thrown around. Is that what you thought? You thought it would be just fine?"

"No, I just ain't have nobody to—I ain't have no way to...what I was supposed to do?"

The top to her pen snapped on quickly and she dropped it and her notebook into this bag on her hip. "There are shelters and churches and DCFS and the police."

"You don't know Ricky—"

"I will make an official report with the court and your lawyer will have access to it. I'll see myself out, Mrs. Morrow." She ain't bother to even look my way as she went toward the stairs. I must have been real disgusting to her because with each creaky step she hurried to get farther away from my truth. How she'd been so close to it and ain't seen it was beyond me.

"I'M A GOOD MAMA! I LOVE MY BABIES! IT WAS HIM...he the one..."

But it ain't matter. She was already out the door. I went out on the porch after her but couldn't think of anything better to say. Just stood there watching as she drove away. That's when I saw it parked a few houses over. The sun was glinting off the shiny black exterior of Ricky's Cadillac.

21

Busy Little Eyes

H I MAMA, HOW WAS work?" Jackie was the first one to stomp up the porch steps, grinning from ear to ear. Don't know why she had to walk so hard. Sounded like a grown ass man coming up in my house.

She'd gotten real good at acting grown but she was still a chile. So, I couldn't answer most of her questions honestly.

"Work was fine." Which was mostly true since I'd managed to stay away from Mr. Bryer for the whole day.

"Hi mama," Nikki and Mya slipped past us and into the house, dropping their book bags near the front door. The two of them took off running. Not long after, somewhere in the back Nat squealed, welcoming her sisters back home.

Jackie stayed with me. Telling me all about her day while she unpacked her book bag.

"Y'all can take a rest, have a snack and then you gonna get started on your homework."

"Okay, Mama. NIKKI, MAMA SAID FIX US A SNACK! AND MAKE IT SNAPPY!"

"Don't be like that."

"Like what?" Jackie shrugged, pretending to be innocent. "Not my fault she stay in the kitchen."

Nikki was exactly where we thought she'd be. She'd laid out bread slices, jars of peanut butter and jelly, and was picking through the fruit basket. I was lucky she was so steady with all the domestic stuff. Just woke up one day and realized she could do damn near everything I could and it ain't seem to wear on her none. Like she was made for it. Pissed me off. I'd spent damn near my whole life in somebody's kitchen and I wasn't about to raise my girls to do the same. But before I could correct the situation Mya distracted me. She popped up in my peripherral vision, arms crossed over her chest. She had a big old band-aid slapped over her elbow.

"What happened to you?"

"She fell." Jackie sat at the table and leaned down to tickle Nat as she explained. "She was racing the fifth grade boys during recess. All of them. She gotta race them because the boys in her grade won't do it no more cause she always win. And then Jonathan Murphy had to go and say that boys are faster than girls so…you see mama, she had to. I woulda raced them too but these my favorite shoes. I didn't wanna mess them up. If I woulda raced we both woulda won. Right Mya?" Jackie didn't pause for an answer. She just kept going. Describing the looks on their faces when Mya came in second. She could've gone on about it for a good ten minutes but Mya looked like she'd already forgotten about it. Her dark stare was fixed on me, thinking on something else.

"What's wrong baby?" I heard myself say just as Jackie was taking a breath.

"We ever gonna get to see daddy again?"

Silence filled the kitchen and all eyes locked on me. Couldn't tell them the truth—that I hoped not.

"What if he sorry about hitting Jackie? Ain't we supposed to forgive somebody when they sorry."

Ricky hadn't been sorry a day in his life, but I couldn't say that either. Besides, Mya seemed real sure of what she was saying...like she had first hand knowledge of his sorriness.

I took a seat at the table and beckoned her over to me. Needed to put my hands on my girl.

"Where's all of this coming from?"

"Daddy say he told you he was sorry but you don't wanna forgive him. He say that you hate him and you spreading lies about him so you can take all his money."

The restraining order said he wasn't supposed to go anywhere near the girls. Not at home and not at school. That little piece of paper was all the protection I had and it apparently didn't mean a damn thing. But I ain't wanna scare them so I smiled and asked, "When your daddy tell you this?"

Mya shook her head. "He didn't." I was about ready to call her on the lie when she said, "Jonathan Murphy did. He say his daddy talked to daddy. And..."

"And what?"

"Nothing."

She clammed up after a double glance from Jackie and Nikki. But it was too late. The nerves that was usually reserved for bedtime pricked at the hairs on the back of my neck and ran up and down my arms. Folks thought I was overreacting when I kicked Ricky out. I was just being overly emotional when I said he beat us. They pittied him and was suspicious of me. How Ricky pulled that off was beyond me. I forced a smile and asked her again as sweetly as I could.

"What else did your daddy tell him?"

"That you umm…doing stuff with your boss you not supposed to be doing. To get money."

⁂

If HELEN KNEW WHICH one of the girls we worked with was Ricky's snitch, she wasn't letting on. She stood at the elevator, pressing the button and giving me that it's-for-your-own-good face. She'd told me a bunch of times to let it go. Said I didn't need to let Ricky get me so worked up. I told her she could advise me on my feelings when her husband was telling her kids that she was a whore.

Helen went up in the elevator and I took the stairs down to the first floor and slipped out the employee entrance into the side parking lot. It was close to the loading dock but a brick wall separated me from the men unloading things and joking around. Customers didn't come through that way so that's where we went to chit-chat and grab a smoke.

I'd just lit up when I heard somebody calling my name.

"Now, what kinda mama take up such a nasty habit?"

Ricky was always real good about scaring the living daylights outta me. He'd find the worst moment in my day to remind me that I was his. And obviously the fact that I was divorcing him didn't change that.

"Since when you start smoking, Pecan?"

My fingers twitched slightly as I took another puff, then I dropped it to the ground and stepped on it. Wasn't none of his business and I meant to say so, just as soon as I found my voice.

"Hope my girls don't take up after you. They see how their mama is and think that's how they supposed to be."

"What you want Ricky?"

He waved his finger back and forth, pointing at the building behind me. "You work here?"

He knew damn well I worked there. He'd pitched a fit at the very thought of it.

"I had no idea. Just came down here to buy some things. So, how's it feel? Being a working girl? It ain't easy like you thought, making the money, is it Pecan?"

"I'm fine. And my girls are fine. You supposed to stay away from us."

He didn't seem to hear me. Just kept right on grinning and stepping in my direction.

"Leave Ricky. Before I call the cops."

But it was too late. There he was, pushing me up against the brick wall. Whispering in my ear about how good I had it and how we could go back there if I just let all this restraining order stuff go. Saying it hurt him that he couldn't be with his family. He said it without an ounce of pain in his eyes while his hands focused on my body.

"Don't you miss me, Pecan?"

"Quit it, Ricky. Stop."

"You still my girl."

"Back up off me!"

"Why? You saying you don't miss me? Don't miss none of this? Hmm? Cause you got that white man all up in between your legs? Huh? That it?"

Mercilessly, the bricks tore at the back of my blouse, making tiny scratches against my skin while I tried to fight off Ricky's touch. I thought I'd won when he finally gave my breasts and hips a break but it was only so he could get a good grip on my neck. One hand squeezing up under my chin, the other latched on to my behind as my feet dangled in the air. The laughter of the men on the loading dock had died down and all I could hear was some pathetic soul gasping for air as she disappeared between the parked cars. I landed hard on the concrete, head first. Dazzed and underneath a typhoon. Ricky mumbled up in my ear how he knew me. How he could tell if I'd been with any other man. He ain't need no kissing or affection to get himself all worked up. Just about any other kind of physical contact was enough.

"Tell me you ain't turned into a slut."

I twisted left and right, wondering why nobody else saw fit to take their breaks at the same time as me.

"Tell me you ain't just giving it away. Tell me Pecan."

He gave up fighting with my knees and thighs and went straight for my panties. Kissing the tears on my cheek. His belt buckle rang in the silence between his words and just for a moment his attention turned from me to himself. Stroking his manhood up under my skirt, reminding me how deep his love went.

"I know you want this."

I didn't. I never did. I wanted love. Wanted somebody to take care of me. But I never wanted him.

"You miss this don't you?" He thrusted into me.

It couldn't be happening, I told myself. Not like this. In broad daylight. Not to me.

"Good girl, Pecan. Yeah, that's it."

Didn't take long before Ricky was done. Panting all up on my neck while he put himself away. And my body finally began to respond to what my mind was telling it. Wiped the tears from my eyes and sucked in the free air again.

22

Gone

MA'AM, WHAT EXACTLY ARE you accusing your husband of?"

The judge wasn't a very friendly man. He seemed bored and angry at the same time. His gavel slammed down, echoing in the courtroom and he declared that I was a liar. A slut. And a bad mama.

Mr. Silverman stood at my side but he was just looking at me with those I-told-you-so eyes. He wanted to know why I didn't run or scream. Why did I just let things happen to me?

Ricky sat on the other side of the courtroom, grinning and counting a stack of bills. He handed some to his lawyer then got up to give some to the judge.

"Mama. Wake up mama. Make us pancakes." Nat stood in front of me, shaking my shoulder even though my eyes were wide open. "Get up, mama." She was just tall enough that she could've climbed into bed with me but she didn't.

I blinked and she was gone.

❦

"MAMA, YOU HUNGRY?" NIKKI balanced a tray with a dinner plate and a tall glass of milk. She slid it onto her daddy's side of the bed and held up a spoonful of mashed potatoes. "Here mama."

Paula sat in the corner, her head tilted to one side as she tried to figure me out.

"You gotta eat mama. Been a whole day. Here."

My friend was all dressed up to go dancing. She laughed and pointed at me, saying I couldn't leave the house looking like that. Helen handed her a dress from my closet and she held it up, considering what accessories to put with it.

"Mama watch me. I made up a dance. Wanna see?" Jackie's braids whirled around her head the faster she moved. "Ta-da!" She finished.

"She need shoes," Helen said and she disappeared into the back of my closet.

"You know you cheated on him," Paula sat at the foot of my bed taking the dress off its hanger. "Adultery is a sin, Pecan."

Helen rose with a pair of black heels and held them against the dress. She shook her head and went back to searching the floor of my closet.

"Mama, I'm gonna sleep with you tonight. Okay? You won't be alone."

⁂

THE MIRROR WASN'T KIND enough to lie. It didn't hold back none of the truth. I'd gone to bed without my scarf so my hair was a mess. I had on my least favorite nightgown. A pink nylon, with tiny holes in the armpit and a bow above my cleavage that had been threatening to fall off for some years. I leaned over to spit into the sink and replaced my toothbrush in its holder. Didn't bother combing my hair. Didn't think about changing my underwear. Fresh breath was more important.

"Mama you up?" Jackie rubbed her eyes sleepily. "What time is it?" She yawned. She'd assigned herself the task of keeping an eye on me.

I took her by the hand and led her back to her own bed. She climbed in and fell fast asleep. It was too early for the girls to be awake. The sun wasn't even up yet.

The stairs creaked under my bare feet as I headed to the kitchen. Flicked on the light switch and pulled the pancake mix out of the cabinet. I had a stack of ten by the time I realized I wasn't alone in the kitchen.

"Whatcha doing?" Mya stood in the doorway. I hadn't heard her on the stairs. Hadn't even seen her in twenty-four hours. "Mama?"

It was obvious. I was making breakfast.

She had a blanket wrapped around her. Same blanket that was normally on her bed. It was so long that it dragged along the floor behind her.

"You okay?"

I was fine. Making breakfast.

She disappeared from the doorway and it occured to me that my girls needed some meat to go with their pancakes. So, I threw some strips of bacon into the frying pan. A chair scraped along the kitchen tile and I saw Mya had returned. This time she had a pillow with her, which she put between her head and the kitchen table.

One thing about Mya, she ain't mind the quiet none. Just sat there watching me. No questions. Just watching. I got the sense she hadn't been to sleep. That she'd been standing guard over all of us the whole night.

"WHAT'S WRONG?" HELEN STOOD in the doorway, holding on to Jackie's hand. She wasn't talking to me but she was looking at me.

"She not talking to us. And she won't stop making pancakes."

Nikki and Nat sat at the kitchen table looking wearily at the fresh stacks on their plates.

Helen's forehead wrinkled and a smile tickled her lips. She thought Jackie was joking.

"Really. She won't stop."

I flipped the last two and slid them both onto Mya's plate. Jackie let go of Helen's hand so I could slip through them and into the hallway.

"Mama, where you going?" They called after me.

All of them crowding into the hallway, watching and waiting for an answer. Helen took a few steps in my direction and stopped when I turned to look at her. I thought it was obvious. The box was empty. I had to get some more pancake mix. I threw on my coat and reached for the doorknob but Helen came the rest of the way, took my hand, and peered into my eyes.

"Pecan, you okay?"

23
Help

RICKY SAID HE WAS gonna take everything I had and he did. Took so much wasn't anything left for him to take. The responsibility had to move on to somebody else. It was the doctors at St. James Hospital's turn. They took my clothes and made me wear their scratchy gray ones. Took all my hair products so I looked like some wild woman. Soon as I got there they started shoving pills down my throat. Saying it was gonna help me see things clearly, help me relax, help me sleep, help me be regular. But I ain't need nobody worrying about my regularness.

This doctor, a woman and black, signed all my forms. She'd point to folks and give the white women orders like it was nothing. Then every day they'd bring me to her office. She sat across from me, putting me to shame with all her schooling and fancy words. She was the no-excuses type of black folk. The ones that thought since they'd

made it—rised above—the rest of us should've done the same thing.
There I was, nothing but a housewife who ain't even finish high school.
Couldn't argue with nothing she said, couldn't even understand half
of it. First she said I was having a breakdown. Then I had something
called Post Traumatic Stress Disorder. She said it was real common in
soldiers that come back from war. Then she finally seemed to make up
her mind that what I had was specific to women who been battered.
I just looked at her. She asked me about Ricky even though I got the
sense everything she wanted to know was already in my file. She just
wanted to hear me say it. So, I ain't tell her a damn thing.

"Belinda? Do you understand how talk therapy works? You have
to say something to me in order for me to help you."

"Where my girls?"

"They're safe. This is a time for you to concentrate on yourself."

What was I supposed to say to that? Mamas don't get to think
too hard on themselves. Everything they got goes to their kids, if they
love them that is.

"Belinda, what are you thinking about right now?" She hugged
the manila file to her chest and pushed the box of tissues closer to me.
"You can tell me."

The box of Kleenex was just going to sit there because I wasn't
touching it. And I wasn't crying, at least I ain't mean to. I loved my
girls. I'd have done anything for them but I ain't tell the good doctor
that. Figured she wouldn't have believed me no way. She looked at me
just like that gray woman from social services did. Thinking she was
better than me, that she could've done better with my life than I had.
So, I kept quiet. Then she told me.

"Belinda, I really would like to help you. We're all here to help
you. I understand it's hard for you to believe that after all you've been
through but the sooner you trust me the sooner you can go back to

your life. To your girls."

They were probably missing me real good by then. I missed them so much they took over all my thoughts. Ain't matter if I was awake or asleep, they were always with me. Saw them the same every time. Just like the last time I'd seen them. Worrying about me.

"Belinda?"

"They ain't with Ricky, right?"

"No. They are not."

Wasn't so much what she said but how she said it. Her short round nose buried in her folder even though she wasn't really reading anything. Just hiding. Hiding the truth from me.

"Where are they?"

"Let's try to concentrate on you."

I ain't wanna concentrate on me. Last thing I wanted to think about was me. I ain't matter. My life was already what it was. My girls were a different story. They could've done things I hadn't even dreamed of. What I wanna talk about me for when I could be talking about them?

"Belinda. I need you to focus for a minute. Focus on me. Alright? Are you focusing?"

"I see you."

She sighed a hard sigh and leaned back against her chair. "Why did you ask me if they were with their father? Does that worry you? That they will someday end up with their father?"

"It'd worry anybody with half a brain."

"Oh? Why's that?"

"Because he ain't right."

"And what does that mean to you?" she asked, scribbling

something down in the pages of her folder. "Not being...right?"

"Mean he don't do right."

"Can you give me an example?"

I could've given her a million examples but I started with just one. Figured that was enough. That I'd start with the worst thing he'd ever done and she wouldn't need to hear no more. Halfway through it I realized it wasn't the worst thing he'd done. It was probably in the top five but not the worst. So, I had to start all over. Kept happening like that. Everything I thought of was the worst thing until I remembered something else. Took me a while to get around to my fall and everything that happened after that. And then him showing up at my job.

"Would you like to speak to the police about it?"

"I don't know. Maybe."

"If you do, it could be very cathartic." She sighed and uncrossed then re-crossed her legs. "But you have to be prepared for what might happen afterwards. From what you say, I doubt Ricky is the type to confess. It'll be your word against his."

"I'm not ready for all that."

She nodded and made a little note. Everything I said ended up on her papers I was sure but I did feel a little better after I said it. Not right away after but a few days later...maybe a week. She said we were making real progress and that's why she wanted to keep me longer. That I could finally be free of all the stuff I'd been carrying around. Said I could stay and work on myself or I could go back. So, it was my choice. I chose to stay. Stayed where I ain't have to worry about Ricky sneaking up on me. There were bars and gates and doors he ain't have the key to. And there was sleep. I got to sleep. No more dreams about Ricky.

Me and the doctor talked about all sorts a things. About me and my daddy. About Aunt Clara, Ricky, and the girls. After a while, she liked my talk about the girls. Always made us smile and laugh. I thought maybe I should go back home to see about them but she shook her head, said they were fine and I should just focus on me. Wasn't no other time in my life it seemed like I just focused on me. But the doctor said I had to, said it'd be good for me and the girls.

Then one day all the pills stopped. I got in line like everybody else waiting for my little cup but the nurse shook her head and waved me off to the side. Said the doctor wanted to talk to me about it. I was in trouble. Ain't know what I did to be in trouble. I talked when she wanted me to. Swallowed what the white women gave me. I ain't cause no problems with the other patients. Most of the time I just kept to myself. So, just sitting there on her little couch, waiting for her to tell me what I'd done, it got me all rattled.

"Well. Belinda. How are you feeling?"

"They won't give me my pills."

She nodded and pulled a chair around so we were nearer to each other. "I asked them not to. We did some tests on you. Do you know what we found?"

"That I'm crazy?"

"No. No. That you're pregnant. Did you know that?"

"No."

"Would you like to have this baby?"

I ain't have one solid answer to that question. I hated Ricky, hated every part of him so I had to hate the baby. But I couldn't keep on hating me. That was the thing the doctor wanted me to see. That I had to love me before anybody else could. And it was my baby. Just like my girls were mine.

"How do you feel about going home, now?"

"So, I can see my girls?"

"So...so that you can resume your life, yes. I'm going to ask that you come to see me once a week. Do you think you could manage that?"

"Yeah, I can do it."

"Good. And after you have the baby we'll talk about anti-depressants. Now." Her chest got all pumped up, arms stretched out in front of her so her hands rested against her knees. She ain't wear regular stockings like most women I knew. She had the kind that looked like they'd stand up to damn near anything. The kind that ain't never rip or run. "I need to discuss something serious with you. Belinda? Are you listening?"

"About the...the baby? I'll have it, Doc. It ain't its fault."

"I'm glad to hear you so confident." She nodded and gave me a little fake smile. "But that isn't what I want to talk to you about. I want you to know that...we, as adults—as parents, we all do the best we can. And the work we've done here was necessary for you and for your kids—your girls."

"Right. So, I can be a good mama."

"Exactly. Exactly. Now, since you've been here with us the girls had to go somewhere..."

"They probably staying with my neighbor. Anise. Or my friend Helen or maybe Paula."

"Yes, well. Things didn't exactly go that way. The court decided not to give custody—temporary or otherwise—to your husband, so DCFS was asked to come in—"

"But my friends—"

"They're not family. Are they?"

Why was she saying that? Looking at me like that? Like I should've known...I ain't know. I ain't know how folks could send me off and then do something with my kids without even telling me.

"Belinda. It's very important that you stay calm now. Do you hear me? Stay calm."

"Where are they? My girls. Where are they?"

"They were placed in temporary homes."

"Who homes? I...don't get it."

"When you were admitted you didn't list anyone as an emergency contact. No family. Right?"

"I don't know...just say it, say what you saying!"

"The girls were put into foster homes. Two. Two foster homes. The state had to be sure that they were safe and I asked them not to notify you. I thought that it would be detrimental to your progress if you knew about this before you were ready."

"Y'all put my babies with strangers?"

"Belinda—"

"I wanna go. I wanna go home now!"

She nodded again, this time to make sure I knew I was heard but it ain't matter. The walls were closing in around me and next thing I knew I was on the floor and she was poking and prodding me and yelling for somebody. They called it a lapse because I went back to not talking. Then I was talking too much, she said. That I wasn't making sense. Made perfect sense to me. They'd stolen my babies. And I'd left them alone in the world. Was both. Ain't have to be one or the other, it was both.

Was another month before they thought I was ready to go home. They gave me back my clothes but wasn't much I could do with my hair seeing as they wouldn't let me have a hot comb. The doctor made sure I had the number to call and told me to use all the stuff we'd been practicing if I found myself getting worked up. To just breathe and count to ten. That I had to protect myself. Stand up for myself. And ask for help from folks that really cared about me.

Was about two in the afternoon when I got back to my house and folks were out tending to they lawns. A few of them looked up to see me but it ain't bother me none. The letter was tacked to my front door. Rustling in the Chicago winds. The official government seal and three lines of typed words. Said DCFS had taken my girls. I was prepared for it. I knew it beforehand. I did. Guess that's why I ain't expect my whole life to cave in at that moment. But it did.

Ain't matter about all the work I'd done making myself better. My phone wasn't working. Light switches just flipped up and down without even the slightest effect. Everything was where I left it but there was this stillness in my house. No fun and games, just toys abandoned on the floor. Nobody'd been there in two months. Thanks to Ricky.

I thought about all the nights I'd slept right next to Ricky. Had him snoring up against me. I could've killed him. Would've been like putting a mad dog out its misery.

24
Wife

WASN'T SURE I COULD just come back after being gone for two months but I walked on in there because I needed the money. I wasn't there for no other reason, just the money. Meant to tell him that too. I would have if he'd been in his office but he wasn't. His secretary ran in after me, trying to stop me but it was too late, I'd already seen it. The boy. He had sandy blonde hair and eyes that changed color in the light, just like his daddy. His pale legs hung over the arms of the chair like it was just for him.

"Mr. Bryer got a meeting. He-He ain't here," she explained even though I could see that with my own eyes.

"I'll wait."

"You can wait out here."

The boy was about the same age as my Nikki. Only she knew better than to sit on furniture like that. And she wouldn't have been shooting little pieces of paper through a straw up at the ceiling like he was. Boy was surely bored out his mind. should've had himself in school. I sat outside the office thinking. Thinking about what it must be like to be one of his boys. All the things they probably ain't have to think about or worry about. Probably had tons of friends and a mama that was never stressed about a thing. That was why he could just lie across furniture, making a mess without a care in the world. Mr. Bryer must have been so proud. He showed up about ten minutes later. His suit jacket making wind behind him as he flew down the hall past his secretaries. Stopped dead when he saw me.

"Belinda?"

"Yeah..." I hadn't managed to get my nerves under control but I could stand alright. "I was hoping we could talk. About my job."

He swallowed hard and heavy, looking over his shoulder at the whispering witches. They ain't have to try too hard to hear every word but he wasn't about to take me in his office. I could see it all over his face. The guilt. It had him all boxed in so he couldn't do nothing. Felt a little sorry for the man right then.

"I wanna come back to work. I expect you and everybody done heard I was...I was in a hospital for a while but I'm back now."

"I had to promote someone to take your place."

"Okay. That's fine. I'll do anything. Not anything—I just mean..."

"I know what you mean. Wait here."

So I did. Stood in the same spot, looking at the witches with their wandering eyes watch me while he went into his office. Wasn't much of a conversation between the boy and his father and a few seconds later the boy breezed by me toward the vending machines with a fistful of money.

"Come in, Belinda. Have a seat."

I'd heard those words a million times before so I knew what they meant. "I'll stand."

"Very well." He sighed, walking around me to close the door.

"Leave it? I just...leave it, alright? I just wanna know about my job." He closed the door anyway. "I need this job. I gotta make money so I can take care of my girls."

"I can't help you with that." He ain't even have the guts to look me in the eye. Just stood over his desk, shuffling things around. "I can give you some references."

"What that pay?"

"What? No. I'm saying I can give you good recommendations if you want to apply for other jobs. I'll tell them how much good you've done here. I just can't take you back, Belinda. It's not personal."

"Why?"

"Why? Because." He sighed. "You know why. I am sorry about what's happened to you, I am. But it's not my fault. I'd like for you to sign this agreement." He pushed the single sheet of paper across his desk to the very edge. "It just says that you won't be suing the company for any reason."

"Why would I do that?"

"Just please sign it."

"Then I can come back to work? I gotta have a job. They're not gonna gimme my kids back if I don't have a job."

"No, now sign the damn paper."

I'd never seen him like that. Never heard him take that tone with nobody. Guess I was special. He'd saved it all for me. Even the way his eyes looked at me had changed. Like I was some pesky little fly buzzing around his picnic. He just had to get rid of me. One of his secretaries hurried past the door and we could hear her fussing over the blonde boy with eyes like him. Asking the boy if he wanted anything to go with his potato chips. And I got mad. First time in a long time, I got real mad.

"No."

"Belinda—"

"I SAID NO! I AIN'T SIGNIN' NOTHIN' 'TIL YOU GET ME MY JOB BACK! And maybe not even then! Nope, not even then. Maybe your boy like to know what his daddy been up to. Maybe it'd do him some good to know..."

"You..." He got so mad he started shaking. Ain't move from around his desk, just stood there—shaking and breathing. "Fine. I'll see what I can do."

"Yeah. You do that. I'll be back tomorrow."

Was a new kinda feeling having the sorta power to make a man do what I wanted. Walked out the office feeling it in every step. Imagined it was cloaked around me so everybody could see. Got all the way home and it was still there. I was going to get my life back. Felt real hopeful about it as I walked down my block. Wasn't even expecting any trouble. Was too high on all my power. Ain't see him until I was right up on my gate. He was sitting on the porch steps, just waiting. The universe sure had a weird way of working things out.

⁂

"I DON'T NEED NO help. I been carrying groceries all my life." But that ain't move him one inch outta my way. Determined. Stubborn ass of a man. I shouldn't of let him in. Should of made him stand out on the porch like all the other folks come around to peek in on me. I was fine. Just fine. Was about to be better than fine as soon as I got my girls back. "I don't need no help."

The winds went howling up and down the street, sending tree branches crashing into the kitchen window. Rattled up against it like a rat trying to claw its way in. Hated rats. Seen enough of them in that horrible little place Ricky and me used to live in. Just thinking about them made my skin crawl all the way up to my ears.

"Belinda."

What he want with me anyway? Wasn't like he wasn't clear from the get-go. He ain't want no parts of me in no real way. It was fine for him to come around and get my hopes all up, though. Him and all his fancy talk about books and dreams and things. Probably said all the same stuff to women all over the city.

"Belinda."

"What?" The top of the bag of flour ripped open and out popped a white cloud into the air. It was a brand new bag and I'd just meant to put it away in the cabinet but since he was standing there watching me so hard I decided to make fried chicken with it instead. "Excuse me. I gotta get in the fridge."

"How are you? Where are the girls?"

"Gone."

"Gone where?" He asked, looking around like maybe they'd shrunk up and was hiding in between the floor tiles. "Belinda—"

"It ain't none of your business. I don't need you all up in it. It's my business. Mine. They mine. Not yours."

"I thought you might still be mad at me. About before...I've been thinking about the...about what to say to you."

He looked the same. Thin. And smart and kind. I hated that

he looked the same. Why did he had to look the same? I ain't look the same. Not that I was some real sorta beautiful to start with but I sure was a long way from where I started. Back in the days when we were together.

"Belinda, I made a mistake. Before."

"You can stay for dinner if you want."

"What?"

"You can stay. I'm making enough. Only because I don't know how to cook for just one person."

"Okay."

So, we sat down to a few leftovers I had in the freezer and some fried chicken. Six empty chairs all around us. And silence. Just chewing and swallowing and the wind blowing against the window. First time Heziah'd been inside my house and wasn't nothing there but me.

"I've been thinking about you. And the girls. I wanted to call but...what happened, Belinda? Where are they?"

"You ain't read the papers? Read how I'm a terrible mama? How I went crazy and them good upstanding folks took my babies?"

"No." Heziah's frown glared down nice and steady on me. "Where's Ricky?"

"With his woman."

"Why didn't you call me?"

"And say what?"

My chicken wasn't as good as it usually was but he ain't know that. Just like he ain't know how to answer my question. Just sat there, chewing one bite after another. What could he say? What was I supposed to say? Tell him how much I missed him and beg him to come back to me? Folks been leaving me my whole life. What made Heziah any different?

"Where are the girls...exactly?"

"Don't know. Can't get the trifling woman on the phone. She always too busy to be at her desk. Guess she got too many kids to steal away."

"Belinda—"

"What?"

"I'm going to help you. Help you get them back."

"You ain't gotta..."

"I know that. But I want to. I...I'm sorry I wasn't there. When you needed me. When they needed me. Wasn't because I didn't care about you. You know that, right?"

Why he couldn't just sit there and eat quietly? Most folks don't necessarily gotta talk the whole time. They can just sit quiet and eat. Ricky used to sit quiet.

"Belinda? You told me you wanted to be with your husband. Remember that?"

"No." Of course I did.

"Well, you did." He looked down at his almost empty plate and pushed some things around. "Wasn't exactly what I wanted to hear but I respected your wishes."

"Mmhmm."

"Seem like if you had wanted to be with me, you would've called...told me you changed your mind."

"And we'd both be dead."

"What's that mean?"

I ain't mean it in no fancy literary way. I meant it just like it sounded. Took Heziah a minute to wrap his head around it. Just

because he ain't know Ricky the way I did. He ain't know Ricky's mind
or his fist. He barely knew enough to pick him out of a crowd full of
people. Part of me wanted to keep it that way. Not for Ricky's sake or
nothing but for mine. I was afraid of what would happen to me if I let
too many things out. I'd have to deal with what Heziah thought about
it all, what he felt. His feelings on top of mine on top of my girls' was
too much. Couldn't take all that and carry it around with me. So, I
scooped up his plate and mine and headed back to the kitchen. He
ain't utter one word, just followed behind me. The rubber bottoms of
his shoes squeaking along the lineolum tile.

"Belinda?"

"I'm tired."

"Alright. Is that your way of asking me to go?"

"Mmhmm."

My back was to him so I couldn't see his face, just hear him
breathing. In and out. And in and out. Until his hands were on my
back, pressing gently like he was admiring it. Breathing in the fabric,
brushing his nose against my hair. And I knew exactly what his face
looked like. Ain't even have to turn around to see it. See what he
felt. My Heziah, honorable as all get-out, he wouldn't let himself get
too close. Was good for both of us. Lord only knows what would've
happened. Crossed my mind, though. Crossed it for a good long while.
Remembering what it felt like to be in his arms, have him loving all
parts of me. Memories, that felt just too real. The dishes slipped from
my hands into the sink and I hurried to turn the faucet on so he
wouldn't notice.

"You said something about going crazy."

"Was just a lot to deal with. That's all. I needed a break. They
ain't tell me I was gonna lose my kids behind it."

"Belinda, look at me."

How I was supposed to look at him and wash dishes at the same time? How I was supposed to keep all them thoughts that was rattling around in my head, keep them straight? He asked a awful lot of me.

"Belinda."

"What?"

"How do you feel about me?"

"Don't feel nothing."

"Nothing?"

"Feel like getting my girls back. Ain't got time to feel nothing else."

"Does it have to be one or the other? Can't you feel both? Feel for them and feel for me?"

"What you getting at?" I shook the water from my hands and turned to go back to the dining table for our glasses. He was standing in exactly the same spot when I got back. Hadn't moved a muscle. Just stood there looking at me with them eyes, only he had. "Stop looking at me like that."

"I love you. I still..."

"Shit." The drinking glasses splashed into the soapy water, soaking the whole front of my dress.

"Belinda."

"I heard you. You say you love me."

"Are you calling me a liar?" He looked like he almost wanted to laugh. "Hmm?"

"No." I figured Heziah ain't do things like that. Lie. Wasn't honorable.

"So, aren't you gonna say something? A man tells a woman he loves her, usually she says something back."

"Like what?" I wasn't trying to be hurtful. It just popped out. Course Heizah ain't know that, crossed his arms in front of him and took a step back. "Heziah, you don't wanna love me. Ain't nothing good ever come from loving me."

"That's ridiculous. Where are you getting this?"

"My daddy loved me. He dead. My girls loved me. They gone. Folks that love me don't get no happy ending. Probably best if you don't."

"I don't buy that. Belinda? Look at me."

Dishes weren't gonna wash themselves so I had to get busy. Drove Heziah crazy I could tell but it was better than saying what was on my mind. What I knew would hurt him. To have me say...no...one more time.

"Belinda, I'm a patient man."

"Just go back to your life, Heziah."

"Why are you trying so hard to push me away? You're not still mad—I could tell if that was it. You're not, are you? Leave the damn dishes and talk to me!"

"What you wanna hear? Huh? That I been sitting around waiting for you to come back to me? Want me to get down on my knees and beg you to save me from my wretched life? That what you wanna hear?"

I was squeezing the dishtowel so tight that I'd rung all the soapy water out of it. Heziah followed me out into the hall, and watched as I took the mop from the broom closet. I whisked it over the puddle until wasn't anything left but a shiny circle.

"I told you. I don't need help. Don't need no saving."

"I heard."

"Good."

"Belinda—"

"No, you know what?" I stood with one hand holding the mop the other on my hip. "All you men think the same way. That a woman don't need nothing outside of you. That we supposed to turn ourselves inside out to keep you happy. Well, I ain't the one! Not no more. I'm done."

"You sound bitter."

"Smart is what I am!"

"And hurt." Heziah reached for me but I stepped back. "Wow. Did I...am I the one that did this to you? I mean..."

I knew what he meant.

"Belinda? I'm so sorry if I..."

But it wasn't him. Wasn't his fault. What happened to me wasn't Heziah Jenkins. It was cowardice. It was failure. It was me being trapped by fear. Being threatened and beat. Thrown against walls and down stairs. It was me becoming a mama when I wasn't even a woman yet. It was the kind of love that left me battered and bruised. And raped. It went by the name of Ricky Morrow.

But I couldn't say all that to Heziah, not to my honorable man.

"It wasn't you."

"It was Ricky, wasn't it? What happened? What'd he do?"

I laid the mop to rest in the corner and left the kitchen behind. Just couldn't stay in the same place any more. I had to move. He trailed behind me to the front door, watching as I double checked the windows. Then on over to the living room where he got a good look at the TV that was still broken. I hadn't had a chance to replace any of the furniture so wasn't any point to staying in there too long. Ended up on the front porch. Was the only place in my house that didn't feel like it was trying to smother me.

"He hurt you. Didn't he?"

He'd never done anything else.

Heziah sighed and pushed against the porch with all his might, dropping his head between his arms. Then moaned real loud as he pushed himself up to an upright position. He hesitated for a split second then wrapped his arms around me, breathing calm into my ear while his fingers ran through my hair. He said I didn't have to say it if I didn't want to. That he was sorry he didn't see it. Sorry that he wasn't there to stop it. He went on to say he never not wanted me. That he'd always loved me, even when we were apart. Ain't shake him none to see me crying neither. He just waited until I was done then told me the real reason he'd come back.

"I love you. And I need you. You make me happy. Belinda, you listening to me?"

"Mmhmm."

"I want us to be together. Forever." His long bony fingers grasped onto my hand and I felt every muscle in his body go tight.

And I finally let out the words I knew he was dying to hear. "I love you too."

"You do?"

"I never loved anybody else."

"Then marry me."

〰〰〰

RICKY AND ME WAS married in a church on a hill in the middle of the week. Wasn't nobody there but me and him and the preacher. But with Heziah it was different. The Cook County Courthouse's basement was lined with couples just waiting to say their vows. When our turn came around the judge took us in a little room that was more like a cross between a closet and an office and he said the same few words he was gonna say to every couple that came through there. Heziah stood all sturdy and determined, watching the man's lips move. And I stood watching him. Ain't seem real as we walked on out into the hallway. Could've been the sour apple colored walls or the floors that looked like they hadn't been mopped in ages but the happiness ain't sink in until we were on the ground level and headed through the revolving doors. While I was blinking and trying to hide from the sun I thought I caught sight of somebody I knew. A man with a strong build and a pretty face. A man I hated. But as soon as Heziah joined me on the sidewalk, he took me by the hand and laid a kiss on me so sweet it could've stopped traffic. For every thought I had about Ricky, I had two about Heziah.

We were starting over. Creating the world as it should've been. He even went around telling folks I wasn't ready to tell yet. His kids. Had them calling me Mama Bell before the end of the week. Told all my neighbors when he showed up with all his stuff, saying he was moving in. Was only right since we were man and wife but it was the way he just went ahead and did it that bothered me some. But that was just me being silly. I knew it and told myself as much.

Heziah taught me all about love that first month we were man and wife. About how it gives and sacrifices and it don't make no conditions. That was how he was. Real loving. Ain't make no difference that the girls weren't his, he wanted them back just like I did and we both worried about it. Made calls, harassing the social worker and anybody else that would listen.

Ain't make no difference that I was already on chile number five when we got married. He just nodded and kissed my hand. Said it was going to be our baby. Course I tried to tell him how it happened but he shushed me, putting his finger up against my lips. Heziah said it ain't matter. Nothing mattered except us.

"You're my wife," he said. "And you're perfect just the way you are."

25
The Visitor

WHEN I FINALLY GOT the social worker to let me see the girls, me and Heziah had our first real test. As wonderful and perfect and loving as he was, I ain't want him there. I wasn't saying anything about him. He was fine. I just needed to see the girls first. Needed them to see me before they saw him. I was their mama. He said he understood and I took that to mean he wanted to understand and I did it anyway. I went by myself. Saw Mya and Nikki first.

The yellow house at the end of the block had a fresh coat of paint on it like somebody was trying to hide something. Other folks might have said it looked fine enough. Like everything that was needed worked. Roof to keep the rain and snow out. Windows to let the sunshine in. I walked up the steps with tears already in my eyes. I ain't know what was going to be waiting for me on the other side. Were my girls gonna be happy to see me? Or were they gonna be mad? If my mama had shown up after being gone so long don't know if I'd of had it in me to be nice to the woman. So I stood there a few minutes thinking about running away. Slid my ring into my pocket and before I could really make up my mind the door flew open.

"Hello. Are you Mrs. Morrow?" I nodded. "I'm Darlene Pratt," she said. "Please come in."

Was a nice house. Not as big as mine but wasn't one speck of dust anywhere. All the wood shined like it was polished daily. And the woman whose name I had to struggle to remember, she seemed happy enough. Wore an apron. I thought that was weird. Who wore a apron if they weren't cooking?

"Come in, come in. We were just sitting down. Mrs. Gibson is on the phone in the kitchen..." She gestured into what was probably they living room and waited for me to enter. Felt like I was being watched from somewhere up on high but there was nothing above us but the ceiling. "This is my husband. The reverend. Reverend, this is Mrs. Morrow."

He was old. Even in his eyes he was old. In the way that only religious folks could be old. And standing next to him, made Darlene look just as old.

"Where's your husband?" Was all he had to say to me. Like I needed Ricky to come with me if I was about to leave the house.

"Alright. I'm back," chimed Mrs. Gibson as she plopped back into what must've already been claimed as her seat. "Mrs. Morrow, I'm so glad you could make it. We were beginning to wonder if you would show."

"I...I had work and...the bus was late." I ain't have no choice but to take the wing chair against the wall. Sun shined so bright through the window it blinded the whole left side of my face. Made it that much harder to think up things to say. The three of them sat perfectly still, not an ounce of sympathy to spare between them. What was so great about them that they were better for my girls than I was?

"Well, the kids will be happy to see you. Mya's been asking about her daddy. Every time I see her, she asks me about him. I've explained that it will be quite a while before she has any visits with him. Have you spoken with your husband recently?" Mrs. Gibson asked, looking down over the top of her glasses.

Guess I ain't answer fast enough because then the reverend added, "Mrs. Morrow?"

"No. I don't talk to him."

"No?" Mrs. Gibson asked like she was surprised. Her pen ready to write down anything I said.

"No. We not together no more. We divorced."

"Oh, that's right! I forgot to mention that. They are divorced now. You'll have to give me the papers so I can make a copy and put it in the file."

"Do you know that divorce is a sin?" It was grammatically a question but something about the way his lips got real tight made it clear he ain't mean it as such. "The bible says..."

The reverend. I hated the reverend. "Where are my girls?"

"They're upstairs—should I..." Darlene moved to get up but with a quick shake of his head the reverend put an end to that. She sank back into the sofa. "Well, they're doing their homework. Since you were late Mrs. Gibson said we could tell them to go ahead and get started. They're so well behaved—and smart, those little girls." She just beamed like a rooster prancing around the hen house.

Should've made me happy, what she was saying about my girls but all I could see was her proudness. Her proudness of my girls. She ain't have the right to be proud of my girls. They were mine. Mine to be proud of.

"They do lack discipline."

"No, they don't," before I knew it I'd snapped at the reverend.

"Yes, miss, they do. Especially the younger one. Always wanting to run loose like a wild animal."

I had to check to make sure I'd heard him right. He'd just called my baby a wild animal. Mrs. Gibson just blinked and kept right on writing in her little worn out notebook. It was Darlene that sorta flinched a little. Made me feel a little bit better to see it wasn't just me that was bothered by his words.

"The reverend doesn't mean it like that. You know men, they talk real hard. We love having them here. They have just brought such joy to our house. Just lightened things up. We take them to church with us on Sundays. Bible study on Wednesday. They say that you didn't really do that sort of thing..."

"We ain't religious folks. Not really. Clara used to sing to them. Sing...some songs to them. Not enough that it be like church."

"Clara is your mother?"

"My aunt. My—Ricky's aunt. She um...she used to live with us. They don't talk about her, huh? They talk...I mean they ask...about me?"

Couldn't make no mama feel no kinda good to have to ask other folks about her kids. How they were...what was on their minds...wasn't supposed to be like that. It was hard to take. Was like pricking my heart on a needle. The tears that had met me at the door came back, this time not bothering to ask permission before embarassing me in front of these folks.

"I...um...you got a washroom?"

"Upstairs. Second door on your left," Darlene stood up, ringing her hands.

Even the banister was smooth. The wood had been polished some time in the last few days, I was sure. They probably never had no accidents where folks fell through the banister. Not in that house. That sorta thing only happened in mine. They had crosses that met you at the door and another right outside the bathroom. Made me wonder what it was they were trying to keep out. Keep evil spirits outside and keep the bathroom spirits where they belonged. In the toilet. It ain't make sense but it was just what I thought. Thinking it was enough to stop the tears from running out my eyes. Thinking about the religiousness of these folks. They were some kinda weird, I could tell. Wiped my eyes and said it to the mirror. My reflection gleamed right back at me, looking just as tired as always.

"Mama?" Nikki's voice wasn't nothing but a whisper. She was wearing a pretty blue dress that looked like it belonged in a Christmas pagent. "Mama." She ran at me, damn near knocking me into the tub.

"Hi, baby." But it hit me like a ton a bricks that she wasn't a baby no more. She was growing fast. Could see the beginnings of her turning into a woman. Only made it all worse. "You okay? Hmm?" Couldn't hear her answer because her face was buried up in my chest. "Nikki. They treating you okay?"

"Mmhmm." She nodded.

"You sure?"

"I'm sure."

"Where's your sister? Where's Mya?"

"In her room. We got our own rooms now." She looked up at me, smiling her biggest smile. "Daddy said that when we come home he's gonna build us two new bedrooms so we don't have to share. Did you know that, mama?"

"You saw your daddy?"

Nikki shook her head then explained that he'd written them a letter. Said he went on for about a page telling them how much he loved us. About how me and him were gonna work things out.

"I think he mean it this time, mama."

FROM THE MOMENT I walked in the door, we talked about nothing except the visit. I told him everything. Everything except the part about Ricky's letters. I was careful not to mention Ricky at all. For some reason I found myself fixated on the new clothes they'd given my girls. Heziah said it ain't matter how many pretty dresses they bought the girls that they were still mine. I wanted to believe him but he ain't see the way they were, sitting pretty like two little dolls all dressed up in satin and bows and shiny shoes. And Nikki couldn't stop smiling.

"She was just happy to see you."

"That wasn't it. She was just plain happy."

"Well..." He frowned in the bathroom mirror, pausing with his toothbrush hanging out the side of his mouth.

"You think being divorced make me a bad mama?"

"No," Heziah spit into the sink. "That's ridiculous."

It wasn't so ridiculous to the reverend. I could see what he thought of me written all over his face. Could still see it sitting on the tub next to me as I filed my nails down. Heziah let me have the washroom first so I was all ready for bed, just waiting on him.

"What about Mya? What'd she say?"

"Not much."

"Yeah? Well, see. I'm sure they wanna come home. They were

just being polite to these folks. That's how you raised them. They miss you. Of course they do."

"They ain't say it..."

"Because those assholes ain't give you no real time with them."

"Heziah!"

"What?" He blinked, suddenly aware of his language. "I'm sorry but they are. Treat you like a criminal...who do they think they are? Nobody could ever love the girls more than you. You're a wonderful mother. You'll be...a wonderful mother." Heziah grinned and dropped to his knees, placing one hand gently across my stomach. It was just starting to poke out a bit but that was enough for Heziah to be thinking happy thoughts. "You think I'll be a good daddy?" He asked and I nodded. My babies couldn't do no better than Heziah. That much I was sure of.

26
Ruined

FOR SOME REASON FOLKS got it into their heads that I had some dirt on Mr. Bryer and that meant I could make him do things other girls couldn't. Girls that had only rolled their eyes at me before were now smiling and asking my advice about things. Technically, I'd been demoted but that ain't seem to matter none. New girls were hired all the time and even though we worked side by side they looked to me to fix the cash register or even relations with customers. And on occasion I was the one that went to management with our concerns.

Mr. Bryer was real careful when it came to me. He preferred to send me messages through his secretary but when that ain't work he'd call me to his office and we'd talk right out in the open where everybody could see us. He'd call me missus Jenkins, never Belinda like he used to and that was fine by me.

It was all fine until it became obvious that I was in the family way. Then folks started whispering again. Maybe I was having the boss man's baby. Maybe I was cheating on Ricky with my new husband. Or maybe I'd cheated on my new husband with some man from electronics. For all the different rumors that was started none of them got close to the truth. I was thankful for that, even if it didn't ease my stress any.

"Ignore them," Helen insisted as she scraped the bottom of her chocolate pudding cup.

Helen knew the truth but she'd never mentioned it. I think she sensed I still couldn't handle it.

"I'm gonna go for a smoke. Come with me?"

She agreed. Tossed her lunch into the trash and followed me to the elevator. "I thought you was quitting."

Heziah wanted me to quit cold turkey and I had, at least when I was around him.

"I'm down to two a day."

"Mmhmm." She smirked as we stepped outside. "Girl, you got more secrets than Victoria."

I felt a faint tug at my cheeks and realized I hadn't smiled in a while. Helen must've known it too because she spent the next five minutes trying to make me laugh. She was just declaring victory when a delivery truck drove past us and onto the street. I glanced over my shoulder at the first rumble of its engine and suddenly I didn't hear it or my best friend. Didn't see them either. All I saw was the brick wall where it had happened.

"Pecan. Pecan, you hear me?" Her fingers brushed against my arm and I gasped in fear. "What? You okay?"

I nodded and let the cigarette butt fall to the ground before pulling a second from the pack.

"You sure you don't wanna look for a job some place else?"

I loved that we were so close but it bothered me that she could read my mind.

"I know it wouldn't be easy but—"

"No."

"I'm just saying it might be better—"

"I ain't leaving this job. It's close to my house and I know everybody here. Ricky don't get to take this from me."

"Okay Pecan. You win."

I hadn't. Not yet anyway.

<hr/>

"How long have you had this firearm?" Mrs. Gibson waited less than patiently for my answer but I ain't have one.

Wondered if all social workers were always too busy to answer the damn phone or if it was just her. So, I was real glad she'd made time to see me. So, I jumped at the chance to have what she called a home visit. Ain't tell me she was gonna be searching my house. Said she wanted to see how things were going for me. My pistol was the only thing she found that was halfway interesting. Sat right down at my kitchen table, looking at me all funny like.

"It's just—I mean..."

"Well Mrs. Morrow? It looks to me like the serial number is filed off..."

"What I know about guns and special numbers? I told you I didn't even known it was there."

"In your dresser?"

"That's right." I ain't care if my lie wasn't convincing. Only thing that mattered was that she couldn't prove it.

"You know that it is against the law to have a weapon without its serial number? If someone were to use this weapon to commit a crime, the police would have some trouble tracking this weapon down. I'll need to see your permit for it."

"I ain't got one. Because it ain't mine."

"And whose is it?" She sighed in that special way she probably saved for me since I was always getting on her nerves.

"Ricky's. He left it."

She ain't look too pleased. But then she ain't never look too pleased with me. "I see. Will you have the firearm in the house if the children are returned to you?"

Hell yes! Was what I thought but I just said, "I don't think so."

"You don't think so? What about when this child is born? Do you plan to keep a loaded pistol in your dresser drawer with a baby crawling around?"

"What you trying to get at? This here baby ain't got nothing to do with you!"

"What exactly did you think was going to happen, Mrs. Morrow?" Her questions always stung worse than any bee sting ever could. "Your children are in state custody. You have another one and we'll be forced to consider taking that one too."

"You can't do that!"

"It's not me. It's the system." She sighed and flipped the page in her damn notebook, writing something else. "Have you spoken to the younger ones?"

I'd had one visit with Jackie and Nat. Just one. That was reason enough to hate this woman. She made me make appointments to see my kids and she was never available for me to make those appointments. Then she got all high and mighty about how much I didn't see them. As my daddy would say, I couldn't win coming or going.

She took a sip from the glass of water I'd given her half an hour before. I'd learned my lesson about offering her anything of value like coffee. She wasn't even gonna get any of my ice.

"Well, I suppose I should update you on their status. They've been relocated to a group home for troubled girls. It's on the north side."

"The north side! You can't just move my babies around and not tell me!"

"Mrs. Jenkins your daughter threatened to kill her foster parents."

"Jackie? She...she just a little high-strung is all. She always been real sensitive. I'm sure she ain't mean it..."

"She pulled a knife on them! I have to put that in her file!"

"Well what they do to her to make her—"

"She thought that threatening violence would get her what she wanted. To go home to you."

At least one of my babies still loved me. But I couldn't say that. Worked real hard not to let it show up on my face either. Mrs. Gibson ain't notice anyway. Her lips kept right on moving even though I'd made up my mind to stop listening. She obviously thought what Jackie'd done was the worst thing and for the stupidest reason. Why in the world would she want to knock to come home to me? She'd given her to a perfectly nice couple. The woman's train of thought was so easy to follow.

"—I can't say that I'm surprised." She sighed. "It happens with children like her that have experienced a traumatic life—"

I just nodded, couldn't find the words. They were jumbled around up in my mouth, making it all dry. "She really is a sweet girl..."

But Mrs. Gibson ain't wanna hear it. She was pissed. Flipping the pages in her notebook with that I-Knew-It-All-Along frown she'd had since the day we met.

"You think we got an endless list of people just dying to take in these kids?" She sighed again, even harder this time. "I had to pull some strings to get her the help that she needs. Badly. Frankly, Mrs. Morrow I am doing the very best I can. For your children. Given what they've been through I'm surprised they've made it this far."

I'd had enough. Every time the woman came around all she did was bring bad news. Bring me down. Ain't matter how close I already was to the ground she always brought me lower.

I stood from my chair and watched joyfully as she flinched as the chair's legs scraped against the linoleum floor. "That it? You said what you came to say?"

"Mrs. Morr—Mrs. Jenkins—"

"That's right! Mrs. Jenkins. Jenkins. You get out my house before I throw your ass out on the curb! You ain't gonna come up in here talking about my girls like...like they anything less than perfect. Looking down your nose at me..."

She got her stuff together in a great big huff but it ain't move me none. I was ready. Ain't matter about my physical state, I was sure I could've thrown her bony ass out if I needed to. She stood straight up like a scarecrow. Her curly short hair standing out on end because of the humidity that was running rampant through my house. Not that I felt bad for her in the least, wanted her to suffer and suffer good for the pain she'd caused.

27
Crazy

WAS A NICE ENOUGH day when it happened. Clouds were hanging in the sky looking all white and peaceful. I took my time going from the bus stop to the store. Enjoying the summer breeze as it tickled my bare legs and feeling warm as the sun shined all around me. On a day like that it's easy to forget things that been troubling you. Or at least put them out your mind for a minute or two. Seem like that's all I got. A minute or two to not worry about my girls or think too hard on the things I couldn't control. One hundred and twenty seconds of freedom from life's burden. Then I heard it. The giggles.

A bunch of girls were huddled in a circle in the side parking lot, some of them coming off their shift and others were just starting like me. But they were good and distracted-chatting and giggling, crowded around some man. Not nearly as worried as they should've been about the time that was slipping away. A couple of them looked up and caught my eye as I got closer. They smiled and nudged each other and before long the whole crowd was looking at me. Didn't make sense until the man they were making such a fuss over stepped out.

"Hey pretty girl."

A bouquet of daisies waved in my direction and Ricky smiled like I hadn't seem him do since before we'd left Mississippi. For a second I thought I'd lost my mind. It couldn't be real. Him standing in front of all my co-workers grinning at me like he ain't know what he'd done to me.

"I brought you something."

I managed to say, "I don't want it," and keep moving to the employee door but Ricky always liked a challenge.

"They pretty ain't they? I got them just for you."

Folks were swooning and giggling behind me. And I just wanted to sock each one of them in their mouths. Then pull my pistol out my purse and point it at Ricky's head. I hadn't made up my mind yet whether I was gonna pull the trigger. I just wanted to see the look on his face when he realized his life was in my hands.

"Pecan, I came all this way to see you. You ain't gonna at least say hi?"

I flashed my left hand at him and said, "I'm married. And I don't wanna see you." I expected the words would at least draw some blood but they didn't. Ricky's smile dimmed a bit but I wasn't telling him anything he didn't already know.

"You looking real pretty there," his eyes dropped to the ground and slowly climbed up my body.

My hands started trembling.

"Remind me of when you was carrying Jackie. Here. Take these."

"I don't want them!" I was shaking all the way up to my ears.

Ricky sighed rolled his eyes and made some comment about how he had no intention of begging me. That he had something more to show me. Shook the bouquet at me, holding it out for me to take. And once again I thought maybe I'd gone crazy. Standing there three feet from the door...from where it happened...holding flowers he said were meant for me.

Ricky pulled out a thin roll of paper big enough to be a map and unrolled it so I could see. "It's blueprints. I got it from an architect. It's for the house. I'm gonna get you a room for you to do all the sewing you want. And the girls gonna get their own bedrooms..."

It wasn't me who was insane. It was him. All this time I'd thought there was something wrong with me. I stood there watching and listening as my ex-husband explained all the plans he had for us. The vacations he wanted to take and family moments he'd never thought twice about before. I watched him go on for a good five minutes until it was just the two of us in the parking lot and I was about to be late for work. The man I'd known my whole adult life suddenly looked different. He was smiling but somehow he still looked sad. And a piece of me felt pity for him.

"Don't worry about Connie. Me and her done. Soon as I saw you—saw your condition, I told her it was over."

"Ricky, we not together no more. I'm married. I gotta husband. And the girls...they gonna come back to live with us. Not you."

"You shouldn't be working—standing on your feet all day. Not in your condition."

I shook my head more outta confusion than in response to what he was saying but Ricky ain't take too kindly to it. Grabbed me by the arm before I could get my hand on the doorknob and turned me back around so I faced him.

"Where you going Pecan?"

I had to have been some kinda fool to pity him. Even for a second.

"We got us a second chance here. We gonna have us a boy. We gonna get the girls back and be a family."

"Let me go, Ricky."

"You love me and I love you—"

"Ricky, stop before I scream."

I didn't want to shoot him. I wanted him to disappear sure enough but there had to be other ways to make that happen.

"You tell him about us?" He grinned, lording it over me like some big juicy secret. "Hmm? He know you having my baby? What kinda weak mothafucka just gonna sit back..." his fingers stretched out against my waist and I immediately felt light-headed. "Mmm, look at my sexy wife."

"I AIN'T YOUR WIFE! AND YOU TOUCH ME AGAIN AND I'LL..."

"Why you acting like this? Cause of him? Think about it Pecan. He can't give you what I can. Can't take care of you and the girls workin' at some rinky dink little carpet shop." Ricky's grip tightened on my arm and his face inched closer to mine. "You know can't nobody get between us. I ain't gonna let them. You mine. Always was, always will be."

He looked at me sleepily, licking his lips, about to make a move to kiss me. No other man would've dared but Ricky was one of a kind. He ain't see the writing on the wall. Ain't see how much I didn't want him. Hints ain't work on my regular old man.

The doorknob was cool to the touch and it turned easily. Before he knew what was happening I was in the doorway. Turned back because I didn't want him to think he had the power to make me run or that I was playing hard to get. I had to be absolutely clear.

"Ricky, I don't love you. I never did. Now leave me be."

❧

THAT NIGHT I GOT home and Heziah wasn't anywhere in sight. His shift ended before mine but he sometimes got home a little after me because of the traffic downtown. So I waited. Kept watch from the bay window in the living room. Watching all over the neighborhood. Nothing. I made dinner. Set the table and poured myself some milk, thinking he couldn't be too far away. An hour passed and I was a mess—working a groove in the floor, ignoring the growls of my hungry stomach, I was about to grab my coat and go down to State Street to see for myself if he was lying in the back alley or something. But then he walked through the door.

"Belinda! Guess what I got!" He was in and then he was out again. Came back in dragging this big box and a smile that was a mile wide. "Look—whoa, what's wrong?" We swayed a bit, me hugging him until I was sure it was real. All of it. He was alive. "Belinda? What is it?"

I ain't wanna tell him because I wanted to handle it myself. Wanted to be able to say I made it go away. That I ain't let Ricky get to me. But just wanting something ain't make it mine. I damn sure wasn't about to risk Heziah over it. So, I told him what'd happened to me on the way to work. He listened real quiet like I knew he would then we called the police.

28
Silver Lining

Ow do you think the girls are adjusting?"

"They fine," I said sniffling and wiping my runny nose.

"Did they ask you to take them home? You mentioned that last week. They wanted to know why they couldn't go home."

"No. That was Jackie. Nikki and Mya...n'all they ain't ask me that."

She nodded like she understood. Couldn't nobody know what it was like. Hurt every part of me to have my family torn apart. Seeing them cry and beg over and over again...seeing them smile and laugh like everything was how it should be. I couldn't be happy either way. Everything had its own special kind of hurt. Her pen went right back to keeping track of whatever I'd said that she thought was important, gave me a few moments' peace before the next question.

"Have you talked to them about your marriage? About your pregnancy?"

The doctor and Helen were the only ones I told the truth to. Heziah didn't want to know and I'd take it to my grave before telling my girls what happened to me. They lived in a world where bodies were fragile. Couldn't add this on top of it. Have one more thing for them to be scared of.

"Well, they might have questions...might feel like they're being replaced. You've been apart now for seven months."

"That's just silly. Can't replace one kid with another."

"Well, Belinda, sometimes children don't fully understand that. Sometimes they have fears—"

"Ain't nobody afraid of that!"

Shut her right up. I was proud too. For all her schooling she didn't know my girls. They were too smart to think anything like that. And I wasn't about to put that in their heads.

"Have you and Heziah discussed it?"

"What? The girls?"

"No," she blinked robotically and waited for me to follow her drift.

I figured most shrinks thought talking was the answer to all their clients' problems. They probably read it in some book.

After a long breath she nodded and moved on. "Have you seen Ricky lately?"

I nodded.

"And what happened?"

"I told him the truth. That I never loved him."

"And what did he say?"

"That the baby got me all confused."

"Why would pregnancy make you confused?"

I shrugged. I'd given up trying to make sense out of Ricky's sense a long time ago. For as smart as he thought he was Ricky ain't understand a thing about pregnancy. He thought that was the reason I did everything he didn't want me to do. Anytime I felt something that wasn't conveient to him, he blamed it on me being pregnant. I didn't even have to be pregnant for him to do it. But it always made him feel better. Maybe because it was a problem that he couldn't do anything about. So, he got off the hook—ain't have to treat me no better, just had to wait until I wasn't pregnant any more.

"Then he blamed Heziah. Said he knew where Heziah worked. That he oughta be careful when he's working late."

"He threatened him?"

The woman was genuinely surprised like we hadn't been discussing the habits of Ricky Morrow for seven months. Was right about then I decided I was done with therapy.

"Are we done yet? Heziah's waiting on me."

⁂

HEZIAH MET ME WITH a big old smile on his face. He said my other doctor, the woman's one, had called to give us the news. Wasn't going to be one baby, was gonna be two. We were having twins. Twin girls.

Heziah acted like we'd won the lottery. Wanted to go out and buy an extra one of everything. Don't know where we got all the money from, but there we were, shopping up a storm. Squeezing stuffed animals and making funny voices, was like we were kids ourselves.

Was a side of Heziah I hadn't seen. Was a side of me I hadn't seen.

"Maybe that's enough. Belinda?"

"I like this. You like this?"

He grinned, leaning forward so all his weight was on the shopping cart. "It's nice, I guess. For a dress."

"I wanna get it."

"Okay. Might as well get two. That way they'll be matching."

That was the point of everything as far as Heziah was concerned. Wanted the twins to have the exact same things. Same bibs. Same towels. Same car seats. We came in looking to get whatever was on sale but turned out they only had one of the sale car seats left. So, we had to get the next cheapest so they'd be the same. Same. Same. Same. He was obsessed with it.

"Should we get toys?" He was peering down the toy aisle.

"No. Be a while before they get any use outta them. They'd just be taking up space." No sooner had I said it than something bright and fun caught my eye. "Oooo look!"

Heziah just laughed and pushed the cart into the toy aisle after me. "We gotta get them some toys that'll make them think, Belinda. So they'll be the geniuses they're meant to be."

My girls were gonna be geniuses. Heziah said it so it must have been true. He went on pointing out different ones he thought were good and explaining why. Some of them he'd gotten for his kids way back when. Said that the good toys ain't never go out of style. They were classic. Ain't make no never mind to me but I liked the way he saw things. Liked seeing the world and all the possibilities through his eyes.

Heziah was sure Nikki'd turn out to be a teacher on account of how good she was at taking care of other folks. I ain't think much of it, in all honesty but it was possible. Heziah said he was sure she would make a good one, said he knew because that's what he wanted to be. Before his ex-wife got pregnant and they got married that is. Said he was all set to get his degree and everything but life had happened instead.

"What about Mya? Think she'll be a teacher too?"

He chuckled and guided the cart into the check-out line. "No, that is definitely not her path. Something a little more big picture... yeah." I wanted to ask him what big picture meant but then he moved on. "Now, Miss Jackie is gonna be a politician. Can't you just see her up there, convincing folks to do it her way? Standing on a podium, making her case?"

"Yeah..." Made me smile just thinking about it. My baby was gonna be just fine. They all were. "And Nat'll probably be right there next to her. You know she don't go nowhere Jackie ain't."

"I think she might just surprise you."

Heziah dug around in his wallet, coming up with the money for all the things we'd piled into the cart. "Louis used to be like that with his sister. They're still close but he doesn't feel the need to follow her around like he used to when they were little. You'll see. He's gonna come up here in a few weeks. Did I tell you?"

"No."

"Before the school year starts again. You don't mind, do you?"

I shrugged and went back to setting the the toys and things in front of the salesgirl. She looked real bored by our conversation, just sat there smacking on her gum. Made me hungry but damn near anything made me hungry. "Fine with me."

"You ain't gotta worry, you know. He's gonna love you. Not like I do but..." Heziah's lips brushed sweetly against mine and we ignored the salesgirl for a good minute.

29
Best Interests

L OUIS JENKINS WAS JUST like his daddy. Tall. Thin. A brown-
skinned gentleman. Opening doors and saying yes, ma'am and
no, ma'am. Laughing and reading and doing what Heziah called
debating. Where I came from it was called arguing. But Heziah, he'd
play along. He wasn't mad, just listened then went about pointing out
things that Louis hadn't thought of yet. They were enough alike that
you'd think they belonged together and just different enough to keep
things interesting. I made myself comfortable on the sofa and watched
the two of them going at it. Was how I learned about the economy and
that folks weren't too happy with our president. Saying his way was just
keeping poor folks down. Hard working folks that ain't did nothing
to nobody and he was calling them things like welfare queens. Wasn't
really sure what that was but it ain't sound like a compliment. Least

that's not how Louis took it. Had him all worked up. Couldn't even sit all the way on the chair, just on the edge of it like it made his reasoning that much better.

"White folks on the rolls outnumber us three to one but that isn't what you hear when they wanna talk about food stamps, is it?"

"No." Heziah answered carefully.

"Because who would love the man that wanted to string up poor little Shirley Temple and her blonde, blue-eyed mother? Nobody! But put a black woman on the chopping block and they all fighting about who gonna get to tighten the noose!"

Heziah just sorta smiled in that way I'd only just come to figure out. Wasn't a happy sorta smile. Ain't mean he liked what he heard but that he was proud of his son. Must've been a real intelligent sort of debate I figured.

"Belinda, what do you think?"

"Oh...I don't know." I wasn't just being modest. I really ain't know but guess they ain't pick up on that. The two of them just sat there, watching and waiting for me to add something just as smart. "I think everybody needs some help sometime."

"Good point," Louis nodded, sucking down the last of his coffee. The boy clearly drank more of it than he ate. "And you know what?"

"What?"

"Rich folks get all the help they need and more and nobody says a thing. That's why I want to work for legal aid. Soon as I get my law degree..."

I left them up debating about something else. Heziah was tired too but he worked real hard not to let on. Kept on nodding and coming up with good points that would get Louis to stop and think. Don't know how long the two of them was at it but by the time Heziah came to bed was like a great big weight had been lifted off his shoulders. Could feel him smiling all up against my shoulder, even in the dark. Smiling that satisfied smile. He was a real good daddy, my Heziah was. I could see it just like I'd always known it. Louis had come out real good. He was a thinking man and he cared about folks. Just like Heziah. Made me feel all warm inside, caught myself smiling too. I could see where every bit of Louis came from. Could see all the times he'd watched Heziah be nice to some complete stranger—maybe he'd changed some woman's tire who was stranded out on the road somewhere and Louis had watched from the safety of his daddy's car, or maybe he'd seen how his daddy would talk to damn near anybody... give them some words of encouragement.

Then it hit me. Reason all that mattered to me so much...it wouldn't have if it was in me the same way it was in Heziah. But it wasn't. I was different. I'd spent too much of my life hiding from folks. Hiding so they wouldn't see my brokenness, my bruises, my faults. What things had I left my girls with? What would they take from me?

❦

HEZIAH SPENT TIME EVERY day working on the bedrooms. Had the girls' rooms freshly painted and all the things they'd left behind put away nicely. And the nursery. Was something real special about it. So much love in it. Would've been my favorite room in the whole house if I let it. Heziah'd made the walls this weird color that was a cross between purple and blue. Was a real pretty warm color, just lit up when the sun hit it. And everything we bought had its place in the nursery. Heziah'd look up at me from the floor as he unwrapped some toy or something. He'd smile so full of pride. He ain't notice I couldn't bring myself to go in there. Had to just stand in the doorway, smiling back at him.

More time he spent working on our future less time we spent

together. Was things I couldn't tell him. Things I couldn't tell nobody. Like how Ricky kept showing up. At my job. At my doctor's appointments. How he sent me flowers the first Monday of every month. Heziah ain't notice that either because I'd sign for them then push them deep down in the trash before he could see. Heziah just kept on walking and talking and dreaming about how things were going to be. He ain't see Ricky's car parked at the corner or trailing behind us real slow. He ain't know what to look for, not like I did.

I told the social worker that I got rid of the gun. Told her it was gone so she couldn't hold nothing else against me. I'd held enough. Everything had been my fault. I'd married Ricky. Had babies with him. Let him make me into this scared thing that couldn't even open up her mouth. Wasn't nobody else to blame. Just me. And as the days turned to weeks I got even surer that girl was gone. The fear that Ricky had worked so hard to keep growing inside me had grown quiet. It ain't rule me no more. Not my smiles or my decisions. I saw things clear, saw all the angles and possibilities. I knew what Ricky was capable of but that ain't change how I was gonna live my life. I had been blessed with strong beautiful girls and a man that loved me in a real way. All I had to do was love them back. Shelter them from the storm that was brewing. The old Pecan hadn't been strong enough to do it but she was gone. And I stood in her place.

"I bet they're gonna be real beautiful just like their mama." Heziah's fingers danced across my huge belly. "And smart too. Just like their sisters. Whatta you think, hmm?"

"Maybe."

"Maybe?" He threw his head back against the pillows, laughing hard. "Let's talk about names. They need strong names that mean something." I nodded but kept my eyes on the open window. Hated to leave a window anywhere in the house open but Heziah liked having fresh air. Didn't matter if it was the cool sort that came right before winter, right after the sun went down. He needed it so I got used to going to bed with a chill. "Belinda? You listening to me? I said what about Hera? She was a Greek god—well goddess. Married Zeus. You know who Zeus is?"

I nodded. The leaves had turned a crisp golden color and littered the ground all around the house. Didn't need to see them from the bed to know they were there. Could picture them in my head. Fluttering down real soft like, turning over, like they were talking to each other. Was the way of the world. Nobody questioned why the leaves had to fall. They just did.

"How about Joyce? That's a nice, sturdy name."

Didn't ask nobody's permission just did what they were supposed to do. Making way for the next bunch of leaves to come out. Out with the old, in with the new. Was the way the world worked.

"Or...hmm..." Heziah studied the ceiling for a minute then sucked in one deep breath. "I got it. We should give them matching names. What you think?"

I wished I was down there. With the leaves. Walking through them in my bare feet and nightgown. Hearing them crunch under my feet.

"You don't like that idea, huh? You're probably right. Too matchy-matchy. Well...if you want we could name them after someone. After your mother maybe?" Heziah's feet shuffled a bit under the covers and he turned to look at me. "I ever tell you about my grandmother? She was a tough old broad," he said with laughter under his tongue. "She raised all seven of her kids and ten grandkids. We could name one after her. Lilly Jean. I know it's a bit old fashioned...Belinda? Where are you going?"

"Uhh..." My feet had hit the floor before I'd even made up my mind. "I'm going downstairs...to get some water."

"I'll get it for you—"

"No, I wanna do it."

Bothered Heziah, I could tell, but I had my reasons. Took my time going down the stairs. One step at a time. Holding onto the banister and the wall. Had to come up with new reasons to get outta bed every night. Wasn't no sense in having both of us worry. I flicked on the lights and checked each window on the main floor. Had to wait until bedtime because Heziah was in the habit of opening a window every time he went into a room but most of the time he forgot to close and lock it. Wasn't his fault. He just ain't know like I did. I knew better than to leave anything open or unlocked. We'd gotten the locks changed but Ricky Morrow wasn't the type to let a locked door stop him.

"So? What do you think?" Heziah was sitting up in bed, waiting patiently for me to return to my side. "Name one Lilly and the other Jean? Or did you wanna name one after your mama or daddy?"

"Calvin? Can't name no girl Calvin."

He flipped back the sheets and helped me ease into bed. "No, but we could try to combine them...like...um... Cal-Jean. Caljean. Or um...Cal-Lilly. Callily."

"Callie?"

"Hmm?" Heziah fluffed his pillow, yawning into the night. "What you say?"

"Callie. Goes with Nikki. And Jackie. And Natalie."

"Hmm." Heziah thought it over for a few seconds then nodded. "I like it. But it sounds like a nickname, though." Was the same thing Clara had said to me some ten years before. He couldn't of known so he just smiled as I laughed. "What? What I say?"

"Guess I like nicknames."

"Well, I guess the next one should go with Mya then. How about Jenna? Get it? My-a...Jen-a? See how I did that?" He laughed.

Heziah was so easy to please. Just a few smiles here and there did wonders for him. So, of course that's what I concentrated on.

For everything else I had my journal. I found it in the grocery in the aisle with all the magazines and books and stuff. Was nice. At least it looked that way to me. Brown leather that felt real soft against my finger tips. And the pages were blank and had gold running around they edges. Was the only one left. Wasn't on sale but I got it anyway. Told myself it was for my girls. Something I could leave them that they could treasure. Something good. And the next time Heziah went deep into nursery mode, I pulled out my special book with the blank pages and thought long and hard about what to write. Just figured I'd start from the beginning.

30

Brave

M RS. JENKINS." SHE'D FINALLY gotten the hang of calling me by my new name. "How are you?" she asked but her eyes stayed glued to my stomach like she couldn't wait to get her hands on what was inside.

Mrs. Gibson's office at DCFS wasn't much to look at. Folks were more organized at my job than hers. They ain't have a real waiting area, just folks walking in the door and passing each other to get to their desks. She pulled up a brown metal folding chair, the kind with white specks on it that was supposed to be decoration and gestured for me to sit there. I did. But I wasn't sure I was gonna be able to get back up again.

"I'm glad you could make it. You didn't have any trouble finding the place, did you?"

Our appointment was scheduled for 1:15, right in the middle of my lunch time. Wasn't like I got a whole hour like some folks. Had to take a taxi just to get to her office in time. Was probably gonna be late getting back but I tried not to think about that.

"How're my girls? They okay?"

She nodded but touched her glasses like she was trying real hard to find something negative to say. She hated giving me good news. Couldn't say that they were doing better or nothing like that. Only wanted to tell me what was wrong.

"Mrs. Jenkins, I wanted to give you an opportunity to enroll in a parenting class."

"Well, I don't need a parenting class."

She sighed and pressed the tip of a blue pen so the ink made a perfectly round dot on the yellow lined page that sat on her desk. "It would go a long way to showing that you are serious about getting your kids back."

"Fine."

"Good." She handed me a sign-up sheet. "Can I assume that your new husband would be open to joining you?"

"He doesn't need a parenting class either. But yeah, he'll come if it'll get us the girls back."

"Good. We have one starting on Friday. Oh. Wait. No. That's probably not a good idea..." But it was too late. I'd already seen it. The sign-up sheet for that Friday had a good number of folks already signed up. Seventeen to be exact. In the box marked thirteen was his name. Ricky Morrow.

"Mrs. Jenkins? Can you give me that sheet back? I'll get you one for the other class."

"Ricky going?"

"To the Friday night classes? Yes. Here's one for Tuesday nights. Just sign on the...the box numbered five. You can sign your new husband up as well."

"Why?"

"I thought I explained this to you." She sighed looking over my head as a lady passed by to get to the desk next to us.

"No, I mean why's Ricky going? Wh-What you promise him?"

"I didn't promise him anything. The court requires that we at least try to reunite children with their natural parents. If he gets some help for his anger issues and takes some parenting courses..."

"You what? You'll give them to Ricky?"

"Mrs. Jenkins. Please."

"You can't do that! What in the world is wrong with you? You stupid?"

"Mrs. Jenkins. That is enough! Contrary to what you may think I don't spend my days thinking about how to make you miserable. I am simply following the rules. And despite your many outbursts and what I personally consider to be erratic and unstable behavior, I doubt that your ex-husband would be a better choice. But I am obligated by law to work toward a resolution that is in the best interests of the children. And according to the law, returning them to their natural parents is the goal. Now, if you would like to be taken seriously I suggest you and your new husband be on time to each one of the classes."

"You can't give them to Ricky. You can't..."

"Right now we are only working on visitation. If that goes well... then we'll see...perhaps the two of you can learn to work together to parent your children."

In the fourteen years I'd known Ricky Morrow, he hadn't learned a thing other than how to throw a better punch. And I knew what it was like to parent with Ricky. Knew about all the things he didn't think were important, how hard it was for him to just be nice to folks. Knew all the signs that he was pissed off about something. Ain't matter if you'd done it or not, if you were there...he was coming for you. I didn't even wonder why he was the way he was or spend any time blaming myself for it, but I couldn't pretend like I ain't know what I knew.

⟨⟨⟨

LOUIS WAS WAITING FOR me on the porch when I got back home. We'd enjoyed him so much the last time he visited that he decided to spend Christmas with me and Heziah. It was good to see him, even though I was sure his mama probably missed him something terrible. He met me at the gate, taking each step with me real slow like the snow wasn't trustworthy.

"I'm okay."

But he just nodded, his cold fingers wrapped nice and tight around mine. Had that way just like his daddy where he could see what I needed despite what I was saying. Louis explained that Heziah had called and said for us not to wait up. So, it would be just me and my stepson for supper. Ain't stop us from having what I call a real supper—fried chicken, yams, collards, and potato salad. Wasn't sure what Louis was used to but figured it was the least I could do.

Everything was so quiet. Too quiet. My house already felt like it was two sizes too big and it just got bigger when we sat down to eat. Felt like I needed to apologize for it because Louis ain't know what it was supposed to be like. He ain't know about when it used to be filled with music and laughter. Felt like I'd invited him in and ain't give him the best impression.

"You think the girls'll join us for Christmas Day? I'd sure like to meet them."

We hadn't told the girls anything really about Louis or Hazel but I just nodded and said, "They wanna meet you too. But I don't know if it'll happen any time soon. The social worker, she made it sound like they were busy."

"Too busy for family?"

Wasn't nothing to say to that so I just concentrated on my plate. They were still my girls, just not so much in person. More so in my head. In my head, they'd always be my girls. With their messy braids and scraped knees and the sweetness they could've only got from me. Didn't matter where they were in the world, my girls had my whole heart.

Snow was coming down real good about then. Wind went from whistling to howling up against the windows and doors.

"Mama Bell, this is the best fried chicken I ever had." Louis ain't have his daddy's smile so I figured it came from his mama. Was big and wide, showing all his slightly crooked teeth.

"You ain't gotta call me that. You can call me Belinda if you want. Or Pecan. Don't nobody call me Pecan no more."

"You don't like Mama Bell?" His smile up and disappeared in the blink of an eye.

"No—I just mean...I ain't exactly old enough to be your mama so..."

"If you don't want me to...I can call you whatever you want."

I watched as he stabbed his fork into a piece of yam and chewed it without looking up. The quiet had come back. Things were going so well then I had to go and mess them up. Make him feel like he wasn't mine. I wanted to take it back, was thinking it through when this hardness started raging up against the front door. That right there should've told me who it was. Only one person would've shown up and started banging on my door like that.

"You expecting someone?" Louis looked confused more than anything. And he got to his feet before I could get the words out fully. "I'll get it," he rose from his chair.

"No..." Poor Pecan raised her damn head, muffling up my words. Had to get to my own feet before I could really get it out. "LOUIS! Don't."

"Why?" He looked back at me then at the door. He'd made it all the way to the hall. Then we both heard it. The quiet.

"See. They're gone. Just...just come sit back down. Finish your supper." But Louis was curious. He walked down the hall anyway. And I held my breath as the front door creaked open, snow flurries and that cold Chicago wind came blowing in. Maybe a second passed but it felt like forever before he closed the door again. Couldn't exhale until I heard him throw the lock. The brand new one we got just so I ain't have to worry that Ricky still had his key.

"Hmm." Louis strolled down the hall, still confused. "Guess it wasn't important. You okay?"

I nodded, noticing for the first time how my fingers had latched on to the corner of the wall.

Ricky's bouquets had started coming more frequent and the last few came with phone calls. He said he was checking on me. Wanting to know if I'd made up my mind yet. Asking me how his baby was doing. And reminding me that his love for me wasn't gonna stop. Not ever.

Heziah wanted to call the cops again but they weren't much help the first time. I wasn't surprised. Ricky's fans were everywhere, like a cult of mindless followers. Watching me and doing him favors. But even Ricky wasn't gonna be a match for my pistol.

I was just about ready to convince myself of that when the noises started at the kitchen door. Louis took off in flash. The phone was in the kitchen. All my knives were in the kitchen.

"Where she at?"

Louis rattled off something that was more him just trying to be polite than anything but I could tell that Ricky had just brushed right past him. Nervous as all get-out, Louis swallowed hard and tried again. Telling Ricky that it was late and maybe he could come back tomorrow when we weren't eating supper. Would've worked too if Ricky was anybody else. He ain't care about manners or nothing like that. All Ricky cared about was his pride.

"What you doing Pecan? Hmm?" Off came his gloves and he stuffed them into his coat pockets. "I'm done waiting. You coming back to me or not?"

Every one of my nightmares started with Ricky standing over me as I slept. So, I'd left my pistol in my dresser. Seemed like a good idea at the time.

"This thing done gone on long enough. We getting back together before my boy get here. Hear me? Pecan, I'm talking to you."

Louis eyes grew wide and he looked at me like he'd never laid eyes on me before.

"It ain't like that," I tried to explain.

"Why you talking to him? I'm the one you need to be worried about."

The food was cold by then but I went back to my plate and sat down anyway, like I could eat with him standing over me.

"You my wife."

"I ain't. And I never will be again."

"STOP SAYING THAT!"

Air filled my lungs as I raised my chin an inch or two. Me looking him in the eye wasn't how things usually went between us.

"Where is he? He here? Or he still at that little carpet shop?"

Louis didn't take too kindly to that and said, "Look man, you gotta go."

"Who the fuck is this? Who you is?"

Ricky's focus was a deadly thing especially when you were unfamiliar with it. Physically, Louis was better equipped to handle it than me but at the time I didn't see it like that.

"Leave him be." I was up and between them faster than even I thought possible. "He ain't got nothing to do with this. It's between me and you. Not him."

But Ricky zoomed in on Louis anyway, squinting his eyes and flexing his fists. My affection for my stepson didn't help his cause.

"Ricky, we over. I'm married to a good man. Better than you ever was."

"That right?" His mouth twisted up real nasty. "A better man living up in somebody else's house? Huh? Fucking somebody else's wife! A thief is what he is!"

"We not married no more!"

Louis stepped to the side behind me but I moved right with him, determined to keep the peace between him and Ricky.

"Yeah? And what you doing with this young-un right here? Mr. Better Man know about him? You fucking him too? Huh?"

"He's my son!" Soon as it was out my mouth I knew I could've said it better. Louis was so busy looking at me with that fuzzy sorta happiness in his eyes that he ain't even see it coming. Ricky's stare. My regular old man was back and he stared good and hard at Louis then at me. I'd never put too much thought into whether Louis looked at all like me. Not until right then. "I mean—"

"N'all I heard you. He's your boy."

"Ricky—"

His hands, still cold from outside, whipped outta his pockets before I could move an inch and sent me flying towards the dining table. Hit my head on the edge and slumped to the floor. But for once I wasn't getting the worst of it. Wasn't even the real target. Heziah's pride and joy was in the kind of danger you couldn't learn about in college.

"STOP! RICKY STOP!"

But Ricky wasn't done. Louis feet came flying towards my head and missed me by an inch. I crawled underneath the table, flinching with every blow that shook the table above my head.

Trembling I crawled out. I had only been to a few of Ricky's fights but even they ain't get to be that bad. He had Louis by his collar, pulling him forward just so he could slam his head into the table. Watching it, I could feel something inside me breaking. Thought it was my heart. Twisting and burning deep up inside me. Burned so bad I couldn't walk straight as it came flushing up outta me. Grabbed the wall just to find my way to the kitchen. The skillet was just where I'd left it. Chicken bits floating in the grease. Same skillet Clara'd used over and over to get Ricky under control. Now it was my turn. Got a few steps, holding it with both hands and letting the grease drip down to my feet. Then the burning turned to something else. Something I knew all about. Pain. The kind that came with each one of my girls. But I told myself it ain't matter. Birthing pain wasn't about to stop me. Couldn't let it go on. It had to stop. It'd gone on long enough. Ricky ruining everybody around him. Everybody I loved.

By the time I'd made it back to the dining room a pool of dark red blood oozed across my table and long legs swung aimlessly over the edge.

Ricky was all outta breath, that wild look still in his eye. He'd had plenty but it wasn't enough. There was still a good amount of fight left in him. His chest heaved up and down, his nostrils flaring out as he asked me one last time.

"What's it gonna be, Pecan?"

"No."

"WHY YOU MAKING ME DO THIS? THIS WHAT YOU WANT? HUH?"

Fourteen years of walking on eggshells, dodging punches, and surviving moodswings taught me how to protect myself from a raging maniac. He ran at me with evil in his eyes but before he could make contact, my skillet met with his forehead. Ricky's eyes rolled back into his head and he dropped to the floor. And I fell to my knees over him bringing the skilled down again.

"I told you. No."

⟫

I WAS LEANING OVER him, studying that empty look in his eyes when I heard Heziah's voice.

"Belinda, call an ambulance."

He was still wrapped up in his coat, hat was still on his head. He ain't have time to take anything off. He stumbled over Ricky's body and went straight for the massacre on my dining table.

"I'm so-so-so sorry I—"

"CALL AN AMBULANCE!"

The skillet clanged to the floor and I took off back to the

kitchen. Hoping and praying somebody would show up before it was too late.

31
Criminal

"HOW'S HE DOING, DOCTOR?"

I'd never seen Heziah so upset. Ain't matter what answers folks gave him he always had more questions. Scratching his arms one minute and folded over at the waist the next. He sat next to me, holding his head in his hands. Wouldn't let me touch him. Or maybe it was me that wouldn't let me touch him. I just couldn't help feeling like it was my fault. They never would've even met Ricky if I wasn't in their lives.

"Mrs. Jenkins? Would you like me to take a look at your lip?" Was kind of the nurse to ask but I'd forgotten all about it.

Heziah jerked right up, studying me like he hadn't known I was there. "What happened to your lip? Did he do that?"

"I'm okay."

"Let her look at you."

"But I'm okay. I wanna stay here with you."

"No. Go. Go with her."

Wasn't no kind of goodbye. He couldn't even look me in the eye. So I went. Let the nurses fuss all over me. Ask me endless questions. about what had happened and about the babies. If I felt them moving around. If I felt my water break. I told them I ain't feel nothing. Wasn't specific to my womb, though. Just in general. Was like my soul was just plain numb from it all. Ain't even care that they'd decided to hook me up to some machines. I was lucky to have found Heziah in the first place. And it was damn near a miracle that he came back to me in the second. But now everything was going to be different. Ricky'd found a way to ruin everything good in my life.

"Ooo, looks like somebody's in labor." This big cheesy grin spread across her face and she pointed to the machine. "Contractions?"

"Can you get my husband?"

"Sure. I'll be right back."

A million things went through my head, waiting for Heziah. Things I hadn't said or hadn't said enough. To him. To my girls. Had a fresh start with the twins and I wanted to get things right. Do it right. Was a difference between doing it right and doing the best I could. But all that vanished soon as I saw Heziah's face. He was at my side, holding my hand just like he said he would.

"It ain't time yet."

"But the nurse said—"

I shook my head but couldn't help but smile a little. "How's Louis doing?"

"He's okay. Doctors say he's got a concussion and a broken nose.

He's resting."

"You sure?"

"That's what they said, Belinda. Now you just concentrate on this."

"I'm just lying here. Ain't much to concentrate on."

The nurse breezed back into the room, saying she wanted to check some things and Heziah's back straightened with the quickness as she dropped down between my legs. I ain't think it was possible but I loved him that much more. Was stupid of me to think he'd stop loving me just because of Ricky. He squeezed my hand, not paying my face no mind. Too curious and worried probably.

"Heziah?"

"Yeah. Just...just stay calm. It's okay."

"I need some things from the house."

"Mmhmm."

"Can you go get them?"

"Now? You're having the babies."

"Nope. Not yet." With a finishing pop, the nurse's blue plastic gloves rolled off her hands and into the trash. "Two centimeters. It could be a while."

"See." He ain't want to. I could see it all over him but I really did need some things. "Please. I need my uhh...my gown. Toothpaste. And uhh..."

"A change of clothes. She'll need that for when you all leave the hospital."

The nurse was trying real hard to be helpful. I just ain't need no help. I knew what I was doing. All that stuff I figured Heziah could've thought of on his own. The thing I really needed. What I really wanted was something he ain't know I had.

"Is that all Belinda?"

"Well um...there's this book. It has leather around the outside. Brown leather. Not fancy or anything. Just something I picked up at the market. Could you bring it to me? It's under my side of the mattress." He nodded.

Heziah wasn't gone more than thirty minutes before they put me in my own room. Not long after that an unfamiliar face in a blue suit found his way around to my bedside. Introduced himself as A.D.A somebody. He used big words and came flanked by two police officers, wanting to know all about Ricky. About what had really happened. What had started the fight? What did Louis say? What did he do? I told him Louis ain't do a damn thing. Having Ricky flip out didn't take any coaxing on anybody's part. But the nice blue suit just nodded and kept going with his questions. Asking if maybe I was holding a grudge or something against Ricky. Grudge wasn't what I would've called my feelings toward Ricky, my lying cheating husband that beat me every day of my life. N'all grudge wasn't the word.

"Not my fault the way he is."

"Was. Ma'am." The serious man and his cold eyes moved closer to my bed. "He was pronounced dead upon arrival at the hospital. The D.A. hasn't decided whether to press charges against you or not."

"Press charges?" Heziah dropped a small bag at the door and marched into the room ready to do battle on my behalf. "For what? My wife didn't do anything wrong. He's the one that—"

"It's not up to me." The fine blue suit explained with a slight wave. "I'm just following orders." He nodded to the young men in their dark blue uniforms and one took hold of Heziah while the other handcuffed me to the bed.

"You can't do this! Get those things off of her!"

Just then Mya's face flashed before my eyes. She was gonna be mad at me. Might even hate me. Jackie wouldn't. Nat probably wouldn't even understand. And Nikki—she'd mourn him like a good girl but then she'd get over it. Mya was really the only one I had to worry about.

"Ma'am? Mrs. Jenkins? Do you know if your ex-husband had an insurance policy?"

"I ain't paying to burying him if that's what you asking. His ass can rot in a pine box for all I care."

Panic flashed across Heziah's face. Panic at my words and the way A.D.A somebody would take them.

"You...You can't talk to my wife without her lawyer. Belinda just be quiet. Okay?"

But the birthing pain was back so I wasn't gonna be saying much of anything anyway.

⋘

As SOON AS THINGS started happening with the twins whatever thoughts on Ricky that were still hanging around got pushed to the back of our minds. We were focused on two things. Callie and Jenna. They came like a freight train, both of them screaming their heads off. Heziah started crying. Kissing my head, moving the sweat from my forehead back into my hair. He acted like he was doing more than just moving it around and I ain't have the heart to tell him he wasn't really helping. Just laid there looking up at my honorable man.

One bundle for him and one for me. Heziah started laughing from the second they gave him his bundle. The doctor said the girls were identical but we took our time comparing them anyway. They had the same hands and feet. Same mole on the crook of their left arms. We'd picked out names but wasn't sure which name fit which baby. Spent a good hour trying to find some way to tell them apart.

Then the nurse came in with paperwork for us to sign.

"What is it?" Heziah was too busy spreading his affection from one baby to the other to pay attention to the clipboard I was holding.

"Just regular stuff. Birth certificates."

We locked eyes for a moment. It had never needed saying before and wasn't no need now. The twins were only gonna have one daddy—the honorable Heziah Jenkins.

—————

THE COPS AGREED TO trade handcuffs for a policeman standing guard outside my door. Heziah took it as a good sign but I knew better. Knew better than to expect the good folks who ain't offer me one bit of help to all of sudden be filled with sympathy.

Looking out over the hospital parking lot, I took a break from writing and wrapped an extra hospital gown around me, tying the tired string into a bow across my chest. It was the first quiet moment I'd had. The twins were in the nursery and Heziah was making phone calls. The doctors said we would all be released tomorrow. We weren't sure yet if I was going home or to jail.

"Belinda?" A knock at the door announced Mr. Silverman. He waited for me to reply before pushing it all the way open. "How are you?"

"I'm good."

Twenty-four hours before I'd pushed two human beings out of my body after bashing in my ex-husband's head and I looked better than he did.

"You look worried."

Mr. Silverman had real concern for me. He liked me. He'd wanted to do more for me and I suspected he blamed himself for the way things had turned out.

"From what I've gathered from the prosecutor, I don't think he's feeling too sympathetic. Given the attention that this will generate... Well, I'm afraid he's more interested in making a name for himself than anything else." He sighed and took a seat under the television. "We've got two options here. We can make a claim for self-defense or..." he paused to take a long breath, "...Or we can argue in the affirmative."

"What's that mean?"

"You weren't in the right mind. You didn't know what you were doing."

"You wanna say I'm crazy."

"I want to keep you out of prison." He rose and met me at the window. "I feel I should tell you that criminal law isn't my specialty. I can refer you to someone else if you like."

"No. I trust you. Which one you think is best?"

"You have a strong case for cognitive insanity."

I nodded, wishing I had a cigarette. "But I wanna be the one to tell Heziah. And my girls."

"He certainly won't hear it from me but I can't make any guarantees about the girls. Their foster parents and the social worker will have the final say there."

32
Lost and Found

HE TRIAL WAS QUICK and weighed more on my people than it did on me. Jackie had a hard time with the kids in her class. Kids could be so mean but my girl was tough. She called me almost everyday. Nikki and Nat were doing pretty good. They were more adaptable than Mya and Jackie. Clara said she wasn't surprised because of their personalities. Jackie and Mya were both stubborn, in their own ways. Jackie would tell you straight out that no matter what she wasn't changing her mind. Mya wouldn't use those words. She wouldn't use any words. She'd just give folks a look and they got the point. She'd given me that look on a few occassions.

"She doesn't hate you," Heziah had said. "She just needs time."

I ain't have no choice but to give it to her. The judge had ordered me to spend thirteen months under direct care. So, Mya got thirte months.

"Mrs. Jenkins? You wanna put your journal away? You've got a visitor."

Nurse Betty was just a few years older than me but she acted like she was old enough to be my mama. Not that it bothered me any, I just smiled and set my brown leather book on the nightstand. Betty and all the other nurses gave me special privileges that the other residents didn't have. Once folks found out why I was there, their attitudes became real accomodating. They came by to chat with me, telling me about their kids, husbands, and boyfriends. Felt more like living with a bunch of friends than being locked up in the looney bin. Of course that ain't change the fact that I missed my people. Heziah brought the twins by as much as he could and every full moon or so the social worker brought my girls to see me.

"You excited?" Nurse Betty cleared off my tray of what was left from my lunch. "Today's the day. We'll miss you around here."

"I'll miss you too."

"You all packed?" She looked to the suitcase that stood in the corner then stood back with both hands on the small of her back. She smiled at me. "That's a really nice dress."

"Thank you hun."

"You take it easy, okay?"

She slipped out the door just as Heziah's frame filled it. He wore a brown pinstripe suit and held a dozen red roses.

"Well Mrs. Jenkins, what's it gonna be? You ready to blow this joint?"

"With you?"

"Were you expecting somebody else?" He grinned. Gestured for me to come to him and wrapped me up in his arms. "I've got a surprise for you. In the hall." His eyes danced for joy. "You're not gonna ask me what it is?"

I didn't need to. I already knew. There was only one thing I wanted after my freedom. My girls. They filed in one at a time in order of birth and surrounded me in a hug of giggles and tears. Nikki, as a teenager, had thinned out some but the chubby little girl I gave birth to was all I saw. She cried the loudest, hugging me gently then making way for her sisters. Nat and Jackie held the twins by the hand and the four of them rushed ahead of Mya. She tried to smile, wanted to smile I could see, but it didn't come easy to my girl.

"Stop crying mama," Nat laughed and tried to hoist her baby sister onto her hip like she saw Jackie do. "This the good part. We're all together again. Now everything's gonna be perfect."

Dear reader,

Thank you for choosing my novel! I truly appreciate it. If you purchased the book online please return to that website to leave a review. You can also leave reviews at websites like goodreads.com.

Here are a few more ideas to make leaving a review fun:

- **Take a "selfie" with the book and pin it on Pinterest.** Include your review in the text area along with the hashtag #HowToKnockABravebird.

- **Tweet your favorite line or chapter title.** Use the hashtag #HowToKnockABravebird

- **Act out a passage and upload the video to YouTube.** Don't forget the infamous hashtag!

- **Got a prediction? Share it on the book's Facebook page.**

If you'd like to drop me a line to tell me what you thought of this novel, you can email me at dbryantsimmons@bravebirdpublishing.com.

You can also find me and the book on the web:

www.dbryantsimmons.com
facebook.com/howtoknockabravebirdfromherperch
plus.google.com/+Themorrowgirlsfanclub/

Hope to connect with you soon!

D. Bryant Simmons